AKOREN

Book Six of the Lissae Series

R. Lennard

Akoren

First published in 2024 by R. Lennard

All books in the Lissae Series are written in **UK English**.

Edited by Anna at CREATING ink.
www.CREATINGink.com

Published by Rebecca Lennard.
lissae.com

Check the trigger warnings by scanning the QR code below:

A catalogue record for this book is available from the National Library of Australia

To Corin,
Never in all the realms did I think that
'a table made of water' would turn into a 700k+ saga.
Thank you for the many different ways you continue to change my world.

Prologue

Summer 4050

Terrance Thorne shoved the Guardian harder into the trip-wire, as it sliced like butter through the teen's armour and skin. Red bloomed bright.

It wasn't enough.

Gripping Jonathan Buan's bowstring, he pulled the man up and back, making his eyes widen like he was worried.

As *if*.

The upstart had the job he wanted, the one he'd worked for. And if little Jonnie Buan with the fisherman's lilt ended up cut in half, well, maybe Terrance could courageously shoulder the mantle of Guardian. After a suitable mourning period, of course.

The others scattered in a frenzy—stuttering fools who only saw what they wanted to see. Then the whole patrol group shifted and was standing under the statue of Kay'imi, watching the Guardian as he faded into the Spirit Realm.

As if Kay'imi herself had reached down, Jonathan's organs started to knit back together. Blood seeped from paling skin to return to his body, and there was the faintest shimmer of silver before the Guardian sat up. Gasping for breath, Jonathan Buan was hale and whole once more.

Biting back curses, Terrance let the others think that the tears dripping down his face were from relief.

Mad at the Realm, Terrance followed Edward into the Quiver and Quill Tavern, trying to hide his agitation from his father and failing.

Arilla, the blank, smiled genially and waved towards a free table. "Be with you in a bit."

Comfortably seated, Terrance tried not to sneer as Father put up a silencing ward.

"Are we going to talk about what happened last night?" Edward asked.

"I fell," Terrance said. He'd lost count of how many times he'd told the lie. Movement flashed out of the corner of his eye, and he turned his head. The daughter of the blank was walking their way, bundles of cutlery in her hands.

"And I'm the Altoriae." Edward scowled.

The child tripped and silverware clattered from her hands, the knife landing with the tip embedded in the seat of his chair, having barely missed his leg.

Startled, Terrance jumped. When he had sufficiently recovered, he peered down his nose at her and said, "You need to be more careful."

The girl muttered something that could have been an apology or could have been: "So do you."

Considering the incident with the trip-wire might have played with his head more than he'd realised, perhaps the better part of valour to endure the rest of Father's presence in silence and ignore the girl entirely.

Spring 4059

He'd been in the tavern the day the rumours started flying, about Shari Dawn being the Altoriae.

Terrance knew better than most that there was no way Anika held the mantle, despite what her parents wanted the Realm to believe. But the blank who stammered through his order and tripped over nothing? He'd rather eat his textbooks than believe such drivel.

The Wisara shared Terrance's reservations. He joked with his friends about how ridiculous the whole thing was.

Until it wasn't.

And there was an U'tan in his face, waving zir tentacles around in a menacing fashion.

Terrance did what he'd trained for, and sliced his broadsword through the primary feeding tentacle, only to have the upstart Altoriae tell him off in front of his patrol group and shift him away from the battle, putting him beneath the children who were hiding in the castle.

Beneath the children.

Like he was *less* than them.

Fuming, Terrance slumped in the corner of his holding cell. Thought she was better than him, did she?

He'd show her.

He'd show them all.

CHAPTER ONE

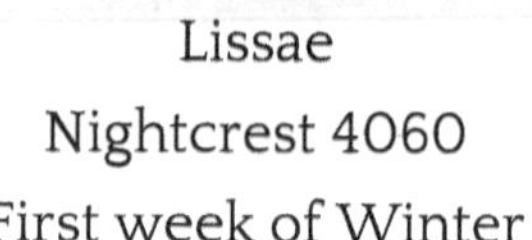

Lissae

Nightcrest 4060

First week of Winter

Shari was in someone else's dream.

Most times, it was easy to tell whose dreamscape she was in, but this one was shrouded in darkness and fear so thick she could feel it on the back of her tongue.

She longed to spit it out.

Crouching, she watched and waited. It took an age, but eventually a door opened and a figure started clicking closer on thick-heeled shoes. A high, tittering voice uttering nonsense words grew closer. It wasn't until her hair flashed in the dim light that Shari jolted.

Chamele.

"Come out, aberration," the imperious mainlander ordered. She seemed ten feet tall and held an object which sparked menacingly in one hand.

Whimpering came from the pile of blankets to her right.

Chamele's teeth gleamed like dental tools in a macabre parody of a smile.

Shari fought a shiver.

Slowly, the blankets moved, and a girl no older than six emerged.

Cruel, talon-like fingers grabbed the child's arm, and the thing in Chamele's hand snapped around the thin neck.

"When I call for you, you come," Chamele said. She held her hand out, and an unseen figure placed a towel on it. Wiping her hands and sneering down at the child, the mainland elder then flicked the cloth to the side, where it burst into flames.

The fire was mirrored in the girl's eyes. "You didn't say my name."

The collar sparked, and the child shrieked, writhing.

"Your name? Aberrations don't have names." Chamele sounded bored, as if children shivering at her feet were a daily occurrence.

Shari's hand tightened on the hilt of her sword. After Jonathan's report today, she knew this was more of a memory than a threat. Still, she longed to run the blade through the shrivelled organ posing as Chamele's heart.

"I'm not an ab-err-ation," the child snarled. "My name is..."

Sound faded out, but Shari could read lips. *Lissa.*

Coloured clouds swirled around Chamele's head as she seemed to inflate even more.

Dread curled in Shari's gut. Dream or not, she burst from her hiding spot and wrapped herself around the child, ripping the collar from Lissa's neck as it started sparking again.

Plasma-like pain raced up Shari's arm. Biting back a shriek, she flung the collar at the elder. Folding herself more tightly around the child, she was abruptly pulled from the dream.

Only to find herself wrapped around Grace.

Who promptly screamed in her ear.

Scrambling away, apologies fell from Shari's lips.

Someone else in the room was panting. *Skye.*

Suppose she doesn't wake up to screaming very often, Shari thought as she twisted out of stabbing range.

Grace lunged again, the sweat beading her brow obviously not impeding her.

"Where were you even hiding that?" Shari hissed as the metal glinted in the light of the two moons shining through the window.

"Out!" her cousin demanded.

"Grace, I'm sorry—I didn't mean to..."

Green eyes flashing, Grace stabbed in her direction.

Shari had to shift out of the way, landing at the foot of Skye's bed.

"Altoriae?" Skye mumbled, rubbing sleep out of her eyes.

"Grace had a dream, and I ended up in it," Shari said, ducking around one of the wooden pillars and letting it take the blow.

"I see," Skye said, as if having someone trying to redecorate her rooms with the blood of another was a regular occurrence.

With Grace as a roommate, it may well be.

"I was trying to protect Grace," Shari yipped as Grace's blade got a little too close to skin.

Grace clambered straight across Skye, careful not to cut her, and fairly flew at Shari, the tip of a too-sharp dagger extended.

"Who has been giving you weapons?" Shari asked.

The door opened, and Shari bolted for it, spinning Yessna around and standing behind the Ferah's back.

"That would be me," Yessna purred.

Slamming to a stop on the other side of the cat woman, Grace peered over Yessna's shoulder and growled at Shari.

"The Altoriae was trying to protect you from the things that hide in your dreams," the Ferah said, holding her hands out placatingly.

Grace's growls died down. "Why?"

"Proximity, and blood, I'd say. You two are close," Skye volunteered from the bed.

"No," Shari and Grace denied at the same time.

Meeting the Altoriae's gaze, Grace nodded and slammed the door.

As if the whole matter was settled.

Shari blew a chunk of hair away from her damp forehead. "Perhaps I will leave the dreamscapes in your capable hands."

Yessna laughed. "The two of you are more alike than you realise."

Contemplating the closed door, Shari wasn't sure if the former leader of the U'sala was trying to flatter or offend her. With Yessna's penchant for a sharp blade, Shari took it as a compliment.

"Thanks."

Laughing again, Yessna tipped her head and strode down the hall.

Elani leaned back and looked up at the castle with a grimace. Shari may have saved them all again, but between Grace, the mainlanders, and the Xanderri, Ronah had sustained significant damage, and the guild were making themselves useful.

Elani patted Talofa on the back. "Excellent! Just remember to breathe when you lift the wall or you'll end up with the hiccups."

Talofa wiped the sweat from her brow and grinned.

The Returned were fixing up the bulk of the buildings, so the former candidates were tackling the castle. The ancient Innarn woven into the very fabric of the building was proving tricky to work with. A few of Ronah's residents had seen the struggle and had come to offer their help. Only now, one of them was filling the air with noise, instead of Innarn.

"It was all blown to the Nine Hells a few days ago. Don't we deserve a break?" one of Ronah's residents complained.

'Terrance,' the island sent.

Fingering the blade strapped to her thigh, Elani wished she could just give the guy another hole to breathe out of. Mu caught the movement and shook his head.

"Really?" Mu said to Terrance and pointed to Talofa, the tiny nine-year-old who's four arms were all straining as she lifted the side of training ground and used her Innarn to wield it back together. "You're going to stand around and mope? Your energy could be better spent."

"Well, where's the Altoriae then? Shouldn't she be out here fixing it as well?"

Wiping the dust from his black clothing, Raven stepped up to the man and stared him down. "Where were you when the attack happened?"

"I... well, I was..."

Someone else on the clean-up crew sniggered, and Terrance flushed a mottled red.

"Perhaps a little more work and a lot less talk." The words might have been a suggestion, but the tone was one of command.

Terrance lowered his head and huffed but started sweeping.

"Do you think it's too soon for Shari to patrol?" Samuel asked, pushing open the double doors of the museum. "She's likely to get antsy. The Altoriae may feel better going on the offensive for a while."

"I think," Jonathan said, stepping through into the hall. "that she's just relived a trauma no Innarnian would be able to..." He broke off and stared at the definitely-taller-than-Pala Ducibus. "Well met," he said.

Samuel's gaze swung to the new Ducibus. The grey cloaks hid all of zir features, from head to toe. He frowned. "Weren't you shorter before?"

'Pala is... indisposed.'

There was something about the hesitation, the inflection of the words that had Jonathan once again thinking that he knew this being. "We've met before, haven't we?"

'Of course... Guardian.'

Another, shorter Ducibus appeared next to the new one, gnarled staff gripped in a grey, trembling hand.

Even without seeing under the hood, Jonathan recognised zir. "Pala?"

A swirl of Innarn from the taller being helped Lissae's Ducibus to stand. 'Well met, Guardian.'

'Can we help?'

Pala made a dry, wheezing sound, which rapidly turned into a hacking cough. The taller Ducibus hovered by ze's side, gloved hand outstretched to catch the other should ze fall.

'Thank you, Guardian, but my kin will see me healed. It will merely take time.' The send was dry and reedy, and so very unlike the vital Ducibus.

"What happened?" Samuel snapped, worry clouding his expression.

'The Xanderri,' the taller one replied.

Pala whacked ze with the staff, and the taller one yelped.

I know that voice. Jonathan stared hard, trying to make out anything under the cavernous hood.

'Return to Lissae for the night, Guardian. We shall warn you if anything untoward is happening.' Pala's thought patterns were muddy, but the message was clear.

"As you will it. Please know that Lissae owes you a great deal, Pala, and we would be honoured to help."

The Ducibus bowed zir hood, but the disjointed thoughts he was broadcasting told a different tale.

"You did not fail," Samuel said, crossing his arms and peering down his nose at the being who, on a good day, barely came to his waist. "The Xanderri are no more."

'They should have never entered Lissae.' Pala sounded more like zirself.

"And you think one, lone being—even one as strong as you—could have stopped them?" Samuel scoffed. "They fed on your Innarn, on your life force, and," he uncrossed his arms and bent, trying to peer into the hood, "you survived. They didn't."

Pala bowed zir head. 'There is still guilt.'

"Oh, there's plenty of that to go around," Samuel said. "The Altoriae is feeling it particularly strongly."

'*Shari has nothing to—ooof!*' the taller Ducibus groaned as Pala's staff connected again, this time with ze's stomach.

'*The Altoriae,*' there was a pointed glance between Pala and the other, '*is not at fault.*'

"By that logic, neither are you," Jonathan said. "The fault lies entirely with the Xanderri."

Once more, Pala bowed zir head. '*I am grateful you feel this way. I feared I would have to give up my post and my... associate is not yet ready.*'

The taller Ducibus slouched, and there was that uncanny feeling again—that Jonathan knew the being, even though he was sure that this particular Ducibus was new to the hall.

"You have been a staple of the portal since I was a hatchling. I forbid you from giving up your post," Samuel said.

'*In that case, it appears I'm here to stay.*' Pala's send was slightly stronger than before, even though Jonathan was almost certain it was meant with a hefty dose of sarcasm.

"Good," Samuel said and stormed through the double doors.

"I'm glad you're still with us," Jonathan said, resting his hand briefly on Pala's shoulder before he trailed after his apprentice.

His apprentice?

Swinging around on Lissae's side of the doors, Jonathan gaped at the taller Ducibus, who was in the act of pulling the doors closed.

The being paused, and the Guardian of Lissae got the distinct impression that the taller Ducibus winked at him.

Jonathan's jaw dropped.

His apprentice.

However soft the cloth felt to her fingers had to be a lie. Chamele raised a shaking hand to where the sandpaper-lined veil had irritated the skin of her ruined face.

"The tailor needs to be replaced," she snapped.

"Of course," the head guard replied.

I really need to learn his name.

There was noise in the hall, leading to her rooms and getting closer. "Elder! Elder!"

Chamele sighed and sat back in her chair, flipping the rough veil back over her face.

The head guard made sure she was settled, then opened the door.

An aide stumbled into the room, puffing and red faced. "Elder, I have news."

Lifting a brow, Chamele waited.

The aide just stood there, chest heaving for breath.

Realising that the thrice-damned veil hid her expression, Chamele bit out, "Well?" Another, more appropriately demure aide, handed her a cup of tea.

"Captain Rappen's body has been found," the man blurted.

Teacup clinking on the saucer, Chamele froze. "What?"

"The captain. Two old fishers at the port saw something floating in the water. It was an open box, and the captain's body was inside. Gave them a proper fright to row out and see that. The healer took a look and reckons it can't have happened that long ago. Maybe a day or two."

"Were there clouds near him?"

The aide wrinkled his nose. "No, Elder. The sky was clear."

After placing her drink to the side, Chamele gripped the arms of the chair. "Are you sure?"

He glanced out the window at the clear blue sky. "Not a single cloud."

"Very well."

Bowing, he then scurried out of the room.

Taking a breath to steady her hands, Chamele picked the cup back up and carefully sipped.

He had one job. One. And now?

No clouds.

Screaming, she threw the cup, watching in some satisfaction as an aide jumped out of the way of the scalding splash of liquid.

Collapsing back in the chair, Chamele groaned.

The head guard barked orders for the aides to clean up the mess, to get her another cup of tea, and to stand closer to the windows and make sure that the doors were guarded.

For the first time, Chamele felt all alone.

"Found it!" Remmy said, holding aloft a... button?

Collis rubbed the sleep out of his eyes. "Found what?" Centuries of practise had his body up and moving before his brain was engaged. He glanced at his hand, quietly miffed as to why his staff had appeared.

Laughing, Remmy clapped him on the back.

Safe, Collis thought and dismissed the staff. Feeling bereft without it, he shuffled to the kitchen to splash water on his face. "Remmy, it's early. What exactly has you so excited that you had to bust into my home and wake me up?"

'*The crystal tap.*' In his excitement, Remmy switched to sending.

Straightening, Collis glanced over his shoulder, water dripping down his chest unheeded. '*Did you...?*'

'*Use it? Yes.*'

Licking suddenly dry lips, Collis raised his brows.

"No reply, yet." Remmy slumped.

"That could be a good thing," Collis said, eyeing the tap. The small device was easily disguised as a button. When they'd all come back to Ronah, the Returned who'd wanted to resettle on the mainland had agreed to use them.

"Somehow, I don't think no reply is a..." Remmy broke off, staring at the tap as it vibrated in his hand.

Collis froze, waiting and watching Remmy's face as it slowly went pale. "Remmy? Who was it?"

Lifting his head slowly, Remmy said hoarsely, "Joana. She's been captured."

CHAPTER TWO

Inthday

Second day of the first week of Nightcrest

hifting in her seat, Tania tried hard not to fidget. Zana kept flicking little spikes of Innarn, trying to get her to stay focused, but it wasn't working.

"You're a ball of energy today," Oakley said.

Chewing on her lip, Tania squirmed. "I can't help but think about what's going to happen during the joining."

Zana raised an elegant brow. "That is rather the purpose of our meeting."

"No, it's—" Tania rose and wrapped her arms around her middle. "When we met with Rakemyst, the Chirea attacked. Talhan, the Crystal Intelligence tried to take over everyone, and Cantash, the Altoriae went missing. When we joined with Ginorti, the mainlanders fired Innarn dampeners on us! What could possibly—?"

Fenix lunged forward, clapping a hand over Tania's mouth, their eyes wide. "Don't you dare voice that thought! We will not tempt the deities to mess with us even more."

Tania licked Fenix's hand.

"Ew!" They pulled away, shaking their arm as if the saliva would fly off.

"I have five siblings," Tania said, deadpan. "What did you think was going to happen?"

Cyrus chuckled and turned the noise into a cough when Cantash's Linked glared at him. "To be fair, the Altoriae went missing *after* the joining with Cantash," he said. "And despite not wanting to tempt the deities, it is a good idea to plan for the worst."

"What could possibly be worse?" Fenix shrieked.

"A horde of Q'Aralides descending..." Zana paused. She'd obviously said the first thing that came to mind.

"The now extinct race, whose remaining members helped us hold off the mainlanders and reside on Ronah?" Tania said, unimpressed.

Zana sighed. Tania had the impression that if she'd been alone, she would have banged her head against something. "Fair point. The stories of the Q'Aralide are hard to overcome, even after seeing them in person."

"The stories are real enough," Cyrus said, fiddling with the scrap metal on the table.

"If they aren't a threat anymore, what are we facing?" Oakley asked. Ginorti's Linked was a picture of solid calm amongst the flaring tempers.

"The hantra," Tania said, loud enough to almost drown out Cyrus's protests that the Q'Aralide were still a threat. "Last time the Wisara were on Ronah, they raised the hantra."

"I think we have more to fear from the mainlanders than the Wisara," Zana said.

"And how do we protect against them?" Cyrus asked, his tone bitter as he flipped goggles over his eyes. Fire Innarn shot out of his finger in a controlled beam that he ran over a seam in two of the metal parts, welding them together.

Tania slumped back into her seat and looked around. "I don't know."

Arilla shrieked with laughter as Calem chased her into the back room of the Quiver and Quill Tavern, snapping a dish towel at her.

"What do you think you're doing?" she asked, breathless as he caught her around the waist.

"Kissing the most beautiful woman in the Realms." He peppered her face with kisses as she giggled at him.

After catching Calem's head between her hands, she gave him a solid kiss then pushed him away. "We're going to open late at this rate." She was only half-joking. The walk from Rakemyst took more time out of their morning than from their house. She smoothed the frown from her face.

Giving her a cheeky grin, Calem flicked his fingers at the crystal pot.

Nothing happened.

Ordinarily, the pot would begin to bubble and Arilla would be able to add in the meat for the stew of the day.

"Tired, love?" Arilla asked.

"Hmmm?" Confident in his power, her husband had already moved on to the next step.

"The pot's being stubborn today."

Calem used the towel to wipe his hands clean and turned to peer at the pot, resting his chin on her shoulder. "Must be." Brows drawn together, he flicked his fingers again, and the water sluggishly started to bubble.

Arilla kissed the side of his jaw and went to gather the vegetables, her thoughts in a whirl.

Perhaps now SilverCloud was in the Spirit Realm, they could move back to their cosy house and have a bit more time to rest? Glancing at Calem and the dark circles under his eyes, she nodded to herself. She'd bring it up as soon as the stew was done.

Tania smiled as Collis intertwined his fingers with hers.

"I'm glad you waited for me," he said as they walked.

"Well, Ronah did want to shift me home, but I thought we should talk," Tania said, bumping his arm with her shoulder.

Collis stiffened. "Talk?"

"About the soul-match. Everyone else has had a say, but I wonder what you think about it?" she blurted. The question had been rolling around in her mind ever since Zana's test.

He relaxed and smiled down at her. "I couldn't find a better soul-match if I had to wait another three hundred and fifty years."

Tania froze. "Wait." She looked up at him, eyes wide. "You're... I'm such a fool!" She slapped her palm onto her forehead.

"What do you mean?" Collis asked, a tingle of Innarn taking the sting of the slap away.

"You're three hundred and sixty-six years old," Tania squeaked.

Collis grinned. "Three seventy-five, actually. We were in there for a while."

"But I'm... I'm about to turn seventeen. I'm about three hundred and fifty years too young for you."

"Who says?" Collis asked, his grin disappearing.

"My mother, probably," Tania grumbled and clung to his arm.

"Surely she would not deny you your best chance of happiness?" he asked gently.

"Mum doesn't have the best track record with older men." Tania scowled into the distance.

"You are not your mother," he said, stopping under the shade of the trees before the bridge back to Ronah. "And if I could forget the years I spent away from Ronah, I would. All of us would choose to do so." Collis gently rubbed her upper arms. "I look, as Remmy so nicely likes to remind me, all of seventeen again. Perhaps with a bit more ink on my skin. Maybe your mother will see the outer shell and not worry about my age?"

Tania's frowned deepened. "What if I'm worried? How can I possibly be interesting to you?"

He smiled at her, tugging gently on her hand to start them walking again. "You are the breath of life and normal that I've always longed for. You are endlessly interesting to me," Collis said as they crossed the bridge.

"Sickening," a voice drawled.

Hand to her heart, Tania just about jumped out of her skin. "Temira!"

"He's telling the truth. You are life, although your lack of awareness of your surroundings does little to indicate you care to keep yours intact." The bald, blue-skinned technomancer glared at the pair, two mechanical B.I.R.D.s flittering around her head. She glanced at the second one. "Did you forget something?"

Leaning against Collis, Tania sighed. "I'm sorry. I didn't think to bring Flutter with me."

"Flutter?" Temira asked, her glare replaced by confusion.

Whistling, Tania tried to hide her giggle as Flutter zoomed towards her head, chittering at her. Pointing at the B.I.R.D. Tania repeated, "Flutter."

"You named one of the most advanced pieces of technology on the entire Realm 'Flutter'?" Temira asked, her expression set into the deadpanned stare that told Tania she was unimpressed.

"Well, what's he doing?" Tania asked as the mechanical creature fluttered about her head.

"Hovering."

Collis covered a chuckle with a cough.

"Hovering isn't a very good name for a bird, though," Tania said.

Temira sighed and looked at the ground as if expecting it would provide the response she required. When it was clear none was forthcoming, she turned, her coat billowing out dramatically behind her as she left.

"Tea next Adonday?" Tania called after her.

'*Of course*,' Temira's send echoed in her head.

Tania grinned and waved after the technomancer's retreating figure, even if she didn't turn around.

"How is it that you are able to befriend the strongest of us?" Collis mused.

"Sorry?" Tania asked.

"Idle thoughts," he said and kissed the top of her head before they set off once more for her house.

Shari stood, hands on knees, panting. "Why," she asked between breaths, "did you let me think Temira's training device was a good idea?"

"I believe you were the one who convinced me," Jonathan said mildly, despite being soaked in sweat as well.

The sound of pounding footsteps was the only warning they got before the doors to the training ground were fairly blasted off their hinges. Samuel stormed through the doorway and froze. "What in the name of Cylanthar is going on here?" he bellowed. Zoomer, tongue lolling and chest heaving, stood by his side.

"Training," Shari said, straightening up. If she could pretend that she wasn't injured in front of her parents for years, she could do it for five minutes now.

"With that?" Samuel asked, thrusting a finger to point at the gently smoking B.I.T. devices the technomancer had installed at the far end of the training ground.

"What else?" Shari said, shrugging.

He stormed over to her, trying to use his height to intimidate. "The last time you fought one of those, you died."

Zoomer whimpered.

Poking his chest with one finger, Shari pushed him back. "This one has been modified," she said, her voice low.

Jonathan took a large step backwards.

"I don't want you using a machine to train," Samuel said.

Jonathan took another step.

"Last time I checked, you weren't the Guardian. And he said it was fine," Shari shot back.

Samuel's scowl deepened, and he pointed a finger at Jonathan's retreating form. "Stay. Right. There," he said through gritted teeth, never taking his gaze from her face. "The next time even the thought of training with that hunk of junk crosses your mind, you come and get me. Or I will make it my personal mission to ensure that every last one of them becomes scrap metal."

Zoomer, traitor that he was, yipped in agreement.

Burying his fingers in her palon's fur, Samuel scowled one last time, and man and palon shifted away from the training grounds.

Any ounce of grace left with him.

Shari plopped to the ground and sighed. "That was intense."

Joining her on the dusty ground, Jonathan nodded. "He's always been a bit like that. I suppose he was hiding a lot of it from you."

Glancing at him out of the corner of her eye, Shari asked, "Was he like that when you first met him?"

"Worse. He was in full Q'Aralide priest mode and called me morsel. I thought he was going to use my shin bone as a toothpick," Jonathan admitted.

A white wisp behind Jonathan caught her attention, and Shari swore glowing eyes were peering at her. She blinked, and it was gone. "Terrifying," she said, and meant every syllable of it.

CHAPTER THREE

Kerday

Third day of the first week of Nightcrest

The base of Chamele's cane clunked as she gingerly made her way down the stairs. Legs trembling, she paused. Reaching the bottom step, she teetered for a moment, balance lost as she came to the end of the banister. The head of her guard rushed forward and hovered, useless.

"Elder?"

"Take me to the aberrations," she snapped.

Something shuttered in his eyes. "Yes, Elder." Turning on his heel, he led the way farther into the dungeon.

Following, Chamele tried to ignore the little voice in the back of her head that wondered when she had become the kind of person who had dungeons carved out of ziom underneath her home.

The guard up ahead opened a door, and a breeze blew the veil into the sensitive skin of her face.

She half-expected this aberration to be like all the others, huddled in the corner, cowering from the light spilling through the open door.

This one, with ink on its skin, sat serenely in the middle of the room, eyes closed, hands resting on the knees of its crossed legs. Bruises covered the exposed skin, and dried blood trickled down from the swelled lip. Needle marks dotted the arms from where they'd tried to inject medicine to cure the creature, with no success.

It didn't even have the courtesy to open its eyes.

"Get up," Chamele snapped, her free hand wrapped around the doorframe so she wouldn't topple over.

As battered and bruised as it was, the aberration smoothly rose to its feet.

Chamele's vision narrowed, pulsing red at the edges.

Striding forward with a strength she thought she'd lost, Chamele then wrapped her hand in its shirt, the buttons digging into her skin. "Why won't you break?" she shrieked into its face, spittle striking mottled skin.

It blinked at her.

Enraged, the elder shook the aberration, and underneath her hand, the button pulsed.

She froze, wondering what sort of horrid sorcery was at work.

For the first time since its capture, emotion flicked across the aberration's face.

Fear.

Beneath the veil, Chamele's melted skin twisted into a smile. "Well, well. What is this?" After shoving the dirty thing to the floor, Chamele snapped her fingers, and guards poured into the room.

"Elder?"

"Hold its arms," she ordered.

The aberration scrambled backwards, but there were too many guards. Before the thing could even shriek, the guards held it fast, with two gripping each arm.

Chamele teetered forwards, reaching out a hand to pluck the button from its shirt, when the creature slumped between the guards, forcing the men to stagger in order to hold it up. Coming closer, Chamele stretched farther, not wanting to sully herself any more than she already had.

The aberration's legs snapped up and out, slamming into her chest and throwing her bodily across the room. Chamele's head smacked into the ziom wall, and she collapsed, watching in a daze as the aberration ripped the button off with its teeth and bit down on it.

In the darkness of the ziom cell, the Realm went white.

"Best behaviour," Samuel reminded the hatchlings.

Jetonyx looked mildly offended, as if he were incapable of anything but being good. Tormorylth blinked at him innocently, but her flicking tail gave away her excitement. Kemanyr's tiny golden face peered down at him from where she'd perched, upside down, claws digging into the ceiling.

'*Why?*' the youngest Q'Aralide sent.

"Because you have the capability to cause great harm, we will ensure that not a single hair on Lizbeth's head is damaged while she is in our presence, especially as a visitor in our home."

'*She brings sweets. She must be protected,*' Tormorylth nodded.

"Not just because she brings sweets," Samuel protested weakly.

Jetonyx narrowed his three eyes at him, his massive black form looming as he got closer. '*Is she your new mate?*'

Sneeze took an interest and sat upright, his razor-sharp claws leaving new dents in Samuel's skin. '*Mate?*'

"What? No! Lizbeth is the first being who was ever kind to me, just because she chose to be," Samuel said. *When did this become my life?*

'*Friend?*' Sneeze seemed almost sad.

"Yes, Lizbeth is my friend!" Samuel said, louder than he meant to apparently, as the hatchlings all fell back.

"I'm glad to hear it," a voice from outside floated through the door.

Groaning, he ran a hand over his face in a movement reminiscent of the Guardian. As he'd always suspected, it did nothing to calm him down.

"Well met, Lizbeth," he called. "Come in."

Sure enough, when the door swung open, the tantalising smell of rutenberry pie reached out to tease him.

Then Lizbeth stumbled as she crossed the threshold.

Stumbled.

In all the time he'd known the blind human, she'd never shown such weakness. He could hear the pounding of her heart from the opposite side of the room.

"Lizbeth?" he asked.

"Oh, I'm fine." She waved him away. "My Innarn has been a bit off lately."

Samuel frowned. Tormorylth rushed forward, her slight body still small enough to slip under one of Lizbeth's arms, propping her new friend up. Together, the unlikely duo headed for the long, cushy lounge, where their guest took a seat.

Tormorylth sat beside her, expectantly.

Lizbeth did not disappoint. "Seeing there's more than one sweet tooth in the house, I baked a few different treats to try."

Jetonyx edged closer, Tormorylth sat up even straighter, and Kemanyr dropped from the ceiling to perch next to Lizbeth.

"I don't know why you're all excited," Samuel grumbled. "I'm the one with all the sweet teeth. You lot only have fangs."

'*Rude!*' Jetonyx gasped.

Laughing, Lizbeth reached into her basket and began pulling out packages wrapped in brown paper. "There's enough for every sweet tooth *and* fang in here. And a few new things to try." She laid all the parcels out on the low table and started sorting through them.

Sneeze peered at the proceedings from his perch, while Samuel tried his best not to drool.

Cookies, a brown slab sliced into squares, cake, and a gently steaming pie.

"You spoil us," Samuel said.

Reaching forward, Lizbeth snagged a cookie and nibbled on it. "That's what friends do."

Tormorylth leaned in closer and breathed in deeply enough to syphon the crumbs from Lizbeth's shirt.

"I know what you're doing," Lizbeth said.

'Me? I'm helping to clean.' Tormorylth was the picture of innocence. It caused Samuel to do a double-take, as he'd never seen that particular expression on a Q'Aralide before.

Kemanyr blinked at Samuel as he placed a piece of pie in a bowl.

"No," he said, holding it to his chest.

Cocking her head to the side, the youngest hatchling blinked again. Quicker than he could see, she sprang forward and shoved her snout straight into the pie.

"Kemanyr!" he roared.

Lizbeth laughed even as the guilty hatchling flailed her head, sending rutenberry filling everywhere, before leaping towards a safer perch. Jetonyx caught her by the tail and pulled her back, trapping her in relative safety underneath his claw.

'Finish while I stand guard,' the eldest hatchling sent to Samuel. *'I'll take my payment once you're done.'*

"And what will you charge?" Samuel asked.

Jetonyx looked at the spread on the table. *'A piece of the brown.'* He tipped his head towards the slab.

"A fair deal," Lizbeth said.

Samuel scowled, but any ill thoughts were banished at the first taste of the pie. There was a reason he'd been feared through all the Realms, but in this moment, it was easy to forget why.

Anika dipped her head but refused to look away from her opponent's hands.

"Good," Arilla said, sword held at the ready. "Now try to land a strike." A rumbling growl came from the stands of the training grounds. Arilla sighed. "I'm safe, Grace. Anika needs to practise, and she's fast outpacing the others."

I need to, Anika thought, and brought her fists up.

Arilla froze. "Did you forget something?"

"This is the new design I was talking about. I showed Grace last night." Anika flicked a glance at the stands and had a fleeting glimpse of the grumbling Innarnian.

"You can't bring fists to a sword fight, Anika," Arilla said gently.

"I know," Anika said. Aiming away from her trainer, Anika twisted her forearm, and the short blade strapped to the inside of her arm sprang forward, the narrowed hilt smacking perfectly into her hand.

The mother of the Altoriae gaped at her. "By the life of Lissae." After sheathing her sword, she carefully reached forward, pushing up Anika's sleeve and examining the contraption. "This is brilliant!"

"I still have a few kinks to work out, but I think the base design is there," Anika said modestly.

"This could change how we fight," Arilla breathed. "Innarnians wouldn't expect us to have anything like this at all." She traced a fingertip over the flat of the blade. "Well, let's see how it holds up. Can you reload it?"

Nodding, Anika re-seated the blade and shook her sleeve down to cover it. Holding up her fists, she nodded. "Ready."

Arilla picked up her sword and bowed again. Moving slow enough so Anika knew where the strike would land, she waited.

Twisting her forearm again, the sword sprang into her hand, and Anika blocked the blow, grinning up at her mentor.

Grace growled when Anika's second blade, a dagger, slipped into her hand.

Using the two to push her mentor back, she laughed. "It works!"

Slowly, aware of their prickly audience, the two moved through the set patterns, blocking, striking, and defending until Anika's arms ached so much she doubted she'd be able to lift a needle.

"Well done," Arilla said, sheathing her sword and wiping the sweat from her brow.

Anika dipped her head. "Thank you for taking the time to test this with me."

"Any time," Arilla smiled. "I should get back to the tavern for now."

Grace was at her side in an instant, the skirt of the blue gown Anika had designed for the odd girl flaring with the force of her shift.

"I bet you want pants like Shari does," Anika said, refitting the blades into their holsters. Grace snarled at Shari's name and ushered Arilla away.

Waving over her shoulder, Arilla yelled back, "I'll see you at training tomorrow morning. Bring the new blades."

Anika grinned. The others would be so surprised.

With a bounce in her step, Anika made her way towards home, so she could get ready for school. Rounding a corner, she slowed, the bounce leaving her stride.

"Why are you so happy?" her former best friend, Maeve, sneered at her.

Biting back a snappy remark, it took everything Anika had not to curl in on herself. She hadn't realised quite how mean she'd been to others until Maeve turned the same spite and fury in Anika's direction. "It's a lovely morning," she said, trying to smile.

"Humph." Maeve glared and strode past, stilettos clicking on the path.

Anika chewed on the inside of her cheek and kept walking, careful not to brush against the other girl.

Home safe, she hastily showered and redressed into something more stylish than her training clothes. If anyone had something bad to say, it wasn't going to be about how she looked.

Finally ready, Anika slipped through the house.

Her father was waiting at the door, a frown on his face. "What are you doing here?"

Screwing up her nose, Anika said, "I was just leaving, actually."

Woodenly, her father nodded. "For the best," he said.

There was a clattering sound from her room. Anika's jaw dropped as clothes streamed past, packing themselves neatly into bags and boxes that materialised just outside the front door. Her makeup, jewellery, and shoes followed. "What's going on?" she hated how her voice trembled.

"You're leaving," her father said.

"For *school!*"

He frowned. "Not for good?" Rany Thorne sounded disappointed in her, yet again.

"Not yet," Anika said, swiping at the tears streaming from her eyes. "But if you're so keen to see me go, I can make it happen." She pushed past him, gasping and rubbing at her face as the breeze outside blew against her tears. "I'll make sure it happens," she said bitterly.

The door closed behind her with a *click.*

Anika slumped and let the tears fall.

Jonathan ran a hand through his hair and glanced at the mirrored wall of the Hidden Vine. Nestled in the top of the tree canopy, the restaurant was discreet and catered to clientele who valued their privacy. Hanging greenery tangled together, making walled-off spaces for couples to get cosy and giving larger groups room to move and talk.

It was the perfect place for his second date with Zac.

Shari was at school, Samuel was busy with the hatchlings, and Asterion was organising the paperwork he would complete this afternoon, leaving Jonathan free to relax.

A tousled-haired man entered the restaurant from the other side, and Jonathan's gaze snapped to the figure.

Zac.

Moving slowly, Jonathan stood, admiring the cut of Zac's jacket and trying desperately to ignore the rapid beating of his heart as the other man drew closer.

"Well met, Jonathan," Zac said as he stepped into their private room.

"Well met, Zac." Jonathan took a deep breath, burying away the scent of pine and zest that could only be Zac.

Sitting, he gestured to the seat opposite and grinned when Zac shook his head. A tingle of Innarn, and the seat below him expanded to be just big enough for two people. Zac sat next to him, their thighs touching.

Reaching for his drink, Jonathan blinked as it was swiped out of his hand.

Zac met his gaze over the rim of the glass as he took a sip before handing it back.

"So, are we still friends?" Jonathan burst out.

"Well, that depends on–"

Under their seat, the limb of the tree vibrated, and Jonathan's glass fell from senseless fingers. He grasped his head as Ginorti's voice travelled through the timber and reverberated all around them. '*Akoren! Akoren! Akoren!*'

From the feel of it, Akoren was under attack. When Ronah took up the chant as well, Jonathan ran a hand over his face.

The Shifting Islands couldn't converge fast enough.

CHAPTER FOUR

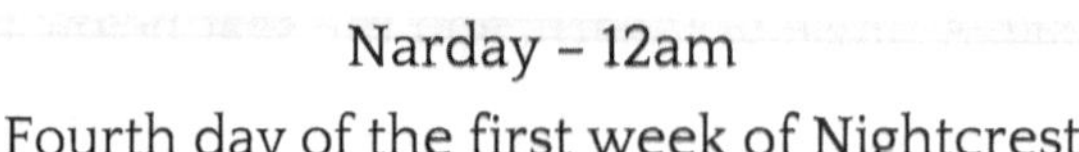

Narday – 12am

Fourth day of the first week of Nightcrest

hari ran a shaking hand through her sweat-soaked hair. Closing her eyes, the image of white bones falling from a coloured cloud seemed burned into her memory. The dream was quickly fading, but her hands were still shaking.

A knock at her door had her looking up, a sword appearing in her hand before she was consciously aware of it. Innarn probing outwards, she banished the weapon when she realised who was on the other side.

"Yes?" she asked, impressed that her voice was steady.

Silently, the door opened.

"Rough night?" Jonathan was leaning against the frame, a study of forced casualness.

"You could say that," Shari said.

"I have a proposition for you," Jonathan said.

Shari's eyebrows rose, and a dull flush dusted Jonathan's cheeks. Buried in his thoughts was a voice much deeper than her own saying the same thing. For the first time in memory, Jonathan pushed her out of his mind.

'*Shari!*' he chided. "Thought you might like to burn off some energy and go patrolling."

"You're setting me free?"

"Assuming you're ready?"

After swinging her legs out of the bed, she rose, her leathers settling into place with just a thought. "Beyond ready."

"Earra has been having some difficulties near the gateway."

A *Grey Realm. How convenient.* Shari nodded and tightened the straps on her bracers to avoid her Guardian's gaze. "Easy," she said, hoping he'd ignore her trembling fingers.

Taking a deep breath, Shari closed her eyes and shifted, landing on the other side of Lissae's double doors. She slumped against their familiar wood and tried to catch the breath that suddenly stuck in her throat.

'*Well met, Altoriae.*'

Shari glanced down, blinking when she saw Pala leaning heavily on a walking stick.

'*Well met, Pala. Are you well?*'

There was a dry chuckle. '*I have been worse. My apologies, Altoriae, for not fulfilling my duties to you and to Lissae. I fear I have grown old.*'

'*What do you mean?*'

The hood bowed, leaving Shari to stare at an intricate stitching of six arrow heads portending from a silver circle. *Lissae's symbol,* she realised.

'*The Xanderri overpowered me and gained entry to Lissae.*'

Shari's mind felt like deep winter snow. Frozen to the bone, to her very soul, she glanced at the hood of this tiny being who'd guarded Lissae's gateway so faithfully for aeons. "We are alike," she rasped, forcing her voice through iced-over vocal cords. "We survived them, and they will *never* hurt us again."

'You wish for me to continue?' Pala asked.

"Do you know the only reason I can sleep?" *However infrequently that is,* Shari added in the privacy of her own mind. "It's because I know you guard the gateway. Because Jonathan will back us both up, and Samuel will make sure that anyone who threatens us doesn't exist long enough to do it twice. All of us keep Lissae safe."

Pala bowed. '*I will continue to do so, Altoriae.*'

Nodding, Shari strode off, doing her best to look confident, when really she was debating heading back to bed and hiding under the covers.

A whisper, which sounded like Pala, but wasn't, brushed against her mind. '*I will ensure you return home.*'

Shari glanced around. A wisp of white shadow with glowing eyes at the centre had her sprinting for Earra's gateway.

Pounding through the portal, Shari slammed through the wooded door with the big metal circle in the middle of it. For the second time that night, she stood with her back to a wooden door, trying to catch her breath.

Had it been real?

Chest heaving, Shari took a long moment to regulate her breathing. There was something about that wisp that seemed familiar, but still terrifying. Possibly because it so closely resembled the Xanderri.

'*You want to make sure I get home?*' Shari sent towards the creature. '*Show your true form!*'

Huffing, she pushed away from the door and went to see what the beings of Earra needed help with.

Earra

Narday – 1am

Fourth day of the first week of Nightcrest

Hidden in the shadows, Jonathan placed his feet carefully. It wouldn't do to let Shari know she wasn't as alone as she thought. Especially after her mad dash through the Ducibus' Portal.

He'd seen the glowing eyes of a creature fixated on Shari and had been tempted to poke at it with his Innarn. Shari had been too fast, and he was more concerned with making sure his Altoriae was safe than the mystery being.

Lissae

Tiny puffs of hot air were escaping Jetonyx's maw every time he breathed out in his sleep. The eldest hatchling had taken to sleeping against the door so no one could get in, or out. Samuel would never admit to it in public, but the Q'Aralide equivalent of snoring was comforting.

Tormorylth was curled up in the nest she'd crafted on the opposite side of the wide room, with Kemanyr sleeping between her older sibling's claws.

Despite the domestic scene, Samuel was restless. He'd been about to settle down for the night, retreating to the semi-privacy of his room with Sneeze, when Jonathan sent a message saying Shari was patrolling again.

It took everything in him to not follow. The big black body blocking the doorway helped as well. After flopping onto the squishy lounge, he let his head drop backwards, staring at the ceiling sightlessly.

The draci on his shoulder curled his tail tighter around the back of Samuel's neck, breath tickling against exposed skin. He had yet to figure out what he could do with the tiny dragon when he patrolled.

What would he do when Shari needed him again?

There was a subtle *twang* to the wards, an old pattern he hadn't heard in decades playing out. Someone was walking around the perimeter, poking at his protections.

Someone he knew.

'*What do you want?*' Samuel grumbled.

'*To enter,*' Yessna replied.

Heaving a sigh, Samuel rose from his spot on the lounge. Making his way into his bedroom, he shifted the Ferah in without giving warning.

'*Rude,*' Yessna hissed.

'*Jetonyx is blocking the door,*' he sent, pointing at the hatchling in question.

'*Fair.*' Yessna smoothed her fur down from where the sudden shift had ruffled it.

'*Did you ever have young ones in the U'sala?*' The thought escaped his mind before he could censor it.

Yessna stiffened. She took her time running her paw over the already flat fur, her whiskers quivering. '*Yes.*'

'*How did you leave them when you had to fight?*'

'*Why?*' The Ferah tilted her head, ready to slash his skin at the wrong answer.

'*I feel responsible.*' He stared out at the two tiny hatchlings curled together. '*There are no others to care for them, and even for those who might be able to, it is unsafe. Q'Aralide young are not the easiest beings to raise.*'

Muffling a laugh with her paw, Yessna shook her head. '*The young of any species are not easy to raise, and yours have seen neglect and trauma enough to make them even more dangerous than they already are.*' She paused, tail flicking. '*We set wards. Someone was always charged with watching them. Often they weren't ours, but more refugees needing aid. They'd seen trauma too.*'

Samuel had the impression that once, a long time ago, Yessna had been one of the young.

'*Sometimes it worked. Other times, we'd come back and they were gone. The guard slaughtered. It was rare, but occasionally one would survive and stumble back into the camp.*'

'*And if you were here, in my place, how would you protect them and the Realm at the same time?*'

Yessna's tail flicked again, and she stared at him as she tried to parse his words. '*I'd ask for help.*'

'*If I asked, would you give it?*'

Her ears flattened. '*I am not good with young ones. Ask the Ulnan— your middle hatchling wants to be friends.*'

Samuel sighed. '*This is not why you came by tonight, is it?*'

Ears raising again, Yessna shook her head. '*I came to see if you were settling in.*' She took a long look at the three sleeping Q'Aralide. '*It is hard to think that you are the last of your race. That your Realm is gone.*'

Sucking in a breath, Samuel turned his head away. '*We may not be the last. There were a few who were banished.*'

'*You four are the last.*' Yessna's send sounded so final.

Samuel felt like the blood froze in his veins.

'*Don't ask,*' Yessna pleaded.

The hot breath of the little draci helped to centre him again. '*My thanks for the news.*' His send was hollow as it must have sounded, if the look the Ferah gave him was any indicator.

'*I am...*'

Samuel shifted her away before his temper escaped him.

'*... sorry.*'

Striding back into the room, he changed form. Sneeze grumbled at the sudden movement, and sleepy heads rose. Three bodies crowded around him, and he covered them all with his wings.

Keeping the last of his kind close.

Earra

Earra's gateway came out atop a cliff. Shari stepped farther onto a broad, paved platform which showed the inhabitants were frequent enough travellers. The view was stunning, a winding river separating them from what looked like a major city. The cliff faces were sheer drops downwards, towards what looked like water from a glacier.

To her left, a man stood slumped over, leaning one elbow on the windowless counter in a small wooden hut, with a bored expression on his face. "Name and rank?" he droned as he picked up a writing implement.

"Shari Dawn. Altoriae of Lissae."

He scribbled something in the book next to his elbow. "Purpose?"

"You tell me. I was summoned."

He lifted his head and gazed at her for the first time since her arrival. "Wait. Altoriae?"

She nodded.

He said something about faecal matter, cursing as he struggled to get into a standing position. Arms by his side and chin raised high, the portly man said, "Welcome to Earra, Altoriae. Our council is waiting to receive you."

"Why?" she asked.

"Err..." He looked at her. "They don't really tell me much."

"Really?" Shari asked, making sure to keep her voice light. "You must have some idea, though?"

Scratching the bristles on his cheek, he said, "Rumour has it that they're wanting to go to war. Could be wrong, a'course."

"Who do they want to go to war with?" Shari asked. She'd eviscerate the Realm now if the next word out of his lips was Lissae.

Leaning forward, he said, "Luerix."

"Let your council know that the doorway to Luerix has been shattered. Repairs are estimated to take a millennium or two." She was exaggerating, but hopefully by the time the Ducibus had repaired the gateway, the feud between the two Realms was forgotten.

"Really?" he asked, eyes wide beneath frowning brows.

"Yes, the Sky Mother shattered it."

"Well, I'll be blowed," he muttered.

"Will you pass on the message?"

"Oh, they won't believe me," he said, waving a hand between them. "Hold on." After picking up a small cube, he raised it to his face. "Ruthford here, calling for the council." As he stared into the device, his eyes almost crossed.

Shari's hand fell to the hilt of her sword. The last time she'd seen anything like the cube, Lissaens had died thanks to sentient crystal.

"I got the Altoriae here, and she's some news." Ruthford turned the cube around and nodded at her encouragingly.

"Well met, council." Shari felt ridiculous. "I am saddened to inform you all that the Sky Mother recently shattered the gateway to Luerix."

Tinny voices overlapped as beings in a faraway room yelled across each other.

"If that is all, I shall be on my way." Shari gave a short bow and made for the handle of the door.

"Wait, Altoriae," Ruthford called.

Shari sighed and turned back to face him.

The guard was holding a long tube in his free hand. "Sorry," he mouthed. "The council wants to see you. In person," he said aloud.

"Why?" Shari eased her hand away from her sword. At this range, it wouldn't help against a projectile weapon.

"Says you might have information on other Realms."

Looking over at the peaceful town, the paved bridge, the spires on the other side of the river almost touching the sky, Shari sighed. At first glance, it appeared idyllic. Peaceful. But it appeared their council was as warmongering as any other.

"Do you have a family, Ruthford?" Shari asked.

"Yeah. A husband and wife waitin' for me to get home. Two young ones, and a third on the way." His chest puffed out even more.

"I'm sorry." Shari's Innarn snapped out, Plasma hitting the cube in his hand.

Ruthford shouted and dropped it, shaking his stinging hand, the tip of the tube dipping down. He looked at her with wide eyes, the tube clattering to the ground as he raised both arms in the air.

"Tell them I knocked you out," Shari said. "And that we're closing off the gateway."

"Ye...yes, Altoriae."

She paused, hand on the handle. "And Ruthford? Hug your family close. Don't ever take them for granted."

"Never, Altoriae. They're my world."

Shari nodded and slipped away.

Heading back through the museum, Shari grinned. It had been a pretty successful patrol. No one died or went to war. And now maybe, she'd have time to sleep. Without the nightmares.

Lissae

Narday 3pm

Fourth day of the first week of Nightcrest

Tania looked out over the crowd. They'd all settled into a large classroom at the Vitreus Academy on Talhan, just so they'd all fit in.

Vren, head of the academy, stepped forward and cleared his throat. "Well met, one and all. Many thanks for our Altoriae, the Linked of our Shifting Islands, our elders, and the Altoriae's Guild. You are all invited to our illustrious academy in order to prepare for the joining of our islands to Akoren and Vannali. Allow me to introduce Zana, Rakemyst's Linked, as she guides us through this exciting time."

Trying hard not to look at Cyrus or Fenix, Tania tried to stay composed. She was relatively sure that Vren hadn't drawn a single breath during the whole introduction. If she glanced away from Zana's back towards the other Linked, she would break into nervous giggles.

"Well met, all." Zana stood serenely before the three-hundred-strong crowd, with the other Linked fanned out behind her on the academy's stage. Shari, Jonathan, and Samuel stood on one side of the stage. The bulk of the Altoriae's Guild and the elders looked up at them. "Our thanks for meeting with us. As you have noticed, each time our islands join, we face unforeseen difficulties and challenges. These last two joinings, resulting in a complete convergence, promise to bring more danger than anything we've seen so far."

The weight of Innarn sending was heavy as the guild swapped theories and concerns.

"We are aware of the threat already within our borders. The mainlanders are proving to be," Zana paused, as if she were searching for the right word, "tenacious. It is in our best interest to come up with a plan to keep them at bay with minimum loss of life, on both our side and theirs."

"Why?" asked a voice from the crowd below.

Zana's spine stiffened. It had been the one point she'd been unwilling to bend on. "Many are fighting because they have no option, not because they believe in the rhetoric of their leaders. Aim to incapacitate, not to kill."

"And how do we get them back to the mainland?" asked another being.

"We have the transport Innarnians dotted across our islands," Zana said, her voice firm.

"Altoriae?" someone asked.

Shari strode across the stage to stand next to Zana. They looked like day and night, Shari in her black leathers and Zana with her white wings tucked neatly in.

Tania held her breath. She'd been unsure of what Shari would say, having only run the outline of their plan past the Guardian.

"I have seen enough beings die. I'd prefer to never watch another take their last breath again. In my role as protector of Lissae, I do not have that luxury. In this fight, against our own, I do. We do. We must at least try," Shari said. Suddenly, her head tilted, and she looked above the crowd. "And we will have our chance sooner than we thought to practise mercy. Scouts have reported a fleet of mainlander ships waving white flags and heading our way."

"Do we believe them?" someone shouted.

"The scouts, yes. The white flag? I'll be ready, but I'm not going in Innarn blasting." Shari made to step back.

"Altoriae!"

She stopped and looked towards the voice.

"Is it true you invited blanks into the guild?"

There was movement off to the side, and Eva's blue hair flashing in the light as the girl tried to make herself smaller.

"Anyone who can fight is welcome," Shari sighed. "Provided they agree to the pledge. And the blanks amongst us can wield weapons better than most Innarnians."

Murmuring broke out, rushing through the crowd like Cantash's moving buildings. Shari stepped back, leaving the stage free for Zana.

"Who the Altoriae wishes to invite into the guild is not the discussion for this session," Zana said. "Now, about the defences..."

Shari sighed. '*How is there still prejudice against blanks?*' she sent to Jonathan.

'*Because the Realm is rotating?*' Samuel shot back. '*Beings fear what they do not understand, and for one born with Innarn, to be without it is incomprehensible. The same for one born without it.*'

'*I know, but I wish…*' Shari sucked in a breath.

'*You can protect them, so they are free to make their own choices,*' Jonathan said.

Shari nodded. '*Sometimes, their choices suck.*'

The two men on either side of her hummed in agreement, the sound lost amongst the mass exodus as Zana released everyone back to their duties.

"Wait!" a voice called.

Samuel tensed as Shari turned.

"Anika, now isn't the best…" Shari started. A bag was thrust in her direction, which Samuel intercepted.

"Here," Anika said. "That's for you three. Try not to wrinkle it any more than it has been." She turned to the Linked and shoved a larger bag towards Zana. "That's for all of you. I'm sure you'll be able to tell who belongs to which outfit. Now, if you need me–" Anika sniffed and looked away.

Frowning, Shari took a long look at the other girl. Her makeup was smudged, tear tracks lined her face, and her hair was tangled. "Anika?"

"I have to go," she said. "I haven't figured out what I'm going to d… do." Anika sank to the floor, arms wrapped around her middle.

The Linked converged around the two girls as Shari knelt next to her former tormentor.

Samuel's words stopped everyone in their tracks. "Who do I have to kill?"

Anika looked up, a frown marring her features. "What? No. It's just… My father kicked me out." She hiccupped and scrubbed a hand across her face.

"Right," Samuel said.

'*Wait*,' Shari shot at him, reaching out blindly and wrapping a hand around his calf. Samuel froze. Sneeze peered down at her from his shoulder, giving her a gummy grin.

"What happened?" Zana asked, waving a hand a finger's length away from Anika's face. Her makeup cleared and resettled, masking the upsetting day and hiding it from any further bystanders.

Taking a shuddering breath, Anika settled a metaphorical mask back in place. "He asked me to leave this morning and packed all my things into bags. I tried to go home after school, but he refused to let me in. Now I've nowhere to sleep. Nowhere to sew." Anika looked and the Altoriae's heart broke.

"You can stay with me," Tania said. "Or there's rooms at the castle, and Samuel's old house is free. One of the refugee families was going to settle there but said it felt too dark for them." Tania glanced at Samuel. "Sorry," she added.

"It would be perfect. You can decorate it with your father's hide," he added.

Shari dug her nails into his leg. Sneeze leaned up and bit Samuel's ear.

"Or not," he added, prodding Shari with a jolt of Innarn.

She dug them in more.

"I appreciate the thought, but I'd rather not have a reminder." Anika paused. "I may take you up on the offer later." She batted her eyelashes at him half-heartedly.

"Very well," he said stiffly. Shari released his leg, patting the spot and sending the darkest healing Innarn she had his way.

"How many bags do you have?" Jonathan asked.

"Just a few," Anika said. "They're at the school."

Shari reached out and found the small mountain of luggage leaning against the side of a bereni tree at Ridden Hall. She shifted the bags to the side of where they were standing, having no desire to be crushed. "Want an escort?" she asked.

"Shari," Jonathan warned. He knew as well as she did that by escorting Anika, someone now shunned by her family, the Altoriae would be making a very public statement.

'You're going to let him get away with this? He was horrid to me, fine. But kicking his own daughter out? Rany Thorne deserves every bit of shame heading his way.'

"You're going to need a hand," Jonathan sighed. "There's no way you can carry everything by yourself."

Samuel picked up a bag in each hand, Jonathan grabbed another, and Shari one as well. The Linked each grabbed a bag, and a few of the Returned joined in, with Collis silently stepping up next to Tania. With Anika's belongings gathered, the group set off. Jonathan, Shari, Samuel, and Anika leading the way.

As they trooped through Talhan and over the bridge, curious beings joined in, wondering what the Altoriae and her Guardian were doing with all the bags.

Jonathan broke the silence, his voice carrying through not only their group but the gathered residents of Ronah as well. "Did you know I was six when I was kicked out of home?" he said. "There was just enough time to scrounge a change of clothes and a few ziom beads. I think you'll fare far better than I did."

"I didn't know that," Anika said softly. "It's odd to think I have something in common with the Guardian."

"More than something, I'd say," Samuel rumbled. His Innarn was fairly lashing around him. Others were giving him a wide berth. Shari created a subtle shield that contained the Dark Innarn without dulling the menace he was exuding. "You're both stubborn, resourceful, and good at making friends, even when you aren't aware of it."

Anika blushed.

They walked by a group of her former friends, all of them gaping at the spectacle and tittering behind raised hands.

"I'm not so sure about that," she said, ducking her head.

"You have talents outside of mere mortals. You'd have to, to get Shari into a dress," Jonathan said, nudging Shari gently.

"Hey!" she protested. "He's not wrong though."

Raising her head, Anika blushed harder.

"Here we are," Jonathan announced cheerfully.

The Linked and guild members poured into the house to drop the bags off, each saying a quiet, kind word to the shocked girl.

The crowd following them had swelled in size. Standing at the head was Rany Thorne, fists clenched.

Shari crossed her arms and stared at him. It was Samuel's turn to shield the others from her Innarn, although he made a show of it, wiping non-existent sweat from his brow.

Anika stood just behind Shari, hesitating in the doorway of what was now her home. Shari felt the weight of Anika's gaze on her father.

Rany stared.

The crowd wasn't helping as they looked between the two to see who would say something first.

Terrance, Rany's brother, stepped up to him, clapping a hand on his shoulder. With one last look, the man who had raised Anika turned away.

"Don't you dare let them see you cry," Shari hissed at Anika. "If you do, I'll... I'll split a seam."

Anika gasped in mock outrage. "You wouldn't dare," she laughed, loud and bright.

Rany froze, his shoulders bunching beneath his jacket. He made to turn, but Terrance shoved him forward, and he kept walking.

The crowd gradually thinned out, a few of the elders promising to bring meals or food over later for the displaced girl. Anika thanked everyone and quietly slipped inside.

"Will you be alright?" Shari asked from outside the threshold.

"I will now," Anika said. "That's twice you've saved me."

"Does that mean I get to skip the dress this time?" Shari grinned to show the other girl she was joking.

"Oh, maybe," Anika laughed. "Thanks, Shari."

"I bid thee well." Shari dipped her head and waited for Anika to close the door before she left. Flicking a finger, she put up the strongest wards possible around the house and set off to find her parents.

Leaving Anika in her new house, Tania beamed to find Collis waiting for her outside.

"Well met," she said, wishing the heat rising to her face would go away.

Collis caught her hand and bent down to rest his forehead on hers. "Well met. How are you feeling?"

"Glad that we were able to help Anika." Tania took a moment and breathed him in. Out of all the beings in the Realms, Collis was the only one who felt like home. Linking her fingers through his, she tugged him in the vague direction of the bridge to Ronah. "We've got everything sorted for the joining, although part of your magnificent wall will have to come down. I was thinking we could make that into a big reveal. I swear, planning a joining is much easier than what Mum wants me to do."

"What does she want you to..." Collis broke off.

A lanky guy carrying a towering pile of books as tall as his torso had his nose buried in the top one and was barrelling down the dirt path, right towards Tania.

Books clattered to the ground as he bounced off a broad chest.

"Collis!" Tania reprimanded.

"I should let you get hurt?" He glanced over his shoulder at her.

"No, but, well. You're a rather unmovable force. I could have just stepped out of the way."

Sighing, Collis reach down and heaved the fallen guy to his feet by his collar.

Eyes wide, he blinked owlishly at Collis then caught sight of Tania.

"We've met before, haven't we?" he asked.

She nodded. "I'm Ronah's Linked."

"Well met," he said. His skin shifted and twisted slightly, pulling back into the lotus roots most Wisara favoured. "I am Akoren's Linked, however, most call me Domic Iabor. My apologies for missing the planning meeting. The Elder Weavers had requested my presence on a matter relating to the joining."

Something about his tone indicated that Domic was not about to answer questions as to what he had spoken with the Elders about. "Well met, Domic." Tania smiled, holding out a hand to help him up. "I'm Tania Bryant."

"Tania Bryant?" Domic's gaze slid to Collis's towering form behind her. "Not for long, I'd wager."

She blushed at the other Linked's smirk and turned, catching Collis's gaze.

He was unashamedly looking as if she'd hung both moons in the sky. "Not for long," he whispered.

Tania cleared her throat. "Um, what brings you to Ronah?"

"The joining. The Guardian gave me some reading material about elemental bridges. I haven't had to practise in a while." Domic looked rather bashful about the whole thing. "Want to make sure I'm prepared. We're only hours away."

Hours. Tania's chest felt suddenly tight. "Suppose we'd better rest up then," she said with false cheer.

Domic gave her a grin. "See you soon, Ronah's Linked."

"Soon," she echoed softly.

Hefting the books higher, Domic strode off down the street seeming confident and at ease.

Would he feel that way knowing what had happened at all the other joinings?

Terrance Thorne cursed the Altoriae.

She'd made his family look stupid once again. Rany had meant to ask Anika to leave, and then welcome the girl home with open arms once she couldn't find a place to stay.

Instead, the upstart just had to jump in and save the Realm, one blank at a time.

Stalking past the Tavern, he spied Arilla scrubbing a table.

How many times it would take before the Altoriae just couldn't keep saving them. What would it take to incapacitate the Altoriae once and for all?

Maybe he'd have to find out.

CHAPTER FIVE

Rasshday

Fifth day of the first week of Nightcrest

aeli's head bobbed above the water. At the edge of the horizon, a shimmer appeared and a faint plume of smoke rose from the towering volcano. The reeds of her face stretched into a grin, and she turned, preparing to dive.

At the last moment, she spotted something else on the horizon. Due west of her position, clouds of a darker smoke were staining the sky.

Mainlanders.

Grin disappearing, Caeli dived under, swimming hard for the elders. Through the seaweed forest, she twisted away from the snapping guard eels, reaching out to stroke along the back of her favourite. The water was clear now, and she swam harder. Schools of fish darted around her before hiding in coral groves. Diving, Caeli followed the glowing line of Akoren's underbelly, trailing her fingers amidst the lit-up creatures and poking a few to help light her way through the darkness ahead.

The water turned the colour of the night sky at the deepest points under the island, and the glow-worms guided her. Swimming on, Caeli suppressed a shiver as she passed through the glacial-cold water. Gills flaring, she kicked harder, and within moments, the water grew lighter, and she was free of the cold. Rubbing her arms, Caeli paused for a moment, the Wisara's city sprawled out before her.

The buildings nestled against the rocky bottom of their island, with the bigger ones encircling the outside and the smaller homes positioned closer to the middle. Lights from angler fish or the glow-worms dotted the water outside, but beneath the cove, the morning sun made the water sparkle. Wisara of all shapes and sizes were scurrying about, getting ready for the joining.

Shaking her head, Caeli swam on. Admiring their city could wait until the Altoriae arrived. She had to tell the elders about the boats.

Laughter pulled Shari from her dreams. She woke sluggishly, glaring at the door which had come ajar in the night. A pair of bright green eyes peered through the gap, scowling at her before disappearing just as quickly.

Groaning, she swung the covers aside but took a moment to lay in the bed. Today was the joining with Akoren, and she was sure that there would be yet another epic fight by the end of it.

"Was it like this for you?" Shari asked aloud.

The ghost of Kay'imi sighed, and Shari rolled her eyes. "The more things change," she muttered. After heaving herself off the bed, she used Innarn to splash water on her face and air to dry it.

From the other side of the bed, Zoomer gave her a baleful look and hid his face under a paw.

Shari chuckled. "You'll have to sleep for both of us," she said and blew him a kiss. "Right now, I think I need a cup of Jonathan's azehal."

Stumbling from the room, Shari wandered towards the kitchen and paused on the threshold to take in the utter chaos.

Dealon was flicking Raven with a towel, trying to get him out of the kitchen. The normally uptight Elani had collapsed in a fit of laughter, and Talofa was, for some reason, hanging from the light fixture with two hands, the other two holding a baking tray aloft.

Dealon yelled up at her, "Those are for breakfast! There are plenty there—you can't have them all!"

Poking out her tongue, Talofa scooped something up from the tray and shoved it in her mouth.

Jumping up to swipe at her feet, Dealon missed, and Talofa giggled at him. He scowled and jumped again, causing her to fumble the tray.

The tray slipped from Talofa's hands, and it fell as if in slow motion. Food spilled out and Dealon, who was too busy trying to gather his efforts with his Innarn, forgot about the vessel containing it.

It clattered to the benchtop, and Shari flinched. Each strike of metal on the stone threw her back into a different battle; scenes of death and destruction burned into her eyelids.

Breath caught in her throat, Shari stumbled backwards. Elani's worried face was the last thing she saw before she shifted out.

Panting, she took a moment and glanced around the back garden of her childhood home. Falling to her knees, Shari dug her fingers into the earth and was reminded of that morning, so very long ago, when Lissae asked her to protect the Realm.

She'd barely hesitated before saying yes. Glancing towards the kitchen window, she'd seen her mother, who'd almost been crushed by a minotaur, and all doubts had disappeared.

Chancing a look at the same window now, Shari froze.

Her father and mother were there, arms wrapped around Grace.

It should be me.

Tears welling, Shari dropped her head. She'd never felt so alone.

Straightening the gorgeous robes Anika had made, Tania pulled herself up to her full height.

She was standing amongst the Linked as they spread out between Ronah and Ginorti's shores, ready to weave the bridges and underwater tunnels she'd created. Temira had said it'd been two-hundred-odd years since the last time Air Innarn had been used to make tunnels, and Tania figured that there were only a handful of beings old enough to remember. The other Linked had agreed, and although Tania was still sad it wasn't an original idea, she was very glad to know that it had worked in the past and she wasn't dooming half the Innarnians to a watery grave.

Even as Akoren approached, the smoke from the persistent mainlanders grew closer. There were a few mainlanders that she considered fit for a visit to the bottom of the ocean.

'Tania,' Ronah chided.

'*They hurt you,*' Tania sent back. '*And your siblings. Surely you agree?*'

'*Remember the plan. All you squishy beings deserve a chance at life. I don't think many of you can breathe water.*'

Sometimes, she found it hard to deal with how forgiving Ronah was. '*Alright. As you wish it.*' She sighed. '*But if they hurt you again...*'

'*We shall move them back to their land where they can't reach me or the others.*'

'Fine.' Tania said and stroked the sole of her shoe over the ground to show she wasn't terribly upset. '*How are we going to safely remove our problem?*' Tania sent to the other Linked.

'*Every joining makes waves,*' Zana replied.

'*We amplify that and send them back to the mainland.*' Cyrus, standing next to Oakley, looked grim. He had metal bits on over the top of Anika's robes, and Tania gulped. He was armed. When they'd met, she'd thought him gentle and goofy, but one look at him now and it was clear he would do everything in his power to protect Talhan.

Akoren was coming closer, his pace gentler than that of some of the other joinings. A figure was standing on the shore, alone.

"Ready?" Tania asked aloud, shaking her fingers out.

Standing just behind her, Shari hummed in agreement, and Tania felt the net of Innarn sending spread. Beings all across the joined islands held their weapons at the ready. The amount of Innarn in the air had the fine hairs all over Tania's body standing on end.

As Akoren drew closer still, the being standing all alone became clearer. It was Domic.

"Where are the others?" she whispered.

'Guarding the underbelly,' Zana sent back. 'Watch the waves.'

With Akoren looming before them, it was hard to see the waves flowing from the sides of the landmass, but Tania caught sight of more than one green-tufted head ducking under the whitewash.

"Ready?" she asked again as Domic's features became distinguishable. Glancing to the side, Tania noted the ships were billowing smoke, struggling to get closer. 'Can we do something about them yet?' she sent to Collis.

'Of course.' Her soul-match sounded so confident.

The ships froze in the water, the sound of straining metal reaching the ears of those on the shore as the engines struggled against Innarn.

'Bridge!' Zana snapped.

Tania pulled her attention back to Akoren, her hands shooting out in front of her as Plasma coiled around her wrists and flared from her fingertips. Next to her, Zana's Air Innarn weaved into the start of the structure.

'Altoriae?' Zana asked.

A breeze kicked up behind Tania as Shari, Jonathan, and Samuel all shifted across to different points on Akoren.

Standing shoulder to shoulder with Domic, Shari cut an imposing figure in her leaf-embroidered jacket. Despite never meeting, the two worked in tandem, saltwater rising and becoming solid as it rushed towards the Plasma and Air to bridge the gap between islands.

'*Is it just me, or did Shari hesitate?*' Tania frowned, pouring extra effort into her side.

Across from her, the ocean spray flicked up, and Shari flinched.

The ice on the bridge cracked for a moment, water seeping through the gaps. Gasping, Shari snapped her hands out and turned it solid once more.

Jonathan, standing across from Fenix and Oakley, chanced a glance back at Shari. Tania's eyes, laced with concern, flicked to the Guardian. He'd felt it too.

Samuel faced Cyrus, who stood on the bridge between Ginorti and Ronah. He froze but didn't stop. Together they had to breach the biggest gap and combine the new bridge from Akoren with the old one. Ice met crystal.

As the last of the bridges connected, the first fat, white flakes of snow fell from the sky.

Raising her head, Tania laughed, the joyous sound ringing out across the gathered beings.

Shari stood rigidly next to Akoren's Linked, who was panting. She, Jonathan, and Samuel had let Domic guide their Innarn in the shape of the bridges he had wanted. They had been mere vessels for his wishes, and from the sweat he wiped away, it had been a strenuous exercise for him.

"Well met, Altoriae," Domic said.

"Well met, Akoren's Linked," Shari replied as Jonathan and Samuel shifted to stand on either side of her. Both men reached out with their Innarn to discreetly support her. She half-felt like slapping them away and half like collapsing in their arms. Locking her knees, Shari stayed where she was.

Across from them, Tania and the other Linked were still hard at work, using Air Innarn to make the tunnels Tania had envisioned. Letting her Innarn unfurl, Shari could feel the tunnels and the trickle of water that was escaping into them. Shoring them up as best she could, Shari turned back to the conversation.

"The leaders of the Wisara wish to invite the Altoriae and her closest companions," Domic was saying, "to explore our city before the others."

Shari wanted to ask, *Why us?*

Jonathan beat her to the answer. "We would be honoured."

Gritting her teeth in a parody of a smile, Shari couldn't decide if she was horrified or scared.

The Altoriae, scared? A mocking voice, which sounded like the Anika of old, echoed through her skull.

Right then. Linking arms with Samuel and Jonathan, more so she didn't run off, Shari followed along as Domic led the way along the edge of the cove to a looming waterfall.

Hoping the others couldn't feel her trembling, Shari shook her head. There was no way she would get near the spray of that thing. From the tensing of their arms, Jonathan and Samuel noted her apprehension. Domic, however, was leading the way and bypassed the fall to a tiny stream with rocks along the bank.

They arrived at a spot that gaped open like a mouth of a giant. The sight reminded Shari of the beast below the waters of Altum, and a quick look at Samuel indicated that he was thinking the same thing.

"Welcome to the hidden entrance of the elders. Occasionally, we don't wish to get quite as wet as travelling through the ocean makes us. On those occasions, we use the cave entrance."

"Does it have teeth?" Jonathan laughed like he hadn't pulled the thought directly from Shari's head.

Domic laughed, a low, watery sound. "Not this one."

'Not *helpful*,' Shari sent to Jonathan.

'*Decidedly not helpful*,' Samuel added.

"Well, in we go!" Domic said and jumped into the hole.

Shari counted to three before the faint splash of his landing sounded.

The hole was too small for the three of them to go at once. Jonathan untangled his arm from Shari. "I'll see you down there," he said. With a reassuring smile, he jumped.

"I don't want to do this," Shari gasped. Her Innarn flared around her for a moment, darker than she was used to. She huddled next to Samuel, taking in gasping breaths.

"Use your Innarn to control the jump. Jonathan is waiting for you," he said gently.

"Can't I just go home?" She felt like a fraud. Her heart was pounding fast enough to escape her chest.

"What was that water Realm you visited recently? The one with the mammoth beast from the depths of the Nine Hells that chased you? This will be nothing like that. And you thought that was fun." Samuel grinned at her. "You can do this."

Taking a deep breath, Shari nodded. Before she could change her mind, she jumped.

Arilla gripped Calem's hand harder when Shari appeared on the shore opposite to them. Standing on Akoren's side, their daughter looked far from the frail, broken being who'd lunged into Arilla's arms when the door to the Realm of Zuefie had opened. Shari was still returning to the girl they knew, but it was gratifying to see the progress she'd made so far.

"Still can't believe my niece is the Altoriae," Wolf grumbled.

Belfar laughed. "She's better suited to the job than any other being on this Realm."

Wolf rolled his eyes but left his arm wrapped around his mate's waist.

A little way in front of them, Ronah's Linked let out a whoop of joy. She was standing atop the rapidly lowering landmass which was morphing and changing.

The mountains that had sprung up overnight along Ronah's shoreline shifted, rocks tumbling towards the water and disappearing without a splash. Someone in the surrounding crowd exclaimed, pointing at the lowest point of Akoren's shore, where the rocks were reforming, keeping them safe once again.

"We're so close," Arilla said. "The joining with Vannali can't come soon enough."

Calem sighed and tugged on her hand, leading her to the tunnel of Air Tania had created. "Every time I think about the convergence, the sense of dread and change gets bigger."

Wolf and Belfar made noises of agreement.

Laughing, Arilla said, "Don't be silly. Ronah will be at her most protected then." She ignored the gnawing feeling of wrongness with practised ease. Keeping her smile in place, she joined the queue for those travelling to the Wisara's city. She shot Wolf and Belfar a look of surprise. "You're venturing under the water?"

"That's where Shari is," Wolf said, a muscle in his jaw twitching. His feathers flared for a moment before settling.

Looks like she wasn't the only one ignoring the uncomfortable today. "You'll get soggy feathers," she teased.

"Bit hard to get crystal wet," Belfar said. "The one benefit of a prosthetic wing."

Wolf chuckled, though his cheeks darkened as his thoughts seemed to wander elsewhere.

Laughing, Arilla took the opportunity to jump into the tunnel.

The water was freezing. Air steamed as she breathed out, and Shari found that being in a cave full of water wasn't quite as terrifying as she'd thought it would be.

Samuel landed with a grunt next to her, the whites of his eyes wide in Jonathan's Innarn light globe.

"Well, the quickest way to get to the city are the air mats," Domic said. "Jump on." He reached into the darkness and pulled out a mat full of air. The sides were higher than the base, and he clambered on, laying down and looking totally at home relaxing in the flowing water. "Once you're on, just push off the side and the current will do the rest." Domic did exactly what he said and disappeared into the darkness.

"Come on." Jonathan gave her a wide grin and wasted no time in grabbing the next mat. He floated off, whooping as he went.

Shari felt like she wanted to heave. Glancing at Samuel, she wasn't the only one. He'd turned a faint shade of green, and his chest was moving too fast.

'*Breathe,*' she sent. '*If Jonathan can do this, so can we.*' She pulled a mat out of the shelf and handed it to Samuel before grabbing another for herself.

'*You and Jonathan both have a habit of nearly dying on Lissae. That's not exactly the pep talk you were hoping it'd be.*' Still grumbling, Samuel waited for her to lay down before copying her.

After counting to three in her head, Shari carefully pushed off, letting the current claim the mat. She half wanted to close her eyes and just wish for the trip to be done. Instead, she tipped her head back, looking at the... glowing ceiling.

"Samuel," she hissed. "Look up."

She heard his indrawn breath and grinned into the dark.

Far above their heads, the ceiling was awash with blue light.

'*You've found our glowers,*' Domic sent. '*It's part of the reason the elders prefer this path. They get to relax and enjoy sights the others don't get to see.*'

'It's *amazing*,' Shari replied.

They floated for what seemed like forever. Clouds of steam lay thick when she breathed out, the glowers removing the fear that would have come from the sight had she been in the light.

'*We're coming up to the drop now. Hold on to your mat. You'll feel your feet angle down. It's safe, so long as you don't rock it.*' Domic's send was gentle enough not to startle her, although the slight splashing from behind indicated it didn't work on everyone.

'*Here we go,*' Domic warned.

Counting to ten, Shari's feet started to tip down. There was a moment of absolute panic, and then she was falling. Water was rushing by—fast. Although she was holding her breath, it wasn't actually touching her. The cave twisted and turned, water propelling the mats along until they were spat out into a wide hall, where the Wisara elders were waiting for them.

Jonathan's Innarn wrapped around her, helping the Altoriae to rise gracefully to her feet in front of the strangers before them. She did the same for Samuel before looking closer at the crowd.

Not total strangers. There was Brayden, next to him was the Lore Teller, and a few of the other Wisara who had fled from Ronah's shores after summoning the hantra.

"Well met, Elders," Jonathan was saying as he bowed his head. Shari copied the movement, feeling Samuel do the same.

"Well met, Altoriae, Guardian, Apprentice. Welcome." Brayden bowed to each of them.

Others from Ronah appeared in the hall, her parents and uncles amongst them. Belfar was shaking his crystal wing, droplets flying everywhere.

"Thank you," Shari said. "I'm glad to be here."

Brayden's eyes flicked to the side for a moment, a wide grin appearing on the twisted roots making up his face. "We are glad you have the time to look through our city immediately," he said.

"Barring any sudden Realm-saving," Fenix said from behind her, their arms crossed soundly as they scowled.

"Perhaps the Altoriae is more comfortable around water than fire?" Brayden hummed and turned before anyone could refute his claim.

Shari ground her teeth together, but a swift shake of Jonathan's head stopped her from saying anything.

Sneeze, comfortably atop Samuel's shoulder, had no such compunction, and a tiny jet of flames shot out towards Brayden. With a practised movement, Jonathan put the flames out before the Wisara saw.

From the big grin Fenix wore, they had noticed.

Twining her arm through Cantash's Linked's arm, Shari set off, tugging the reluctant Daen with her. Domic swept past them with an apologetic glance and caught up with Brayden.

With Innarnians, there was no need for them to tip their heads together to talk in hushed tones. Shari could feel the sending flying between the two as they serenely led the small group towards the water flowing by an invisible barrier.

Domic turned to the group and grinned. "Well, we can give you the tour from here, pointing out all the sights and ensuring you can see your fill of the city, or we can get in the water and show you all what actually lies in the depths of our home. Which would you like?"

Wisara of all ages were creeping closer to the group. Elders mixed freely with tiny children who were still learning to control and shape their bipedal forms. They were all looking at her group curiously.

Shari gritted her teeth and fought to keep her hand off the hidden pommel of her blade. The thought of being covered in moisture again, with no control, was not particularly thrilling.

The smile Akoren's Linked wore started to fade. "Of course, if you don't want to, there's no need." He turned to the barrier, his thin shoulders held high. "On the horizon you can see the..."

"I was taken captive."

The words brought everyone to a standstill.

Blinking, Shari sucked in a breath between her teeth. The words were hers. "I was taken captive," she repeated, stepping away from Fenix and closer to the barrier. "By Innarn-sucking clouds. They would loom over me, dousing me in water until I thought I was going to choke on it."

Sucking in a breath between his teeth, Domic shuddered. Slowly, he turned to face her. "And you are here? Standing in an underwater room, surrounded by unfamiliar faces? You truly are brave."

"Let's take it up a notch, shall we?" Shari asked.

Domic's eyes shone.

CHAPTER SIX

Spyglass pressed to his eye, a sailor shouted from the crow's nest, "We're closing in!"

This tedious journey is finally coming to an end. Indijo sighed and looked at the approaching Shifting Islands. Tiny figures dotted a mountain range. "Could have sworn that was a beach," he muttered.

"Wot?" a sailor asked as he rushed past.

Tommie shook his head. "Nuthin," he said, the accent a perfect mimic of the man who'd spoken.

Without warning, wood creaked and metal groaned alarmingly. Tommie grabbed hold of the side as the ship moved. The white flag above their heads snapped and tangled in the sudden breeze.

The deities had different plans for us, Tommie thought as the land masses on the horizon retreated. Pulling his hood up for the meagre protection it offered from the sea spray, he withdrew, going below deck. Now was not the time to help the surly sailors who were cursing up a storm at their lost prey.

White flag, Na'reh's behind. The sailors had no need for peace when they could plunder instead.

"Ready to get wet?" Domic asked.

Shari nodded.

'There is no shame, Altoriae.' The send sounded like the foam on the top of the waves felt. 'Not all like the water.'

'Akoren?' she asked.

The island above their head rumbled.

Domic grinned even wider. "Well, it looks like someone likes you," he said.

'I might struggle with the water, but I want to learn more about your people. About you.'

'Don't worry, land fish. I'll protect you so long as you're within my waves.'

"Land fish?" she asked Domic.

Wrinkling his nose, Akoren's Linked nodded. "He really likes you."

A shoulder bumped into hers, and Shari turned, expecting to see Fenix next to her.

Caeli, one of the former candidates was there instead. "I might not have sworn the oath as one of your guild members," she said, "but I can still protect you better than they can in the water."

There was a vague hissing going on behind as Samuel tried to get Sneeze to go to Fenix. Soothing thoughts flowed easily as Shari promised to bring Samuel back to the tiny draci.

'Are we doing this?' Jonathan asked.

'Looks like it.' Shari swallowed heavily. "Lead the way."

Domic beamed and took a step backwards, through the barrier and into the ocean beyond. Caeli joined him without hesitation.

Shari controlled her shudder and stepped up to the barrier, Jonathan and Samuel by her side.

'Get in the water,' Caeli sent. 'You won't regret it.'

Closing her eyes, Shari took the final step.

All sound faded the instant she was enveloped in water.

Shari looked around. Domic and Caeli were both mouthing something, but she couldn't hear them.

The Realm was silent.

Jonathan and Samuel broke through the barrier, and with them, sound rushed back in an overwhelming cacophony.

Domic and Caeli were both babbling in terror, their eyes wide and voices frantic as they overlapped each other in a desperate bid to communicate.

Behind them, a dark shape was rising from the depths, getting closer the louder the two Wisara shouted.

'*Enough.*' The send wasn't loud, but the tone of absolute authority made Shari flinch. Their Wisara guides turned and faced the grey-skinned being. '*Show the Altoriae around and see she returns safely to land.*' The being sank, returning to the depths he'd appeared from.

'*Who was that?*' Shari sent.

Jonathan waved a hand, and the entire group of land-dwellers had their heads covered in a bubble, making it feel less like she was drowning.

She shot her Guardian a grateful look.

'*The head of our elders. That he would appear now...*' Caeli sent. Her thoughts were laced with panic and bloodstained water. Apparently this elder had a taste for outsiders.

'*Well.*' Domic's smile was strained. '*Shall we start the tour?*' He turned without waiting and swam away.

With a glance at Jonathan and Samuel, Shari followed, taking in all the sights Akoren had to offer.

The buildings of the city were clustered up against Akoren's rocky underbelly, gel-like barriers keeping the water out of homes and businesses alike. Domic pointed out their library as they went past, the Wisara inside tending to books without any fear of the damp getting to them.

Jonathan, of course, had to stop. "How do you prevent damage?" he asked.

"Innarn," Caeli said drily.

"The books are made of crystal. You merely tap the page to read the next one." Domic sent a chiding glare at the younger Wisara.

Caeli rolled her eyes. "You're just mad cause I'm rereading Everon Castor's latest book, and you can't have it yet," she sneered.

Jonathan caught a smug look on Samuel's face that seemed entirely out of place. Why would he care about Caeli's reading material? Ignoring his apprentice, Jonathan turned away from the library and back to their host. "That's quite similar technology to our newspaper slabs," Jonathan said mildly.

"Come," Domic said. "I'll show you one of my favourite places." He swam on, idly pointing out spots of interest. A school surrounded by kelp, farms of fish and seaweed, homes of their elders, the best cafe in the whole ocean, and the dark, where only the bravest of Wisara ventured.

Finally, they came to what must have been close to the cove, as sunlight was streaming through, warming the water around them. Domic pressed on, until they were bobbing above the waves.

Jonathan cancelled the bubbles around their heads as the group swam to shore. The Returned shifted in to her location, reluctant to leave her protection to those they didn't personally know any longer. They crowded around Shari in their typical arrow formation, making room for Jonathan and Samuel amongst their ranks.

"This is my favourite place," Domic said. When he glanced back to see the Altoriae surrounded, he blinked but ignored the extra bodies. "This is where I spoke to Akoren for the first time."

Shari glanced around, using Innarn to poke at the bodies in her way. Instead of moving, the Returned projected the view straight into her head.

Smoky green leaves against black sand dunes, mountains whose peaks she could see even above Collis's head. A patch, over to the side, perfectly shaded and moulded to fit Domic's body.

The Linked slumped into his hollow and waved a hand. Other spots to sit were created, enough for them all, and vaguely in the same pattern they were standing in. "Come, let us turn away the rest of the day with tales of a fairer kind. I'm sure I can spin something to put a smile on your face, Altoriae," Domic said.

'He's *no Lore Teller yet, but he can make you laugh,*' Caeli sent, pushing past the edges of the Returned to sit close enough to Domic without being intrusive.

Collis sucked in a breath. '*They're soul-matched.*'

Remmy dug an elbow into the taller boy's ribs. '*Looks like you're not the only one matched to a Linked then.*' He stepped forward. The Returned moving effortlessly with him until they were all seated in the shade, a light dusting of snow melting on the black sand.

Shari settled in, grinning when platters appeared all around them.

Domic started to weave a tale of a boy chasing a fish up a tree.

Before she knew it, Shari was laughing along with the others.

Vebaday

Sixth day of the first week of Nightcrest

Jonathan looked at the blank page of *The Altoriae's Handbook*. He could have sworn he'd sent the information about the latest patrol to book, but it seemed he'd done it in his sleep.

It was something he'd often been guilty of doing, but this time, the tactile memory of holding the quill had been real. Rubbing a hand over his face, Jonathan sighed. Maybe he just needed to get some more rest.

Hours later, a knock at the door had him looking up. Leaning back, Jonathan kneaded at the crick in his neck. "Come in," he called.

Asterion's horns rounded the doorway first. "Well met, Guardian. You have a reporter from the *Shifting Island Sentinel* here to talk to you."

Jonathan's eyebrows rose. "A reporter?" he asked flatly.

His minotaur assistant looked at him steadily, the corners of his mouth quirking up as a voice beyond the door said something. Asterion coughed, and Jonathan tilted his head. It sounded suspiciously like his assistant was smothering a laugh. "I, ah, think you might want to talk with this one."

"Really?"

Nodding, Asterion tilted his head and chuckled again. "Absolutely."

"Very well." Jonathan sighed, sitting back in his seat. It wasn't like he couldn't get rid of the reporter if they became nosy. He'd found that Asterion was quite picky with who had the pleasure of his time, which made him curious.

Pale golden hair appeared first. Pointed ears followed, and a freckled face peered at him uncertainly.

"Well met. Please come in," Jonathan said.

"My thanks, Guardian, for taking the time to meet with me," she said, her eyes wide as she took in the room. "I'm Ginna, from *The Shifting Island Sentinel*. I understand you're a long-time reader?"

Jonathan frowned. "I am."

She grinned at him, completely unbeguiling. "Your reputation proceeds you."

Innarn started to swirl around him as Jonathan prepared to shift the reporter away.

"Wait!" Ginna said, throwing up her hands. "Miss Jo from the Freeson Library told me."

"And what were you doing in Freeson?" Jonathan asked.

"Research." Ginna slumped into the chair across the desk from his. "You're an intimidating figure, you know? It's a bit hard to know what to ask if I don't know who you are."

"And who am I?" His Innarn was settling down, but Jonathan found it difficult to relax.

"A sailor's son turned orphan, who somehow travelled halfway around the Realm for a chance to become apprentice to one of the most ruthless Guardians of all time."

"That's not why I did it." The words slipped out before he could censor them.

Ginna sat forward, elbows resting on her knees, a small crystal slab dangling from one hand. "Then why?"

Jonathan laughed, the sound drier than Akoren's black sand. "To tell him off."

Her mouth fell open. "You went from Freeson to Ronah, at seven years old, to tell Guardian Joshua Clemise off? Why?"

"My father had died on patrol. Weeks later, so did the Guardian's Apprentice. There was an article where he used the exact words he had for my father. I thought they both deserved better than a rote reply." Jonathan rubbed the back of his neck. He couldn't remember the last time he'd dredged that story up.

Eyes wide, Ginna asked, "What happened?"

"He made me his next apprentice."

Ginna's hand flew to her mouth. "Did he know? About your father?"

"He did. Joshua was deeply apologetic. The training almost killed me a time or two, but there was really no better way to prepare me for what was to come."

"Was your first meeting with the Altoriae a little less... fraught?"

Jonathan shook his head. "Hardly. The first time I met Shari, she had a gaping wound and dripped blood all over my lounge room floor."

Time flew, and before Jonathan knew it, someone else was knocking. Pushing with his Innarn, he checked who was on the other side.

Zac.

"Who did you just think of?" Ginna asked, tilting her head.

'*I have a guest at the moment,*' Jonathan sent. He gave her a tight-lipped smile. If Zac wasn't ready to face the press, Jonathan would not be the one to push him.

'*Do you want me to go?*' Zac replied.

'*Are you ready for the target that's about to appear on your back?*' Jonathan asked.

In answer, Zac pushed the door open. "Well met."

Ginna swivelled in her seat and eyed Zac up and down.

As always, Zac only had eyes for him. Swiftly, he crossed the room, slid behind the desk, and gave Jonathan a sweet peck on the lips.

The reporter beamed at them. "Congratulations!"

Both men turned to look at her, incredulous.

"Don't worry. Not everything needs to be printed," Ginna said, rising from the chair. "Thank you for your time today, Guardian Buan. I really value it. I'll send you the article I'm putting together before my editor sees it, so you can take out anything else you don't want printed."

"Wait. You're a reporter?" Zac said.

"Yes." Ginna tapped a nail against the small crystal slab in her hand. "I think I have enough to go now. I bid thee well." She turned and strode from the room.

"A reporter?" Zac repeated, staring down at Jonathan.

"I did warn you," Jonathan said.

"Not about a thrice-damned reporter," Zac said gruffly, gathering a fistful of Jonathan's shirt and using it to pull the Guardian to his feet. "You and I are going to talk about the correct way to warn someone that the press is around," Zac said.

"Later?"

"Later."

CHAPTER SEVEN

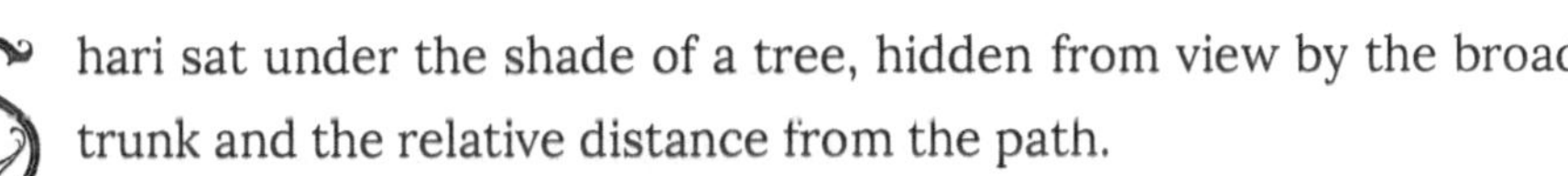

Shari sat under the shade of a tree, hidden from view by the broad trunk and the relative distance from the path.

Jonathan was all concern and caring, tempered with years of knowing which of her buttons he could press without getting a fireball to the face. The members of 'her' guild had all the former and none of the latter, and if she'd had to stick around the castle for one more blasted, *Here, Altoriae, this will make you feel better*, she was going to set them all alight.

No doubt she'd regret it the instant she did.

Their concern, on top of her Innarn acting up, had been too much. Had it been *her* presence in the water that had caused the silence? Or was it some larger, more sinister thing?

The memory of a voice tickled the edges of her consciousness. *Says one of the most dangerous beings on the Realms.* It had been said in a teasing tone, but the sharp edge of truth remained.

Almost as if the thought had summoned the speaker, a scout in a brown cloak flopped to the ground beside her.

"Are we hiding or sulking?"

Shari laughed, but the sound was bitter. "I'm sure Jonathan would say both."

Fiona made a rude noise. "Our precious Guardian wouldn't know his way out of a well-deserved sulk." She picked up a stick and prodded the leaves by her feet. "Maybe if Zac showed him, he'd stand a chance."

The left corner of Shari's mouth tilted up, but she didn't have the energy to do more than that.

"Both it is, then." Fiona sat by her side, and they watched the sunlight filtering through the leaves for what felt like hours. "Do you remember the Chirea? How they caught me, and you thought I was tough? I didn't feel it, not then." Fiona stared into the distance, the stick dangling forgotten in her hand.

By her side, Shari twisted the hem of her shirt between her fingers. "Yeah, I'm not feeling so tough either," she admitted.

"But you are. And I am. What was it you said to me?"

Shari shook her head, too tired to even guess. "I say a lot of things," she hedged.

Fiona sighed. "To be fair, it was more a fleeting thought passed on through Jonathan, than actual spoken words."

Tilting her head back, Shari gave a non-committal hum. "And this fleeting thought was?"

"You've just gone through something that would shatter anyone's confidence, and although it may be an act, you've come out the other side smiling. You are the best of us. We look up to you. I know you won't fail."

Raising a brow, Shari glanced over at the scout. "That's some fleeting thought."

Standing, Fiona dusted off the leaves clinging to her pants. "I may have embellished a bit."

A rough laugh escaped before Shari could stop it. At the sound, Fiona grinned and disappeared before her eyes.

The smile slipped from Shari's face. "You might think I won't fail, but it already feels like I have," she muttered. Lifting a hand, she flicked a finger and a tiny ball of Plasma struggled to splutter to life.

Zoeday

Seventh day of the first week of Nightcrest

Grace reached out and poked Arilla's cheek.

Again.

Eyes fluttered open, and Arilla sucked in a sharp breath. "Grace?" she whispered. She chanced a glance at Calem's sleeping form beside her and struggled out of the covers. "C'mon." Sleepily, Arilla led the way out of the room. She stumbled down the stairs and drifted into the kitchen before slumping at the table.

"What's wrong, Grace?" she asked. Tired eyes glanced out the window, and Arilla sighed. "Please tell me it's important. It's still dark out."

"It's wet," Grace said.

"What is?"

"The sky. White and wet."

"It's snow, Grace. When the weather gets cold, the water in the clouds turns to snow and it falls down instead of rain."

Grace crossed her arms, glaring at the window. "Don't like."

"You don't like it? I'm sorry, I don't think I can stop the snow."

Grumbling, Grace glared harder.

"We have seasons for a..." Arilla broke off, a huge yawn overtaking her words. "... oh, excuse me. A reason. Without them, nature wouldn't be in balance."

"Still don't like." Grace huffed.

"Arilla?" Calem was calling from upstairs.

"Down here," Arilla called back, resting her head on crossed arms.

"Why are you…? Oh. Well met, Grace." Calem casually banished the dagger he'd been holding.

Grace nodded in approval. He should be ready to defend Arilla.

"Are you having trouble sleeping?" he asked, looking at Grace and not his wife.

"Grace doesn't like the snow," Arilla said, her voice muffled.

"And you don't like to be woken up in the middle of the night," Calem said easily, wrapping a blanket around her shoulders.

"No wake?" Grace asked, frowning.

"Most beings need a full eight hours sleep in order to function sufficiently the next day," Calem said. His tone was gentle, and he took care to modulate his words, but Grace still felt them like a slap across the face.

"Arilla not function?"

"Not without sleep, she won't."

"I'll stay away," Grace said and shifted out before they could say anything else.

Skye's nightmares had forced Grace out of their room. She had been planning on walking the streets of Ronah and possibly sneaking over to see the new island and discovering what the fuss was about. The snow had foiled her plans, the freezing droplets confusing. Grace could remember catching them on her tongue as a child, and she had a vague memory of female laughter as someone grabbed her from behind and twirled her around.

No one would dare do that now.

The snow was still falling. It blanketed the town square in white as she huddled under the awning of the tavern. If she was to allow Arilla sufficient rest for the day, then Skye may need time to recover as well. What would she do without them?

Suddenly, the Realm seemed like a very big place.

Anika stepped up to the bridge again, and froze. There was something about the ice that was messing with her head. And although she was sure her mind healer would tell her to look deeper, right now, she really didn't want to. She wanted to see the Wisara. She wanted to travel to their underwater city and discover the new sights and sounds, and she wanted so badly to do it without getting wet.

Others brushed by her with friendly waves and polite greetings, but Anika paid them no mind until someone bumped her shoulder, causing her to teeter uncertainly for a moment.

"What's wrong, niece?"

Anika glared at the newcomer. Terrance was her father's brother. She'd seen him at the constant family gatherings over the years, but the last image of him, leading her father away from her, was stamped into her mind.

"Nothing you can help me with," she snapped.

"Anika?" Arilla was calling her name, the sound louder as she drew closer. "There you are! Thought you'd left without me." The Altoriae's mother wore a bright smile as she slipped between Anika and Terrance, claiming Anika's arm and guiding her away from the other man.

Clearly, she hadn't been the only one to see Terrance with her father.

Rage got her halfway across the bridge before she froze again. Looking down at the ice, she could see through to the water churning below. Gripping Arilla's arm with claw-like fingers, Anika whimpered.

"You can do this. Don't you dare let that mud-puddle of a man think you can't," Arilla hissed in her ear as she forcefully pulled Anika forward another step. "You are stronger than water."

Another step forward.

"Stronger than ice."

Another.

"Look at everything you've done so far."

Every word was another step on trembling legs.

"Look at the mountains. Do you think they cower because others jeer at them?"

Arilla's words ceased to make sense, but Anika kept her gaze fixed on the snow-capped peaks of Akoren.

"And just like that," Arilla said. "You've made it."

Anika looked down. Solid, beautiful earth was beneath her feet once again. She glanced out over the never-ending span of bridge. "And how do I get back?" she whimpered.

"You've done it once," Arilla said, rubbing soothing circles on her back, "and you survived. You can do it again."

A watery laugh escaped. "I don't think that's how it works."

"For this? Of course it is. You covered every step of that bridge with your own two feet. You can do it to get home. I hear you have a training date with a certain member of the guild later?" Arilla teased gently.

As Anika looked back over the bridge, she could have sworn she saw Terrance scowling at them, his hands in fists. Shaking her head, Anika looked again and her uncle was nowhere in sight. Perhaps she'd imagined it.

The chill that raced down her spine said otherwise.

Grace had spent a lifetime watching others. What they liked, what they didn't like, what they avoided, and what they rushed to. As the sun rose, making the town square sparkle, Grace smiled grimly. It was time that she figured out what she enjoyed. She'd gone long enough without knowing.

She wandered the main street of Ronah all day, observing those around her. If someone bent to smell a flower, she'd wait for them to move on and do the same. Others around her age wore clothing like nothing she'd seen before—long, flowing dresses, pants that hugged their skin, and jackets that draped and looked perfect for hiding all sorts of weapons in.

Grace's outfit flicked and morphed as she tried to find the right blend. Loose pants and a flowing jacket to conceal the glint of her blades.

Her stomach rumbled by the time she was happy with her outfit. Thanks to the guild, she'd been introduced to all sorts of new food, but in the main street, there was even more. Fish pie with white sauce and herbs, fresh from Akoren's bakeries, made her mouth water. After snagging one off the tray, she ate it happily, moaning as the flaky pastry dissolved in her mouth.

Food is a good thing.

What else was good? Some flowers were acceptable, but others made her sneeze. Grace felt mildly disappointed when flames didn't appear. Perhaps that was a draci trait?

She wandered past the end of the main street, stopping at a ring of bereni trees. Tiny children were playing some sort of game which seemed to involve kicking a ball and shrieking very loudly. Grace was impressed by the noise they made, and a tiny part of her wanted to join in. As she looked around, she noted there were others who were closer to her age. They were mostly standing around talking, although there were a few with inked skin who were weaving something complicated with their Innarn.

Drifting through the gate, Grace carefully drew closer to them, watching as they wove a mini map of the current islands. Hesitantly stepping forward, she looked down and frowned.

"You like it?" the tallest of the group asked.

"It's wrong," she said.

"Wrong? How?" another spoke. Darker hair, stockier than the first, he was frowning at her.

Grace drew back, wrapping arms around her middle.

"Remmy," the first chided. "Grace, I'm Collis. This," he side-eyed the other, "is Remmy. Who has apparently forgotten his manners."

"Well met, Grace," Remmy sulked.

Grace liked him, despite the Innarn rumbling under his skin.

"How is the map wrong?" Collis asked, voice gentle despite his size.

"No bottom."

"The mainlanders can't attack from beneath," Remmy said. "They don't…"

Below them, Ronah rocked.

"Thank you for coming today, Shari. How are you?" Her mind healer smiled brightly at her and gestured to a chair. As Shari sat, ze sank into the one opposite and looked at her expectantly.

"Fine." Shari crossed her legs, hands clasped tightly, so she didn't fidget.

The healer's smile didn't dim. "And how did you sleep?"

"Fine," Shari repeated. She'd found out during the first session that ze had never been off-Realm—had never seen battle or the insides of a creature before. Ze had had a decidedly green tinge after Shari had described her nightmare in detail. When her whole purpose in life was to protect beings, she found it difficult to burden such an innocent with her troubles.

"No more nightmares?"

"None," Shari lied.

"The Guardian said you had," ze chided.

Shari didn't flinch. "He must have been mistaken."

"I can't help you if you won't talk to me," ze sighed. "This is our sixth session. How can I get you to open up?"

"I won't burden you with my problems," Shari said.

"You aren't a burden," the healer soothed.

Biting her tongue was the only thing that stopped Shari from blurting out the latest nightmare. "Do you know of a healer who has been in battle?" she asked instead.

Ze drew back. "No. Because of the nature of our jobs, mind healers are uniquely unsuited to the battlefield."

It was the sniff at the end of the little speech that did it.

Shari rose. "I thank you for your time. I won't be returning."

"Altoriae, wait!" Ze rose as well.

Freezing, Shari looked at zir. "So that's what this is about. Feather in your cap because you're the mind healer of the Altoriae?" Shari sneered. "Not anymore."

She stormed out of the room, shifting to the highest point of Ronah.

Glowing eyes in a wisp of white flickered as she appeared. Ignoring it, she stormed right up to the edge and screamed.

On the other side of the chasm, where Rakemyst now was, a furred head popped up from the undergrowth.

"Altoriae?" Yessna said.

"I'm going to run through the next being who calls me that," Shari snarled. She swiped at the angry tears tracking down her face.

Yessna appeared by her side. "What happened, little healer?"

"My mind healer." Shari kicked at the snow on the ground and used a blast of air to clear it from a fallen log.

"Your mind healer made you scream?" Yessna tilted her head. "I have not heard of that method. Does it work?"

Shari rubbed at her throat. "Well, I feel better, but my throat is raw. Ze wasn't the one who suggested it." Shari shrugged and looked away. "It kind of just came out."

"You did put a lot of power into it." Without preamble, Yessna sat next to Shari. "Why are you seeing a mind healer?"

"Jonathan swears by them. It's all good for him. But the one assigned to me wanted to treat the title, not actually help me."

Yessna growled low in her throat.

"Said that mind healers were 'uniquely unsuited to battle'—how is ze going to help me if ze doesn't understand what I'm talking about?" Shari threw her hands in the air then slumped, elbows on knees, her head hanging.

"Zir gives us a bad name," Yessna grumbled.

"Us?" Shari asked numbly.

"Not all mind healers avoid battle. Some have no choice."

Shari glanced at her companion. "You're a mind healer?"

"Someone had to be. The stuff we see, the things we do, it needs to be talked about."

Blinking back tears, Shari asked, "Would you be willing to talk to me as well?"

Yessna huffed at her. "Why do you think I call you a healer? You are so much more than a protector, Shari Dawn."

Giving a watery laugh, Shari leaned against Yessna and sighed. Maybe the nightmares would fade properly now.

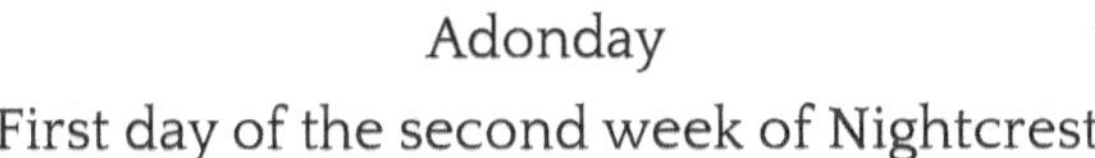

Adonday

First day of the second week of Nightcrest

Shari tapped against the wards of Samuel's new house.

'*Altoriae!*' There was a thundering of giant feet, and a big black head pressed against the window to peer out at her. '*Why are you out there?*' Jetonyx asked.

'*It's polite to ask for entrance, rather than barging in,*' Shari said and waved at Jetonyx.

His head whipped away from the window. '*Shari is here.*' The send was deafening, even if Shari appreciated the sentiment.

'*Come in, Shari,*' Samuel sent as he opened the door.

Stepping through, Shari grinned as she spotted Jonathan on the wide couch. Kemanyr had her back claws on his belly, front paws on his shoulders, and was sniffing his face intently.

Tormorylth was watching from her perch on the arm of the couch, amused. She had put on some much-needed weight and was almost eye-height with Shari now. A vast improvement over the tiny creature who had just been bones and scales when they first met.

'*Well met, all,*' Shari broadcasted.

Jetonyx slid up to her and rested his head heavily on her shoulder. '*You haven't been by in ages. Did you forget about us?*'

'*Never!*' Shari sent. '*Saving the Realm is a full-time job. I would far prefer to hang out with you all here.*' Soothingly, she patted the scales along his jaw.

"He'll hold you to that," Samuel said, flopping down next to Jonathan. Sneeze grumbled from his shoulder, but still lifted his head to shoot flames of greeting at Shari.

A door leading to a room off to the side opened, and Zoomer trundled out, legs getting slightly tangled as he sleepily wandered over to Shari and lent against her.

Surrounded by Q'Aralide, her Guardian, a creature who shouldn't exist anymore, and a tiny ball of black-scaled ferocity, Shari finally felt safe. The tightness in her chest eased, and she drew a full breath. "I do need to come and visit more often."

Tormorylth gave her a sly glance. '*You could move in here. Your island is clever. I'm sure it would be easy to add another room. Or you could share Sanithane's.*'

'*Tormorylth,*' Samuel's send was harsh, but the hatchling just smirked at him, all three eyes glinting with mischief.

"I'm not so sure it would be easy," Jonathan said, gingerly transferring Kemanyr over to Samuel's lap. "Innarn hasn't been working as it should. I've had reports from all over the islands, but this morning, mine started to fail as well."

Shari snapped her gaze over to him, careful not to jostle the Q'Aralide on her shoulder. She sent a gentle probe into Jonathan's mind, but he shoved her out, a blush staining his cheeks.

"I have a witness," he said, refusing to meet her eyes.

"Do you mean Zac finally stayed over?" Shari teased.

"What would Zac's presence have to do with Innarn acting up?" Samuel asked. He grunted as Kemanyr jumped from his stomach to the floor, trilling as she went.

Wriggling her eyebrows at Jonathan, Shari giggled as his blush deepened. Tormorylth was looking between them in fascination.

"It's not Zac who made the Innarn act up," Jonathan said gruffly. He shot Shari an unamused look.

"Then why would…" Samuel started to say.

'They're trying to have hatchlings!' Tormorylth burst out.

Shari couldn't help but laugh, leaning back against Jetonyx.

Jonathan covered his face, groaning.

Samuel frowned. "Two males can't have hatchlings," he idly corrected Tormorylth. Shari saw the instant realisation set in for him. *'This is allowed?'* he sent on a narrow band to Shari.

'Yes. So long as two beings are consenting,' she sent back.

When Shari had first met Samuel, she would have been disgusted that he had to ask, but after seeing a tiny portion of how he'd grown up, she'd gained a better idea of why he thought *any* two beings needed permission. Their whole way of creating the next generation was foreign to him.

Frown turning into a smirk, he nudged Jonathan in the ribs. *'Congratulations.'*

'That's not… we just fell asleep.' Jonathan cleared his throat. "The bigger question is, what is happening with our Innarn?"

"I may have an idea," Samuel said slowly. "But you're not going to like it much."

Jonathan just raised a brow.

"We are all aware that Lissae is the Mother Realm, yes?"

They all nodded, even Zoomer.

"Perhaps she is gathering energy."

"Why?" Jonathan asked.

Samuel's gaze locked onto Shari's. "What do mothers do?"

After sucking in a breath, Shari whispered, "Give birth."

The three looked at each other, the colour slowly draining from Jonathan's face.

Collis raised his brows as Tania stormed out of her house, huffing.

The memory of an aborted conversation struck him. "What is your mother trying to get you to do?" Collis asked. He was standing just inside the fence, Esse pecking at the ground by his feet.

"She wants me to organise a natal day celebration!" Tania threw her hands in the air, huffing.

Collis tilted his head. "And this is a bad thing? Who is it for?"

With her skirts billowing dramatically as she strode towards him, Collis felt intimidated by Ronah's Linked for the first time since they'd met.

"Me," Tania all but hissed.

"Your natal day is coming up?" he asked, heart sinking. *How did I not know my own soul-match's natal day?*

"In a week. There's a *convergence* happening. Surely that would take precedence, but no, apparently turning seventeen does!" She huffed and crossed her arms tight against her chest.

He wanted to hug her so badly. "Perhaps I could help?"

"How?" she wailed. "The Linked are determined to make sure that nothing stands in the way of the convergence, and at the speed we're going, it'll happen sooner rather than later. Probably right when the party is, knowing my luck. Then it's all..." She broke off, her voice muffled against his chest.

Collis had given into the urge, and she practically melted in his arms. "I might not be able to help plan the joining, but perhaps I can help with the party? Relieve some of your burden?"

Eyes wide, Tania looked up at him. "Really?"

"If you so wish." He smiled down at her.

"Thank you," she said and wrapped her arms around his waist.

His stomach sunk. Collis couldn't even remember the last time he'd celebrated anyone's natal day. What if things had changed? What were the current protocols for one of the Linked celebrating another turn around the sun? He vaguely remembered dignitaries coming from all over the Realm for his mother, and tiny, fancy cakes he'd been too scared to touch.

'*Remmy,*' Collis sent, '*how do you plan a natal day?*'

Arms linked, Arilla and Calem strolled towards the main street of Ronah. It was odd, living on Rakemyst now that SilverCloud had gone to the Spirit Realm.

Looking at Calem, she noted the new frown lines. Tugging on his arm, she said, "I think we should move back."

He smiled at her, but it did little to ease the severe expression he wore. "I was just thinking the same thing." His gaze slipped away, and he nodded at Edward Thorne, who was in his garden, tending to Harmony's beloved carrots.

"With your Innarn, we could be home tonight." Arilla grinned.

"Don't count on it," Edward said. "Everyone's Innarn seems to be on the fritz since the battle. Think some of those dampeners managed to get through."

"Why?" Calem asked.

Edward gestured to the hanging pots, the leaves drooping sadly over the side. "Winter's coming. I have a warming charm that's been working flawlessly for decades, but this morning I come in and—" He opened his hand, and in his palm was a smattering of frost-covered leaves. "This shouldn't happen. Figure I'm just tired, though. I'm going to finish up and rest."

"Good idea," Arilla said.

Calem hummed, but his frown deepened. Edward gave his goodbyes and disappeared back inside.

"I hope he and Harmony get a decent rest. Nar'eh knows they deserve it."

"I wonder how many other people are having issues?" he said. "If the best gardeners on Ronah are struggling, who else is?"

Jonathan paced around his office, paging through *The Altoriae's Handbook* to see if it offered any clues. Really, he should get out and go for a walk or head to the training ground to let off some steam. The idea of Lissae giving birth was frightening. He couldn't remember being so terrified since Shari's test to prove she was the Altoriae.

"Guardian?" Asterion knocked on the open doorframe.

"Yes?" Jonathan turned to face his assistant.

"There's a message on your Crystal Send. From the mainlanders."

Perfect, Jonathan grumbled to himself. "What does it say?"

Asterion, lips pursed, held the Crystal Send out to him.

After placing the ancient book onto his desk, Jonathan took the slab and tapped the top corner to activate it.

"Well met, Guardian." A very officious man was staring down his nose at the screen, his eyes narrower than the multitude of tiny bars on his shoulder pads. Vague memory told Jonathan that this meant the man was someone high in the mainlanders' defence forces. "We want to ensure you received our message about the troops who wish to train with the Altoriae. If we are to continue to defend the Realm, we need to guarantee our troops are at their fighting best. In order to do so, ships filled with our finest soldiers are on their way to you now. Please make them welcome and ensure that their training mission is a success."

"That can't mean anything good," Jonathan muttered.

"Nothing good at all," Asterion said.

"What do you make of it?" Jonathan asked, curious.

"A threat worded as a request."

"Me too." Jonathan ran a hand over his face. "And just what does their training mission entail?"

"I am loath to find out," Asterion said, looking out the window of the office. It was high enough that, had the mountain wall not been there, they could have seen the sea. And potentially their attackers as well. "What should we do?"

"Set a watch along the outside of the islands. Divert some of the patrols, perhaps. I think we need to take the threat seriously." Another attack from the mainlanders was the last thing they needed right now.

For the first time since they'd met, Calem saw Collis fumbling with a tray of food. The Returned boy had been helping them at the tavern almost since he'd arrived back on Ronah.

Collis caught it before so much as a drop could be spilled, but it was clear he was distracted.

Calem waited until Collis came back into the kitchen before saying anything. "Are you alright?"

"Not really," Collis admitted. "Tania's natal day is coming up, and I have said that I will organise a gathering in her honour. I'm not sure what traditions have changed since our time away. There is also the matter of a present." He sighed and scrubbed his hands on the dish towel hanging from his belt. "I don't know what to do for either of the things."

"We host parties all the time. Arilla and I would be more than happy to help you out." Calem grinned.

Collis bowed his head, and Calem stifled a grin as the tension visibly ran out of the boy's frame. He remembered what it was like when he'd first met Arilla, and trying to come up with the perfect present for her natal day had been nerve-wracking.

"As for a present, what does Tania like?"

"Innarn," Collis blurted then sheepishly ducked his head.

"Arilla was much the same when we met. I took her on a picnic under the stars and used Innarn to draw shapes in the sky. We still go stargazing now and then." Calem bent to get the next lot of baking out of the oven.

Collis gazed around the room sightlessly, no doubt trying to come up with a similar plan.

Had he ever looked so hopelessly in love? He was sure that Wolf would say he still did.

Grinning as the spark of an idea alighted in the boy, he nodded when Collis muttered, "Thank you," and rushed from the room.

"To be young and in love," he murmured and turned back to the baking.

CHAPTER NINE

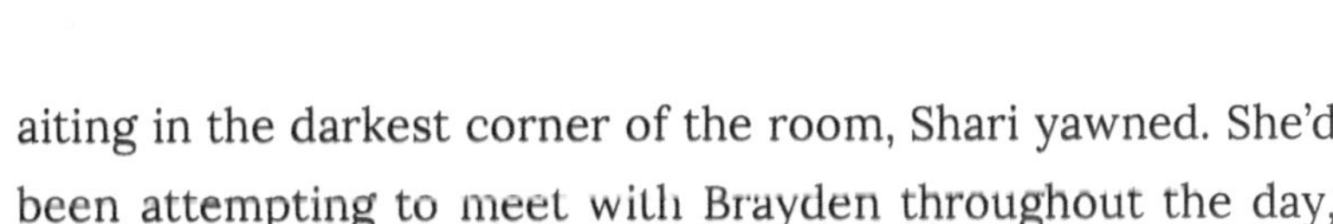

Waiting in the darkest corner of the room, Shari yawned. She'd been attempting to meet with Brayden throughout the day, but the Wisara leader had proved challenging to locate.

Domic had let her in, hours ago if she was any judge of the dissipating light under the water outside.

Brayden's house was surprisingly dry for a submerged dwelling. Decorated in blues and greens, the feel of the inside mimicked the rippling beyond the gel window. A type of coral made up most of the slightly spongy walls. Shari was propped against one. It felt like an age since she'd been able to rest without fear of being stabbed, and she had dozed off accidentally.

Now something had nudged her awake.

Shari's jaw dropped when Brayden crossed the threshold. The roots forming his body sloughed off like week-old sunburn. At the end, he shook himself and sighed, clearly relieved of the burden. He threw a loose robe on and traversed the room to a long bench.

"Is it all a lie?" Shari blurted.

Brayden's features hid his galloping heart well. "Hardly, Altoriae. It is, however, amusing to watch how uncomfortable land dwellers are around those they consider being different from them." He paused for a moment, considering. "It does let us move around the water easier, too."

Shari tipped her head, conceding his point.

"You're here to talk about..." Brayden's lips were moving, but it was as if the sound was sucked out of the room.

It came back in a rush.

Brayden moved to retrieve a glass. Shari noted the shaking of his hand as he poured the drink.

It wasn't just her.

Wriggling a finger in her ear to get rid of the ringing, Shari said, "Silent moments."

Nodding, Brayden said, "The Lore Tellers have often warned of what lies in the silence."

"I must have missed that one," Shari said.

After taking a long pull from his drink, Brayden sighed. "The silence holds menace of a different kind. That we have not faced in our memory. The tales of our ancestors say that in the silence, lies something we cannot escape."

"A monster?" Shari frowned.

"We don't know. I thought the old tales were told to warn us. To listen to even the quietest of sounds. Now I find myself unsure."

"Since the Realm went silent when I entered the water, you mean?" Shari said.

Brayden poured a second drink and held it out to her. "Precisely."

Shari found it hard to be offended when she was just as worried as he was. She took the drink and stared as tiny lights blinked in the swirling blue liquid.

Tossing back the rest of his drink, Brayden then poured himself another. "My people have been demanding to rectify the wrong we did to you."

"When you summoned the hantra?"

"Exactly."

"And how are they expecting to do that?" Shari asked, trying to temper her tone. She failed, by the look Brayden gave her.

"An allegiance ceremony."

Shari choked on her drink.

Inthday

Second day of the second week of Nightcrest

Arilla hummed softly as she moved around the kitchen, getting an early breakfast ready. She'd snuck off to the tavern before Calem had woken in order to get the preparation for the day sorted so she would have time to train her growing class of weapon wielders.

There was the soft pop she recognised as someone shifting. Arilla was sure that Innarnians weren't even aware that they made the noise, but perhaps her lack of Innarn meant she was aware of things they weren't.

"Arilla?" Calem called.

"In the kitchen," she said.

Calem was by her side in an instant, swinging through the serving doors with flowers in his hand. After giving her a kiss, he murmured, "You didn't have to get up so early."

"Training today," Arilla replied.

"Maybe I should join you?" Calem grinned. "It's been a while since I've swung a sword."

"Only if you can keep your feathers to yourself." Arilla smiled at him. Lost in Calem's eyes, she almost missed the front door opening.

He pressed a lingering kiss on her cheek. "I think I can manage that," he murmured.

"Ew," a voice said.

The two sprang apart, Arilla reaching for the sword strapped to her side.

"You're worse than my pare... friends," Anika said, nose wrinkled in mock outrage.

Arilla's jaw fell as Grace dropped from the rafters above their heads, growling at the other teen.

Holding a hand against her pounding heart, Arilla drew in quiet, practised breaths. "If dealing with Shari growing up as the protector of the Realm didn't kill me," she muttered to Calem, "having her cousin hiding in the rafters when we're trying to have a moment to ourselves shouldn't either."

Grace's chuckle was more rusty than menacing.

Arilla glanced at Calem.

He shrugged, as if his heart wasn't beating as fast as hers. "Keeps us on our toes."

Wolf smiled as Belfar flew in a loop around him. Their team had been assigned to fly around the perimeter of the Shifting Islands since the mainlanders seemed to have lost their collective minds.

Who thought attacking those who protected you was a good idea?

Varlee and Charin were up ahead, the others were a little way behind, and he and Belfar were in the middle. His mate had woken up in a good mood today. It was rare enough that Wolf allowed the goofing off, instead of insisting he fly in formation.

Belfar looped him again, playfully creating a downdraft that ruffled Wolf's feathers in the wrong way.

Then he grunted.

His full weight fell on Wolf's back, their wings tangling together.

Mid-flight.

The others were far enough away that they weren't able to catch him.

Wolf reached for his Innarn, shoving his wrists together and slamming his arms out to the side to summon a cushion of Air.

For the first time since he'd mastered the move, there was no response.

Garbled yells from the others and Belfar's panting, too-fast breaths in his ear drowned out the pounding of his pulse. He tried again.

Nothing.

The ground was getting closer.

The team were circling them, desperately trying their own Innarn.

Closing his eyes and ignoring the rushing wind, Wolf attempted the cushion motus again. When they jolted to a stop in midair, he gave a ragged sigh.

Belfar whimpered in his ear. '*I'm sorry*,' he sent, his thoughts whirling. '*My wing just... stopped.*'

'*We're safe*,' Wolf sent back. '*Try again now.*'

Wolf felt Belfar flex and stretch, and the powerful downdraft as his mate lifted off.

Everyone was looking at him.

Tensing his jaw, Wolf drew upright and glanced around the team. They were almost home. He glanced at Belfar, who nodded. '*Why are you still here? We need to complete the circuit.*' Wolf took off, straining to gain height again.

It was difficult to fly with shaking wings.

Chamele had already survived one attempt on her life last week when an aberration had crafted some sort of exploding device and escaped, leaving her feeling weak and dizzy. The back of her head still ached horribly.

She'd upped the guards, making sure there were two at the top of the stairs, another pair in the hallway just out of sight, and the head guard—*What was his name?*—would be right next to the slatted door while she attended to today's attempt at a cure. He was running late, but the man's obsession with her would ensure his arrival.

Turning her attention back to the task at hand, Chamele plunged the stopper from the needle down, forcing the yellowish mixture into the aberration's flesh.

It screamed, the sound dulled by the ziom walls of the dungeon.

"Oh, do be quiet," she scolded. "Or we'll have to gag you." The guards had dragged it into the hall to make sure the others could witness and marvel at the cure.

The beast thrashed out, attempting to kick her.

Tutting, the elder stepped out of the way. "You are bound. What do you expect to achieve?"

From the cell behind her, a voice rasped, "Redemption."

"I'm afraid you're out of luck." Chamele smirked. The quiet tapping of boots on the floor made the elder grin. "See?"

The aberration in the cell flicked a glance over Chamele's shoulder and smiled, showing bloodstained teeth. "Oh, I see."

A chill raced down Chamele's spine.

"All right?" asked the newcomer.

The voice was not that of the head guard. Perhaps she really did need to pay more attention to the man. At least he thought to send a replacement when he was tardy.

"Could be better," answered the aberration in the cell.

The one bound to the seat gibbered, foam frothing from its mouth.

"Get this one back in its cell," Chamele demanded.

"I'd be delighted to," the newcomer purred, far too close to her ear.

Chamele's arms were roughly grabbed and she was shoved forward, slamming bodily against the door of the cell that housed the sneering aberration. Calloused hands turned her around, and the elder gawped at the man who was decidedly not wearing a guard uniform.

The hit to the head must have dazed her more than she'd realised. It took several long moments for things to click in her mind. *He's killed the head guard. Now I'll never find out the man's name.* Chamele frowned at her captor.

"Some things don't deserve to live, Jo," the not-head-guard said, holding her easily in place as he sneered at her.

"It'd be easy, wouldn't it?" 'Jo' said, hands patting Chamele's pockets as it searched. "Snapping her wretched neck and watching the life leave her eyes. Tempting, even."

Trembling, Chamele knew better than to beg. She had never listened when they tried, after all.

"Do you know how many she's taken?" The sneer fell from its face. "Kids. Total innocents. She pumps them full of filth and watches them writhe."

The searching hands had reached her neck, and Chamele froze as they stretched around. Her heart seemed to stop in her chest.

There was a blinding pain as the chain with the keys was ripped away.

"Oh, I don't think we have much to worry about. Her guards are gone. And the Fixed Islands are being overrun by off-Realmers. Under her orders, the mainlanders stopped going to patrols. Now they'll pay the price."

The key rattled in the lock, and Chamele all but fell through the door, falling roughly on hands and knees. The aberration in the cell landed a stunning blow to her stomach, and the elder fell to the side.

A shape crouched next to her. "When they find her, alone and begging, what do you think they'll do?"

There was a raspy chuckle from the former cell inhabitant, and both aberrations were up and gone. The door was closed and locked before Chamele got her breath back.

"Wait!" she called. The sound went no farther than the door.

There was no answer.

Her attackers hoisted the latest experiment into their arms and walk away without looking back.

Chamele cursed and curled around her throbbing stomach.

One of her guards would be here any moment.

Any moment.

CHAPTER TEN

Kerday

Third day of the second week of Nightcrest

Tania dodged a third person as she hurried through the streets of Talhan, wishing she had Collis by her side. At least he would help her avoid all the beings who seemed intent on crashing into her.

The residents of Talhan still had their B.I.R.D.s, the Bio Instructor for Relative Distance to guide them, but there seemed to be some sort of malfunction.

A metallic screech from above seemed to prove that theory, as a B.I.R.D. shuddered to a stop, its person wandering away unsupervised as the machine rocked in place in the sky. Tania watched in fascination, passing carefully underneath the B.I.R.D. as the crowds pressed against her. As soon as she was directly underneath it, another machine crashed into the first, sending them both tumbling from the sky.

Gaping at the flaming wreckage above her head, Tania forgot for a moment that she was an Innarnian. Strong arms wrapped around her middle and whisked her to the side, while an Innarn shield sprang up around the burning B.I.R.D.s.

She turned to look at her rescuer, the ink on his skin glistening slightly under his sheen of sweat. Collis had been running to reach her side but didn't seem to be out of breath.

Shaking his head, Collis tucked a strand of hair behind her ear. "Remember to have your shield at the ready," he chided gently.

"I can do that," Tania said, slightly breathlessly. She stared at him, gaze dropping to his mouth for a moment.

Gently setting Tania on her feet, Collis smiled at her and rubbed his thumb over her cheek. *'Our first kiss is not going to be in the main street of Talhan, jostled by people who have forgotten to look up.'*

Tania blushed and tore her gaze away from his mouth. *'Of course not, I...'*

'I will see you to Temira.' Collis bundled her against his side, and they strode off.

Against the solid press of his length, it took Tania a while to think of anything other than their almost kiss. Three beings in front of them collided and scolded each other, causing the thought to be lost. Safe to observe those around her, Tania noted that more than once, beings were crashing into each other. The tension seemed to rachet up a notch every time it happened.

"Something's wrong," she said.

"Very wrong," Collis agreed.

Tania couldn't wait to see Temira. Maybe she had an idea about how to fix it.

The Techno Centre came into view, a long line of disgruntled beings snaking away from the entrance. Most held hunks of gently smoking metal in their arms, some looking quite distraught.

"Looks like she's busy," Tania said.

'We could shift in?' Collis sent.

'You are a bad influence.' Tania grinned and shifted them to the room where she usually had tea with Temira.

The technomancer was nowhere in sight, but a pot of tea was gently steaming on the table, a cup sitting half-poured as if she'd been called away.

"Maybe she needs a hand?" Tania glanced at the door.

"Maybe she needs the Linked to announce their entry before commencing it," Temira said.

Whirling around, Tania sagged in relief as Temira entered from a door behind them before placing a metallic cylinder with a handle in a holster strapped to her thigh. The bags under her eyes were pronounced, and there was a pallor to her skin that Tania hadn't noticed before.

"Are you well?" Collis asked slowly.

"My Innarn goes to fixing the B.I.R.D.s. Little remains for mundane tasks," Temira snapped.

"Shall I add to the wards Cyrus created?" Tania asked.

Temira sank into the seat to finish preparing her cup of tea. "Yes. Please."

Nodding, Tania got to work. She could feel Collis's Innarn reaching out to her and glanced up at him. He nodded.

Gathering Innarn from both, Tania added to the wards around Temira's room, and the ones around the Techno Centre as well.

The technomancer sighed and took a sip from her tea. "I feel safer."

"That's what family does," Tania said "Keep each other safe."

Temira smiled and set about pouring them tea as well.

With all the things that had been happening lately, Tania was glad to take a moment to rest and reconnect with two of her favourite beings. The falling B.I.R.D.s could wait a while longer.

Rather than face the crushing weight of the water and the many worried eyes, Shari stood on dry land, her toes digging into the black sand of Akoren's beach.

The mountains were in stark contrast behind her, their peaks rising even higher than Cantash's volcano. Before her, the Wisara formed a winding line, following the shore. Behind them, the line stretched beyond what she could see. The refugees who had settled on Akoren were wearing heavy coats and scarves intermingled with long-term residents of Talhan, Cantash, and Ginorti, who were similarly dressed.

'*I don't suppose we could take the chill out of the air?*' Shari asked Domic. There were more than a few bare arms in the crowd.

Domic shook his head. '*It's snow, rain, or in the water.*'

Gritting her teeth, Shari nodded. '*Of course.*' She debated creating a pocket of warmth around them, but the thought of dealing with the slush of melted snow made her reconsider.

Standing just in front of her, Domic was the master of ceremonies, inviting those in the crowd up one-by-one or in their groups to pledge their allegiance to the Altoriae. Jonathan and Samuel stood either side of Shari, the rest of the guild clustered around behind her. Those who had already pledged, including her family, were to the side, nestled up against the base of the looming mountain in conjured seats and wrapped up warm against the chill.

Thoughts about the cold and wet disappeared as Domic waved his arm, and Brayden stepped up to her. Noise rippled through the crowd until all the beings fell silent. The lap of water against sand and the song of hidden birds made Shari grateful that whatever the Wisara feared would not make itself known here.

Brayden stood tall, his white roots gleaming brightly in the morning sun. "Altoriae, the Wisara are many, and our pledges run true. We have already granted a boon to help protect Lissae when you or your Guardian call."

Directly behind him stood Garayen, an elder Shari recognised from their recent visit. He'd been far from happy to agree to the boon Brayden spoke of. Now, Garayen looked tired, lines drawn deep into his roots.

"Today, we come together once more, to pledge our individual allegiance to you and your guild," Brayden continued.

Garayen grunted but said nothing.

"I pledge to stand by your side when what is hidden in the silence comes," Brayden said, his voice amplified to carry through the crowd.

Shari's jaw was not the only one that dropped.

But she was one of the few who heard Garayen's mournful, "No." The elder hung his head, as if defeated.

"I accept your vow, Brayden of the Wisara," Shari said.

Brayden winked at her then stepped aside.

Domic waved the elder towards her.

It was a long minute before Garayen took the three shaking steps forward. "Altoriae," Garayen's voice sounded like dried reeds rubbing together. "My wife died protecting Lissae, long before you began your time as Altoriae. I've watched my brothers and sisters go out on patrol and never come home. I've seen and felt the devastation a family endures when their sole provider dies."

Sucking in a breath, Shari fought to keep her composure.

"So, I will not promise to fight for you or with you. But I do pledge to help the ones left behind. Those who fall through the cracks and require the aid of another need only ask, and I will be there." Garayen bowed his head.

Shari blinked away the moisture gathering in her eyes. "I accept your vow, Garayen of the Wisara," she said. "And thank you for it."

Garayen shuffled off to the side, and the next elder stepped forward.

One by one, those in line stated their pledges, and Shari dutifully accepted them. Promises of healing, aid, cooking, and care from the Wisara.

The Satyrs from Ginorti were next. Shari had been glad that she hadn't had to endure the island elders having discussions of who was first in line, but it was interesting to see that it was General Morrow striding up to her, his long silver hair flowing in the breeze.

"Well met, Altoriae," he said.

"Well met, General." Shari smiled at him.

"It was under a year ago that I found you resting in our glade," General Morrow said. "You took out most of my platoon without breaking into a sweat. Didn't even flinch when I threw my weapons at your feet." He chuckled and shook his head. "Since then, you've faced many more foes." The general paused, and behind him, his troops moved into formation. Squaring his shoulders, the general continued, "For generations, the Satyrs have been Lissae's foremost troops, prepared to fight with blade, bow, and brawn to defend our Realm. But even the strongest fighters need time to recuperate. Not every battle goes according to plan, and there's few of us who have near as many scars as you wear. Altoriae, the Satyrian army vows to join with your guild and take on the battles whenever you need to rest."

Shari tensed her jaw so it wouldn't drop. Her automatic response of, *But I don't need to rest*, felt like ash on her tongue. "I accept your vow, General," she said, voice hoarse.

The rest of the army, grouped behind the general, thumped their fists on their chest plates, the sound ringing through the valley.

The general bowed his head. '*Remember, Altoriae, the vows are there to make use of,*' he sent as he motioned to the rest of the Satyrs to move off.

Digging her fingernails into the back of her leg through the fabric of her pants, Shari nodded and made a show of smiling.

Temira strode up next, a B.I.T. by her side. Shari eyed the machine warily.

Looking somewhere in the vicinity of Shari's left shoulder, Temira, hands clasped in front of her, said, "I vow to ensure you are the best trained Altoriae Lissae has ever seen."

Behind her, Cyrus coughed into his hand.

The technomancer rolled her eyes. "And that if you are incapable of fighting, we… I will supply you and your guild with the tools or healing you need to continue."

"My thanks, Temira. I accept your vow," Shari said.

With a final scowl in Samuel's direction, the technomancer moved off. Other residents of Talhan came forward, with vows of offering strength, crops, homes for the displaced, and words of thanks for stopping the Crystal Intelligence from further decimating their homes.

Shari wasn't sure she deserved the praise. She'd spent most of that battle dead, after all.

The Daen appeared, four of them riding on the backs of their coal-black eobustus mounts, who were shying away from the water. Suspended between the horses was a black box large enough to hold a child.

"Altoriae." Fenix stepped forward. "Not only do you and your guild protect us from external threats but internal ones as well. We vow to aid you in upholding justice and ensure that it is meted out. We also invite you to watch."

The black box rocked slightly, and one of the riders shot a bolt of Plasma at it, a sneer on her face.

"Invite me to…" Shari looked harder at the box. It seemed made of metal, or perhaps ziom, crafted into thick, lattice-type panels. Shari could just see a white tuft of hair.

'Fenix, is that a being?'

The normally happy Linked looked every inch the fierce Fire Innarnian. 'That is the traitor.'

The tuft of hair was replaced with the view of a single, terrified eye.

Milo. The one who'd poisoned Fenix and their mother. Who had cheated and lied with the intention of causing everyone on the Shifting Islands harm. Who'd stolen the golden arrow with the idea that the mainlanders would be able to use it to claim the Innarn of others.

Drawing herself up as straight as she could, Shari said, "I accept your vows, Fenix of Cantash, and on this occasion–" She paused. Her parents, somewhere off to the side, were not going to be happy. "–your invitation as well."

By her side, Samuel cursed suddenly as a white mist appeared before them.

Glowing eyes peered up at Shari, and the fuzzy thought of a send from too far away entered her mind.

'... *watch... rip... tear... teeth.*' The white wisp leaned nearer to her and disappeared.

Shari flicked her hand, freezing everyone bar the two men by her side in place.

Turning to Jonathan, Shari hissed, "Did you see that?"

"I did," Samuel rumbled in her ear. "The Shadow Bringer."

"Did it say something?" Jonathan asked.

"Yes, but it was fragmented." Shari looked at Samuel.

He raised a hand to his shoulder to keep Sneeze from falling off in his time-frozen state. "Shadow Bringers are sent to watch over others. Sometimes to protect, sometimes to kill."

Gulping, Shari said, "Well, it doesn't sound like it's here to make friends. And we have the rest of the ceremony to get through."

"It would be helpful to know *who* sent this one. Maybe then we could figure out why it's here." Jonathan ran a hand down his face.

"It was in Altum as well," Shari said.

Jonathan shot her a look that said they'd talk about it later.

Innarn pulling tight, Shari released the time hold and allowed herself a small sigh.

"We will see you after the ceremony, Altoriae. At dusk, the traitor will meet his fate." Fenix bowed their head, and the Daens moved off.

There must have been some sort of sound-proofing on the box, as Milo didn't make a noise.

Domic watched them go, mouth open.

His expression was exactly how Shari felt.

"I didn't know Fenix was so bloodthirsty," he muttered.

"You try being poisoned for decades by someone who claims to be your friend and see how bloodthirsty you feel," Shari snapped.

"That's why he's..." Domic jerked his thumb in the direction of the retreating eobustus riders.

"Yes," Shari said.

Clenching his jaw, Domic ground out, "I hope he burns."

"I'll ensure it," Shari said, her gaze hard.

Jonathan ran a hand down his face. "That had to be the most interesting allegiance ceremony in the history of Lissae," he muttered, flicking the handbook open.

After dipping the nib of his quill into the inkpot, he set about listing each of the vows. A crystal screen on the wall played his memory of the event back as he faithfully recorded the exact wording from each being.

When the Shadow Bringer came onto the screen, he paused. There was something about the glowing white shape that seemed familiar. Not the look of it. Jonathan couldn't recall seeing a creature with a glowing chest cavity before, but the feel of it.

Scrubbing a tired hand over his eyes, the Guardian sighed. One day, Shari was going to forget to tell him something important.

A knock at the door had Jonathan snapping the book closed. "Yes?"

Terrance Thorne stepped into the room. "Well met, Guardian," he said, his smile jovial enough, but it failed to reach his eyes.

Jonathan slid the book to the side, confident that all Terrance would see was the false cover.

The man came closer, peering at the book. "Getting back to your roots?"

The Sea Tailor's Handbook was scrawled across a boring brown, the white ship barely noticeable.

He hummed uncommittedly. "Was there something you needed?"

"The Altoriae seemed upset today. I was wondering if I could help?" Terrance said. Insincerity oozed from his pores.

"Thank you for your concern. The Altoriae has all the help she needs," Jonathan said. "Did you wish to discuss anything else?" He rose from his chair, scooping up *The Sea Tailor's Handbook* as he went.

Frowning, Terrance eyed the book again. "No, Guardian, thank you for your time. I bid thee well."

As Terrance walked unhurriedly from the room, Jonathan made a note to tell Asterion that Terrance Thorne was not to enter the castle again.

Unless it was for another trip to the holding cells.

As he stalked away from the Guardian's new office, Terrance fought to wipe the scowl from his face. There were too many people in the castle and far too many on the streets of Ronah.

The convergence was the perfect time to make a fool out of Shari, and he had a feeling that the book the Guardian was so jealously hoarding was the key to making it happen.

CHAPTER ELEVEN

Kerday - dusk
Third day of the second week of Nightcrest

Shari stood shoulder to shoulder with Jonathan and Samuel on the rim of Cantash's volcano.

The same four riders who had carted Milo's cage to the allegiance ceremony were making their way slowly up the hill between the rows of Daens who lined the path. Fenix and the other Linked positioned on the far side of the volcano's crater.

Fenix looked serene, their feet almost in the lava, staring over the flickering sparks as if they were thinking of warm water and taking a dip. They held a ziom box in their arms, thick gloves covering their exposed skin.

Tilting her head, it occurred to Shari that the only skin you could see of the Linked was their face. Every other part was covered. Tania, Zana, Cyrus, Oakley, and Domic were the same.

'*Tania, what's going on?*' Shari sent.

'*Promise not to stop it.*' Tania met her gaze over the waves of heat.

'*Should I stop it?*' Shari asked.

'No.'

'*I won't then.*'

'*Cyrus wants a hand in making sure Milo suffers.*'

Biting back thoughts that revenge wasn't healthy, Shari merely nodded. It was not for her to judge the desires of others but to fight for them, so they could choose. However hard that was at times.

The four riders reached the top, and the crowd closed in. If Milo tried to run, there was only one way—into the bubbling lava.

After dismounting, all four riders helped to lower the cage to the ground, and the eobustus were set loose to graze on rivulets of magma.

The crowd moved closer, and someone opened the door to the box.

For the first time since discovering his deception, Shari caught sight of Milo.

His white hair was standing on end, as if he'd been gripping it in his fists. Milo's normally pristine clothing was covered in a fine layer of soot, and he had yellow bruising around one eye.

Running his terrified gaze around the crowd, Milo seemed to realise he wouldn't get help from anywhere and puffed out his chest in a vain attempt to draw attention away from the growing wet patch trickling down the front of his pants.

"Milo, you are charged with five crimes," Fenix's voice rang out, the heat taking away none of the bite. "Three of which were directly against three separate Linked. Two of Cantash, and one of Talhan." Cantash's Linked stepped forward, standing on top of the lava.

For a desperate moment, it looked like their Innarn was failing too, and they teetered. Instead of moving back, Fenix took another step forward and locked their knees, the box held tight in their arms. "The Linked of Lissae have decided that, due to the heinous nature of your crimes, you are to get an additional punishment."

Out of the corner of her eye, Shari saw Samuel's head snap up.

"No," he breathed. Sneeze, nestled against his collar, tucked in tighter, chuffing against Samuel's neck.

In a show of Innarn Shari hadn't witnessed before, Fenix slowly crossed the volcano, gaze fixed on Milo the entire time. Shari felt like melting from the heat, and Fenix wasn't even sweating. Lava bubbled and popped around them, and they didn't flinch or break away. They just continued walking as if they were on solid ground.

"Tell me it isn't." Samuel's gaze was fixated on the box in Fenix's arms.

From Shari's vantage point, she caught the flash of gold when Fenix opened the lid.

Samuel could too, if the litany of curses he was sending was any indication.

After reaching into the box, Fenix pulled out a golden arrow.

Grasping Shari around the waist, Samuel lifted her bodily and placed her behind him, phantom wings coming out to shadow her and Jonathan.

'Zhahyeem, be calm, Samuel,' Tania sent.

'I know very well what that arrow is capable of,' he snarled. 'And you know that Shari and Jonathan are useless at protecting themselves on Lissae.'

'Hey!' Jonathan and Shari sent together, glaring at the back of Samuel's head.

Tania nodded. 'That is a fair point.'

Fenix ignored the ruckus and showed the arrow to Milo, who whimpered.

The sound echoed across the quiet crowd.

"You have been judged and found guilty, Milo of nowhere," Fenix said and stabbed the tip of the arrow into the soft flesh of his belly. They stepped to the side and waved an arm to indicate the traitor's final fate.

Innarn left Milo in a trickle of gold, soaking into the arrow as he contemplated the volcano.

Milo shuffled up to the edge, his legs shackled. Glancing back over his shoulder at Fenix, he looked down at the arrow and up at their face. "I'd do it again," he said, then dove, headfirst, into the lava.

A few beings shrieked, and one fainted before being caught by those around her.

Shari watched until the soles of his shoes were sucked under, a lone bubble bursting where Milo's head had entered.

Fenix tucked the arrow safely back into the box, a lone tear trekking down their cheek.

Slowly, the Daens paid their respects to Fenix before making their way back to their homes, many shaking their heads as they went and muttering about how much their Linked had suffered.

When the last had gone, Samuel stalked towards Fenix and held out his hand.

"What?"

"The arrow," he demanded.

"You can't handle it or..."

"I made the thrice-damned thing," Samuel said. "I know how it works. Give me the arrow and I'll ensure it's disposed of safely."

"That's how you knew the cure," Shari blurted, smacking the back of his arm.

Fenix reluctantly placed the box in Samuel's claw.

He snatched it and the box disappeared between one heartbeat and the next. "Don't play with things you don't understand," he snarled and stalked off, shifting before he'd gotten more than ten steps away.

Jonathan sighed and pinched the bridge of his nose.

Shari patted him on the back. "Would training make you feel better?"

"I think it would," Jonathan said.

Collis stood at the tip of Rakemyst, squinting as the mainlanders' ships drew closer, the setting sun behind them. The endless litany of articles in *The Shifting Island Sentinel* did little to capture the menace the belching ships exuded.

"They remind me of the sedolic packs," Remmy said. "Ready to take a chunk out of you if you breathed wrong."

"What do you think they want?" Collis asked.

"Whatever it is, your soul-match isn't willing to give it to them."

Eyeing the ships, Collis grimaced at the white flag. "At least with the sedolics, you knew where you stood. All of this fakery is the last thing Ronah needs."

"Ronah, eh?" Remmy asked, nudging Collis in the ribs.

Rolling his eyes, Collis motioned to the others, and the Returned spread their Innarn net out, bridging the gap with a ward between Rakemyst and Akoren. Only those without ill intentions should be able to pass through. With Innarn not working correctly, they would still need to be on their guard.

The first ship came to the new ward, the bow passing through unheeded.

Eyebrows raising, Collis poured more power into the ward. From down below, there were a few muffled curses. More than one sailor ended up in the sea after being unceremoniously spat over the railing. A few on deck hurried to throw a lifeboat their way.

On the back of the first ship, a man pushed his hood back and looked up.

Collis flinched, eyes wide. If four hundred years hadn't gone past, he would have sworn that the man was Indijo, his best friend from childhood.

"Remmy, did you see?"

"I did." Remmy's face was pale as he looked over.

Following his gaze, Collis almost dropped his staff. On the bow of the other ship stood Daivi, hair flowing in the sea breeze, face lifted to the wind, and a gentle smile playing on her features.

Collis felt the wards flicker.

"She died, Collis," Remmy said hoarsely. "We saw her body."

"I don't know who is on these ships," Collis said, "and I'm not sure I want to find out."

Jonathan lashed out again, striking where Shari's ribs had been a moment ago.

"Getting slow," Shari taunted him.

He swung again, and she laughed, skipping out of the way.

"Stay still so I can hit you," he grumbled good-naturedly.

"Isn't the entire purpose of training to *not* get hit?" Shari said, smacking his back with the flat of her blade.

"Can't you feel it?" Jonathan asked. He lunged forward, the blade only just missing her.

"Feel what?"

"The rising tension? Beings all over the islands are snapping at each other, and with Innarn failing, it's only a matter of time before it stops working all together."

Shari sucked in a breath then let it go. Lining up her next strike was easy. She hammered Jonathan with blow after blow, making him retreat until his back hit the wall. "Focus on what we can do. We can't change how everyone feels, but we can give them something to hope for."

"I hope you're right," he said.

Shari felt someone come up behind her and ducked to the side, forcing Jonathan to bring his sword up to block the blow.

"Are we talking, or are we training?" Samuel asked. Together, the two men turned on Shari and started advancing.

Dark shadows passed overhead as the remaining Q'Aralide took their places in the stands.

Grinning, Shari snapped her hand down. Bladed glove and sword at the ready, she sprinted towards the middle, throwing a wave at Jetonyx and the hatchlings before turning to face Samuel and Jonathan again.

"What do you make of our newest guests?" Shari asked.

"The mainlanders?" Samuel struck as he spoke.

Shari blocked easily. "Yes. Do you really think they just came to train?"

"Doubtful." Jonathan was quick to flank her.

For a moment, Shari concentrated on keeping her feet as she worked up a sweat blocking blows and delivering her own.

"Do you think we need to worry?" Shari asked, pushing stray hair away from her sweat-soaked face.

'I *could always eat them*,' Jetonyx and Samuel offered simultaneously.

Shari laughed, even if a tiny part of her considered setting them loose on the intruders.

The sound of swords ringing out would help her settle into sleep—if she could defend herself from these two, she'd be able to outlast anyone.

Shari stared down at the knife jutting out of the shield around her ribs. It appeared that Grace had graduated from growling to stabbing at some point. Idly, she pulled the knife free and tutted at her cousin. '*We don't stab others at the dinner table.*'

'*What if they deserve it?*' Grace stared at her, viciously biting into the roll in her hand whilst maintaining eye contact.

Not sure if she should be proud that Grace was finally coming out of her shell, or terrified, Shari sighed. '*Maybe check with Skye if you aren't sure.*'

Nudging the Innarnian next to her, Grace said, "Can I stab the aberat... Altoriae?"

"Grace!" Skye looked between the cousins, horrified. "No! Remember, Arilla would be sad."

"What if she deserves it?" Grace asked. Something about the innocent way she asked it made the malice coating her features all the more intimidating.

Chamele has so much to answer for. Shari bitterly ripped into a roll.

"In what Realm does Shari deserve to be stabbed?" Talofa, sitting across the table from them, asked.

"This one." Grace lunged forwards, knife extended, aiming at Shari's heart.

She batted it away. "I'm not really in the mood to be stabbed this morning, Grace."

Foiled, her older cousin sat back in her seat, almost pouting. "Tomorrow?" she asked hopefully.

"Maybe the day after," Shari said, pushing her chair back and deciding it was probably best she go before Grace changed her mind.

"Day after." Grace nodded.

As she waved farewell to the rest of the guild, Shari bit her lip. What had she just agreed to?

CHAPTER TWELVE

Nanka

After Grace's stabbing attempt, Shari found she couldn't settle.

'*Going patrolling,*' she sent to Jonathan and Samuel.

'*Not alone,*' Samuel shot back.

Shrugging on her jacket, Shari pulled a face. '*You'd better hurry up. I'm leaving now.*' Shifting to the museum, she was in time to see Samuel and Jetonyx arrive in a tangle of wings and limbs.

Shari stifled a giggle and used her Innarn to help untangle them.

'*I'm coming too!*' Jetonyx fairly bellowed.

'*I was going to a Grey Realm,*' Shari said.

"Change it," Samuel growled.

Sighing, Shari thought for a moment. "What about Nanka?"

Samuel nodded and shoved Jetonyx's bulk through the double doors. The hatchling really wasn't designed to remain in the museum for too long.

They arrived at the Nanka's entrance quickly, the Ducibus seeming to hurry them through the portal faster than Shari would have liked.

Pushing through the silver door, Shari teetered on a standing stone that dropped rapidly. Buildings seemed to brush the sky and glowing neon lights lit up the wet pavement that was a long way down. Samuel was swearing as the standing stone he was on dropped as well, landing close enough so he could reach out and touch her. Jetonyx whooped and took to the sky.

The tiny dots of beings far below looked up at the huge shape flying overhead. Flashes of light went off, and Shari hastily threw a shield around the hatchling.

Samuel's eyes were wide as he took everything in. Beings were everywhere, in the street far below, on the bridges of rope and steel which connected buildings like the webs of a metallic spider, and above them, floating on their own standing stones, looking as serene as if they weren't a hundred-odd lengths above the earth.

"Shari," he said hoarsely. "This morning, over half the residents of the Shifting Islands made vows to you. I need you to make one to me—now."

Shari tilted her head. The lights were doing odd things to his skin, making Samuel look both pale and sickly at the same time. "What do you want me to say?"

"That you'll never be alone in the portal again. You will always have someone I trust with you."

"Who do you trust?"

He looked away. "Far fewer beings than you do, I'd wager."

Shari nodded. "Alright. Samuel... Sanithane, I vow to you I will always have someone you trust by my side when I travel through the portal."

Slumping, he said, "Thank you." Samuel looked around again. "Why here?"

"Sometimes the portal just tells me where I need to go."

"And tonight you needed to come here?"

Ignoring the sneer in his voice, Shari said, "Apparently." If she remembered correctly... She tilted her weight forward slightly and the standing stone moved forwards. "Let's find out why," Shari said, and shot ahead.

"Shari!" Samuel yelled and zoomed after her.

Lissae
Narday
Fourth day of the second week of Nightcrest

Humming, Calem wiped the last of the crumbs off his hands and into the scrap bucket. There was a certain sense of satisfaction in cleaning the kitchen, knowing it would be ready to use the next morning.

"Hey, love," Arilla said, coming up behind him and wrapping her arms around his middle. She shivered and pressed up tighter into his back.

"Cold setting in, is it?" Calem asked, turning to wrap Arilla in his arms.

"Just a tad," she said and shivered again.

"Why don't you head up, and I'll make you a warm drink?"

"Mmm, sounds perfect." Arilla leaned a hand against his chest and gave him a kiss then turned and hurried upstairs.

Calem chuckled. When he joined her, Arilla would be huddled under the covers, with just her nose poking out.

After getting the ingredients, he raised his hand without looking, waiting for the cup to leap from the shelf and into his grasp.

Instead there was a rattle then a smash, and Arilla's favourite cup lay in shards on the ground.

Calem stared at the mess. He'd made this drink for Arilla a thousand times before, and never had he shattered a cup.

Using Innarn to sweep the pieces away, Calem then carefully crossed to the shelf and retrieved another cup by hand.

Glancing at where the shards had lain, he sighed. Perhaps he needed to take a leaf out of Arilla's book until the Innarn on the islands stabilised again.

Asterion looked up as the double doors opened. He found it oddly poetic that he was on the Lissaen side of the doors and the Altoriae was the one entering the Realm.

Shari and Samuel stepped through the gateway at the same time.

Asterion opened his mouth to call out a greeting, but no sound escaped. Everything around them was silent, as if his ears had been stuffed full of fur and someone had turned the volume down at the same time.

He shot a panicked look at Samuel, who was too busy ushering his young through the door to pay him any attention.

The Altoriae shook her head and glanced around the room. Asterion felt the brush of her Innarn as it flowed over him. He shivered at the feeling. Fifteen years ago, they had both been in this room, and he'd felt the potential in the tiny toddler back then. Still, he would have never guessed who she would turn out to be.

Whilst the silent moment seemed to have worried Shari, she didn't turn to him for advice. The Altoriae merely pursed her lips, gave him a smile and nod, and shifted away before Samuel could stop her.

Asterion hid a grin as the golden priest cursed the Altoriae and shifted to follow her. He would hazard a guess that Samuel would be concerned about the Altoriae's whereabouts for quite a while.

Jetonyx sighed and looked around. His bulk in the museum was even more concerning than Asterion's had been all those years ago.

Years ago. Something clicked in the back of his mind. In a different lifetime, he'd stumbled across the diary of one of the first inhabitants of Rataeo, the last Realm to be born. There had been something about silence in the diary.

The large black hatchling cleared his throat, shaking Asterion from his thoughts.

'*Would you like to be shifted out of here?*'

Jetonyx nodded, careful to keep his breath trapped behind his teeth.

Dipping his head, Asterion shifted the Q'Aralide out into the freedom of the gardens in front of the museum. Brushing a finger over the tip of his horn, the minotaur frowned. Where the diary had gotten to? It had been such a long time since he'd seen it.

Weaving through the glass cases, Asterion set off for home, determined to find the book.

A knock sounded at her bedroom door, rousing Tania from a half-doze.

"Hey, Tania, are you free?" Alistair asked, poking his head through the opening.

For a moment, it struck Tania how tall he'd become. "Sure, Al." She nodded to the chair at the desk. Rubbing her eyes, Tania sighed and tried to focus on her brother.

Alistair crossed the room and dropped into the chair, lanky limbs spilling over the sides. "I'm, ah... I kinda don't know how to say this..."

"One word at a time is a good start," Tania said drily.

Looking around, Alistair seemed unable to meet her eyes. "Okay. Well, I'm worried about the refugees. I remember what it was like when you came to live with us, and I want to help so no one else will feel that way."

Her heart just might burst. "Al, you can't control how people feel. Sometimes it just takes time for them to settle in. To feel safe."

"Surely there's something I can do?"

"Be there for them, the way you were for us. Ask them the best way to help, because we're all different and they may need things I didn't think of." Tania looked down, tracing the patterns on her quilt. "You have a big heart, Al. Just remember to guard it while you're helping others."

Alistair nodded. "Thanks, Tania." He slipped from the room.

Tania scrubbed at her eyes again. As she lay back down, she shivered. Had she dreamed the whole thing?

CHAPTER THIRTEEN

Rasshday
Fifth day of the second week of Nightcrest

Languishing in a pool of hot water while the snow drifted down around them was not how Tania had thought she'd be spending the afternoon.

Zana had pulled her out of class, apologising so sincerely that her mother couldn't help but cave to Rakemyst's Linked's request for Tania's help to plan the last joining and the final part of the convergence.

The other Linked were lazing in the pool as well, although they weren't idly chatting. Zana was true to her word, the afternoon dedicated to organising the joining with Vannali. Domic had declared that they could do their planning in water as well as they could on land and all but demanded that they use Akoren's hot pools as a way to *relax while they had the chance.*

"Well, I've been wondering," Domic said into the lull in the conversation, "what happens when one of us dies?"

The water around Tania splashed when she abruptly sat up. Tania wasn't sure if she should feel horrified or intrigued by Domic's question.

"Our bodies are entombed within our islands, and our spirits join the ones who came before us. We go on to help guide our island and the new Linked." Zana sounded serene.

"What if we aren't on our island when we die?" he asked softly.

For a long moment, there was only the sound of lapping water.

Zana sat up, water streaming from her feathers. "It's not really an option. If we die and we are not on our island, they will automatically shift us back."

"And with the failing Innarn?" Cyrus asked. "What if they can't?"

"That is an option which doesn't bear thinking about."

"Does that mean we all need to stay on our islands?" Tania asked, her voice small.

"When the threat becomes too great, then yes. I suppose it does."

"Mainlanders have landed," Tania blurted. "Two days ago. The Altoriae's Guild have been keeping an eye on them." She neglected to mention that Collis and the other Returned were spooked by the uncanny resemblance of two of the crew.

"Why are they here?" Domic asked.

"Officially, to train with the Altoriae. Unofficially..." Tania broke off.

"All of a sudden, the threat level is high enough," Oakley said and rose from the water. Fenix flicked a burst of warmth his way, and Ginorti's Linked was gone in a blink.

Tania blew out a breath. She could understand Oakley leaving so abruptly. When Tania had been captured, all she'd wanted to do was get back to Lissae, to Ronah. For Oakley, being on the same Realm but unable to return to Ginorti must have been a special kind of torture.

"We can still send to each other," Zana said.

Nodding, Tania rose as well. "We all need to keep in touch."

Cyrus, Fenix, and Domic made sounds of agreement.

With a last look around the peaceful pools, Tania shifted back to Ronah. Although she had no desire to wander off-Realm again, being able to visit and talk to the other Shifting Islands had been the highlight of her week.

Refusing to give in to the temptation, Tania slipped from the house. She would wander the streets for a bit. Maybe that would help her remember why she had agreed to be Ronah's Linked.

Samuel had escaped the madness of his abode with only Sneeze for company. He stuck to the shadows as he walked through Ronah's streets.

There were a fair few mainlanders gawping at the sights. He doubted they were all hardened soldiers, but Samuel refused to take his chances with the newcomers. It was easy to stay out of their way. Only one or two even noticed him, but with a flick of Innarn, their gaze drifted by like Samuel had never been there. As he wandered, his feet led him towards Lizbeth's house, where the smell of something burning made his nose wrinkle.

Creative curses drifted through the window with a plume of smoke. Samuel was startled that he didn't even recognise some of them. The only thing to do was investigate, he strode up the walk and knocked on the door.

"Don't even start!" Lizbeth yelled. "I'm quite aware of what has happened, and I don't need a busy body from–" The door was yanked open. "Next door. Oh. Well met, Samuel."

"Do I need to eat someone for you?" he said, grinning. On his shoulder, Sneeze perked up, looking around as if to discover where this new prey was.

"Tempting, but no," Lizbeth said. "You can come in, if you don't mind the smell." She was scowling.

Samuel felt a flash of irritation. He did not like that look on her face and wanted to wipe the Realms with the one who had put it there. "What happened?" he asked instead of turning immediately to evisceration.

"I set a timer for the cookies and got caught up in the garden. The timer never went off. I haven't burned cookies in decades!"

"I'm sure they still taste just as good," Samuel soothed. The charred sugar was tickling his nose in the most unpleasant way.

"You don't have to be nice," she snapped, scraping the leavings into the bin. "Just because I can't see doesn't mean my nose is defective as well."

Breathing through his nose was not the smartest choice, but he did it anyway. Lizbeth was one of a handful of beings who was brave enough to talk to him in that tone and survive to tell the tale.

She dropped the pan onto the bench and slumped against the wooden top, head in her hands. "Sorry," she said. "Friends really shouldn't talk like that to each other."

"You must be quite distressed," he said and winced at how stiff he sounded.

"I'm terrified," she countered, her voice so soft, he almost didn't hear.

"Why?"

Lizbeth chuckled. "Innarn is how I *see*. And with it just... not working at the oddest times, well, I can't trust what it tells me anymore. May as well take my niece up on her experiment."

"No," Samuel blurted. "I'll fix it."

"How?" Lizbeth asked.

"I don't know yet, but I will."

As his friend's face lit up, Samuel only hoped that he could figure out a way to keep his promise.

Working at the tavern had a multitude of benefits. The food, the company, and that all newcomers to the island seemed to be drawn to the building.

Counting on this, Collis had asked all the Returned to make sure there were a few of them lounging around the tavern at all times.

His caution paid off when Indijo stepped through the door, arm in arm with Daivi, a group of other mainlanders trailing behind the pair.

Keiran made to stand, only to be yanked back down by Remmy before they held a hissed conversation in a quiet corner of the room.

Indijo and Daivi strolled over to the counter, picking up a menu and glancing through it as if a dozen of their fallen friends weren't sharing the same space they were.

Collis stepped up to greet them. "Well met," he said, too busy trying to catalogue the differences between the not-Indijo and the one he'd known to smile at them. The eyes weren't quite the same—more amber than a lighter shade of brown, and the nose was different. Narrower, rather than the thick bridge Indijo had sported.

Not-Indijo didn't seem put out by his behaviour. "Well met. We'd like to order the stew of the day." He waved an arm to include the entire party.

"And how will you be bartering today?" Collis asked, the words coming out by default.

Not-Daivi laughed, a scornful sound that the woman he'd known would never have made. "Bartering? How quaint. We'll pay with coin, unless ziom beads are no good to you?"

"If that is your wish," Collis said stiffly.

"Aww, did I offend you?" she cooed.

Keiran's chair scrapped across the floor as he rose, fists resting against the table.

Not-Daivi paid the noise no mind, but not-Indijo's hand fell to his hip where a mainland weapon rested. His gaze flicked to the disturbance, brows drawing together when he spotted the intent look on Keiran's face.

"What name shall I put your order under?" Collis asked, loud enough for Keiran to hear.

"Briar," she snapped, "and Tommie."

Collis dropped his gaze, unwilling to let the woman see how she had affected him. "Very well. If you are paying by beads, it will be thirty pieces."

"Thirty!" she exclaimed.

Tommie patted her hand consolingly and reached for the other side of his belt where a fat bag was tied. "Here," he said, counting out the correct amount. "And some extra for a decent drink, if you please."

Nodding, Collis gathered up the beads and turned away, catching Keiran's devastated expression as he went. Despite feeling much the same, he set about serving the mob, ignoring the churning of his gut every time Tommie's amber eyes glanced his way.

In spite of knowing it would have taken more than a miracle for Indijo to still be alive, it hit quite hard to have it confirmed that he wasn't.

After finishing the rest of his shift in relative silence, Collis made sure the tavern was spotless before he left. Locking the doors behind him, Collis then turned towards the castle. He spotted a shadowy figure fugitively glancing around before slipping through a spill of lights from the open doors.

Heart thumping, Collis tried to shift.

Nothing happened.

Cursing, he set off running, sending to the guild as he did so. *'Protect the Altoriae. Protect the Guardian. There's an intruder in the castle!'*

Jonathan sank into the comfortable lounge in his office at the castle, trying to figure out what the mainlanders were after. Tilting his head to the ceiling, he ran through various scenarios, each one less likely than the last.

Closing his eyes, the Guardian sighed. Sometimes, you just couldn't figure out the motives of others until they showed you.

Cold steel touched his exposed neck.

Well, that's one way to find out.

He debated sending for help but figured if he couldn't take out one measly assassin by himself, there was little the others would be able to save him from.

Opening his eyes just enough to peer through his lashes, he spotted someone who looked remarkably like Daivi, minus the ink on her skin and the sneer on her face.

He threw up a ward to prevent his flesh from being sliced, just as his assassin pressed closer with the blade.

The sneer dropped, turning to frustration when she couldn't press forward. "Die already," she hissed.

Jonathan shot upright, startling the woman into scarpering backwards, her dagger tucked close to her forearm.

Showy, potentially not well trained, he thought.

She jumped high, twisting above his head and landing on the seat behind him. Razor-sharp wire wrapped around his throat.

I take it back! Jonathan thought, twisting to the side and jamming the blade Grace had hidden behind the cushions between his neck and the wire.

Of all the beings in the Realm, Anika chose that moment to walk in.

"Guardian, I need you to..." She looked up from the swathe of material draped over her arm. "Huh. Is this another weird training exercise?"

"Not... quite," Jonathan grunted as he grappled with the attacker.

There was a rustle of material and twin clicks. Jonathan managed to flip the mainlander over his head, slamming her to the floor.

Before he could do anything else, Anika lunged forward, burying stiletto blades into both of the woman's shoulder joints.

"Stay," she snarled.

The woman looked up at them, sneered one last time, and bit down on something in her mouth. The assassin started convulsing, foam spilling from her lips, until her eyes rolled backwards and she slumped. Still.

"Is she dead?" Anika asked, her voice only slightly trembling.

Raven burst into the room, bow at the ready. He froze when he took in the scene. "Anika?"

"I killed her," she blurted.

After hurriedly banishing the bow, Raven gathered Anika into his arms.

"She was trying to kill the Guardian." Anika hiccupped. Raven rubbed her back soothingly.

"She chose to end her life. Her death is not your fault," Jonathan said.

Anika pressed her hands together and leaned into Raven.

Collis burst into the room, followed by a pack of others, all drawing to a stop to stare at the dead body in the middle of the room.

"Are those your heels?" Elani asked.

Anika drew herself up and nodded. Everyone ignored the shuddering breath she took.

"Impressive," the Earth Innarnian said. "Come on." She grabbed Raven by the arm, "Let's go get your girl something to take the edge off."

"I needed to talk to the Guardian, anyway." Anika waved a hand dismissively, but Jonathan knew he wasn't the only one who saw the tremble she was trying to hide.

"You'll be alright?" Raven asked.

She gave him a forced smile.

Jonathan grinned. Anika was good for the tracker.

Reluctantly, Raven left the room. The others glanced between them and slowly left. Collis stepped outside and turned his back to the door, leaving it ajar.

"Do you have a sink in here or something?" Anika asked.

Silently, Jonathan conjured a basin with warm water.

"Perfect." Anika crossed to it and dipped her hands in, frowning when the water turned pink.

Jonathan syphoned away the blood and refilled the basin for her.

"Honestly, I thought you'd be more situationally aware as the Guardian," Anika scolded as she scrubbed the blood from under her nails.

Shrugging, Jonathan went to reply and almost jumped out of his skin when a deep voice beside him spoke.

"Unless it's about saving Shari, gnats have more awareness than the Guardian." His apprentice smirked at him. Perched upon Samuel's shoulder, Sneeze chittered angrily at him.

Clamping his mouth closed before he blurted something he'd regret, Jonathan slunk off to the corner.

"You shouldn't let them get to you," Asterion said.

"Where did you come from?" Jonathan hissed quietly.

Not quietly enough, if the twin chuckles from across the room were any indication.

"Hidden door," Asterion said. "It appeared in my room, and a chime sounded. When I opened it, I was here." He glanced down at the body on the floor. "It appears I missed the main event."

"Indeed," Jonathan drawled.

"Me too," Shari said, appearing by his side.

"Bells!" Jonathan said, throwing his hands in the air. "You all need to wear bells!"

They laughed, the tension broken. The mood in the room felt even less oppressive once Shari shifted the assassin's body away.

"Are you okay?" she asked Anika.

The other girl stared at the bloodstain Samuel was removing from the floor.

"I'm not sure," she said. "But I think I will be."

"Some days, that's all we can ask for," Shari said.

Samuel re-entered the Guardian's office, trays of snacks and drinks trailing after him. He wasn't sure when he'd become designated snack bearer, but if it meant being able to snag a bowl of rutenberries all to himself, well, he would not argue.

"I still want to know what the mainlanders are up to," Shari was saying.

"We find ourselves disconcerted," Collis said. "At least two of the mainlanders look like those we know. I don't think the Returned are the best choice for scouting."

Jonathan gratefully grabbed a cup of azehal and drank the boiling brew before it had time to cool. "That's why I've asked some of the Ilutri to keep an eye on them instead."

"Wolf's team?" Shari asked.

Nodding, Jonathan took one of the tiny pies and bit into it, moaning with pleasure.

"What's going on in here?" Zac asked, peering into the room. His eyes widened when he saw the crowd.

Raven and Anika were curled up in the same seat. Collis stood stiffly by Shari, who sat across from them, her legs folded under her in the chair. Zoomer was resting his chin on one of Shari's legs, staring up at her like she'd hung the stars. Asterion hovered behind the desk near where Jonathan sat. For once, Samuel could understand why some beings found the minotaur intimidating. A few of the other Returned were scattered around the room. Yessna had muscled her furry self in as well and was leaning up against a bookcase, picking under her claws with the tip of a blade.

Samuel munched on a berry as he took in the scene, growling when Sneeze bit his ear for not offering his bounty.

Zac crossed the room and perched on the arm of the Guardian's chair, stealing another of the little scallop pies.

Heavy footsteps proceeded a knock at the open door.

"Guardian?" Wolf Dawn called.

"Come in, and well met. What news do you have?"

"There was another of the mainlanders hanging about. A few of the Returned said they recognised him."

Samuel's gaze cut to Collis, who clenched his jaw. "He says his name is Tommie," Collis said. "But he looks like someone we knew from before Anriluka."

"A relative, perhaps?" Jonathan suggested.

The not-so-young boy looked like he wanted to hit himself for missing such an obvious idea. Collis refrained.

Samuel thought about offering to do it for him but kept his mouth closed when Sneeze bit his ear again.

"Either way, this Tommie is looking unimpressed that the assassin has yet to return, which is why..."

There was a grunt, and Wolf's mate entered the room, the bound form of a mainlander draped over his shoulder. The man struggled in his bonds, straining and kicking. Belfar wrapped a steel-like arm around the legs of his captive, wings flaring out behind him.

The bound fool tried to bite into a wing but chose the wrong one. The sound of teeth on crystal scraped through the room, causing most of the occupants to shudder.

"Another upside," Belfar said, shrugging the captive off his shoulder and none too gently guiding him to the floor.

Jonathan stared down at the bound man, and there was a faint shimmer behind him, where the body of the assassin had lain. An outline took form, and it was as if she were back in the room with them.

"Missing someone?" Asterion asked, his voice far more menacing than Samuel had heard before.

The minotaur tilted his head, looking over Tommie's shoulder.

Straining, the mainlander twisted until he spotted the illusion on the floor. "Briar," he moaned.

'Not *Daivi*,' Collis broadcasted.

"Would you have any idea of why Briar was trying to kill me?" Jonathan asked mildly. He put another tiny pie into his mouth.

Tommie looked at him as if the Guardian was mad. "You're eating? With a dead body in the room? What's wrong with you?" he shrieked.

The illusion disappeared.

"What dead body?" Shari asked.

Twisting around, Tommie jerked his chin. "There! That one..." His voice faded as he stared at the spot where his fallen comrade was no longer laying. He whimpered. "What did you do?"

"I'm afraid Briar will not be returning with you," Jonathan said.

"Why not?"

"She tried to kill me."

"No, no, she would never." Tommie shook his head.

Samuel half thought he was going to fall over from the force of it.

"The proof is in the razor wire she held at my throat," Jonathan said blandly.

"But you're still here, right? She didn't succeed. Just banish her back to the mainland. Briar can't hurt you if she's not here to do it."

"How did she get through my wards?" Collis asked.

"Briar is clever. She's managed to trick all sorts of wards into letting her into places she shouldn't be." Tommie looked mildly ill, like the words were creeping up his throat and out of his mouth without his consent.

"Why do you think she wanted to kill me?" Jonathan asked. Asterion gripped the back of the Guardian's chair, a looming shadow who threatened death if Tommie so much as breathed wrong.

Enthralled, Samuel popped another berry into his mouth. It was nice to be an observer instead of the menacing presence for once.

"There's a bounty on your head. With the Travel Innarnians recalled, things are harder now. It's enough ziom to set a family up for the rest of their lives."

The other occupants of the room seemed horrified by the prospect.

It was time to chime in. "I could just eat them all. It would stop the nonsense," Samuel said.

Tommie looked aghast at the suggestion.

For a fraction of a second, it appeared like Jonathan would agree with him, but the Guardian merely sighed. "They'd probably be bad for your digestion," he said. "Banishing them all back to the mainland, minus their ships, is a sound idea, though."

Heaving a put on sigh, Samuel nodded. "If you think it's for the best," he said.

Jonathan wasn't quite quick enough to stop a smirk. "This time, at least."

In the next blink, Tommie was gone, and Ronah felt right for the first time since the mainlanders had set foot on her mountain-covered beach.

Zac whistled as he headed home, a bounce in his step. Jonathan had managed to, once again, foil an assassination attempt, and the perpetrator would never be able to harm him again. The mainlanders had been sent back to where they had come from, and the Shifting Islands finally felt at ease again.

All was right with the Realm.

Until a body bumped into his. Zac's grin fell as hands grabbed his arms in the parody of an embrace.

"Sorry," the man said, a husky note in his voice.

"No harm," Zac replied and stepped back, forcing the stranger to drop his hold.

"I, uh, I've seen you around Ronah recently. It's so good to have you back." He fidgeted with his hair, and once it was away from his face, it was clear exactly who Zac had run into.

"Terrance," Zac said flatly.

"You remember me." Terrance gave a throaty laugh.

Zac glared at him. "Yes, you're the incompetent one who pushed Jonathan into a trip wire."

"Wh... what? No. I... I wouldn't do that!" The colour drained from his face. "It... it was an accident!"

"Keep telling yourself that," Zac said and stormed passed, good mood forgotten.

Yessna returned to the makeshift camp, satisfaction at still being able to sleep under the stars purring beneath her skin.

"The Guardian almost died again," she announced and perched on a log by the fire, accepting the plate Drah handed her.

"How this time?" Wubi asked.

"Mainland assassin with a garotte."

"How unoriginal," Felton muttered.

"I had garotte as the next weapon!" Henot jumped up and down in excitement.

"What? Did someone say something?" Kibon said, stepping over the log and the bouncing gnome and throwing Yessna a wink as he did so.

"I'll show you who!" Henot lunged forward and bit Kibon's ankle, sharp teeth piercing the leather of the archer's boot.

With decades of practise, Yessna pulled Henot away from Kibon and shoved the juicy drumstick of a beast into the gnome's angry hands. "Chew on this instead."

Henot tore into the meat, glaring at Kibon. The two bickered worse than siblings.

Drah sighed moodily, no doubt thinking of his fallen twin, Kerk. Nerina was a talented healer, but even she hadn't been able to heal Kerk after the Xanderri had gotten to him.

"How goes the golden priest?" Wubi asked, handing Henot the stack of coins from their bet.

"Unhappy that the Guardian was targeted, disappointed he can't eat the mainlanders."

"Nothing new then," Nerina said, tearing a chunk of meat off the spit roast with her dagger.

Yessna chuckled, "Exactly." She looked around at the crew. "Do we know which Shifting Island we want to settle on yet?"

"Straight to the heart of the matter," Drah muttered. His ability to speak a full sentence by himself impressed her, considering Kerk usually finished them for him.

"We can't agree. Maybe this last island will be the one, but at the moment, I'm liking Talhan, Wubi prefers Ginorti, Felton and Henot want to live on Cantash, and Kibon likes Rakemyst." Nerina spoke matter-of-factly, but the tight line of her muscles and the way she ripped into the meat showed how upset she was about splitting up.

"And we know you want to stay here, of course," Kibon added.

Nodding, Yessna leaned back. Would be one of the last nights they spent together?

CHAPTER FOURTEEN

Shari woke up with a scream trapped behind her teeth. Her heart was pounding so hard, her temples were throbbing.

Clouds, again. Swarming her, wrapping around her in a damp mist, sucking the Innarn right from her body. And the dead eyes of the former leader of the U'sala staring as she screamed for help.

'Lissae?' Shari sent out as she struggled to sit. Wrapping her arms around bent knees, the bravest being in the Realm rested her head and tried not to cry.

The Realm, once Shari's confident and support, remained silent.

'Please,' she sent. Somewhere between Altum and Zuefie, she'd gone beyond begging.

"I need you," she whispered and let the tears fall.

In the corner of her room, fabric rustled. Shari's head shot up.

Grace emerged from the cloth and shuffled forward, idly tossing a dagger in her hand. "I'm nice," she said, nodding. "You're sad, so I won't stab you today. Even though you said I could."

Shari ran the back of her arm across her face. "Maybe we can give everyone a show at breakfast."

Tossing the dagger one more time, Grace phased through the door, leaving Shari to her thoughts.

A warm glow in the room's corner pulsed, and wisps of white rushed together to form a wolf-like shape. The creature growled, too low for mortal hearing.

Zoomer lifted his head and rose. A long tongue lolled out of his mouth as the palon yawned. Sleepily, he trotted towards the door that led to the castle. Pushing it open with his head, Zoomer sniffed the air.

Hurry.

Wide awake now, the palon rushed down the hall and phased through the door and into the room where Shari sat sobbing on the bed.

In a single bound, he was by her side, nudging his head underneath her arm and letting his fur soak up her tears.

The glowing eyes in the corner hummed at him and disappeared once more.

Vebaday

Sixth day of the second week of Nightcrest

Shari had just put her cup down when the tip of a dagger slid under her chin. She'd been having a quiet breakfast in the castle kitchen before the others awoke.

Of course, after last night, Grace wasn't about to let her get away with that.

Shifting the blade to the kitchen counter, Shari grinned when it wobbled in place, sticking up from the stone. "Thank you for waiting," she said to Grace.

Grace snarled at her and went to pull the blade out. Her cousin pouted when it didn't come free. "Help?"

Raising her brows, Shari tried to keep her expression neutral. "If I help you get it out of there, are you going to stab me again?"

Grace nodded.

"You're on your own then," Shari said as she rose from her seat.

Sighing, Grace looked down, her gaze scanning the table.

Carefully strengthening her shields, Shari kept her eye on Grace as she eased out of the room.

Swinging around to find Shari had almost left, Grace picked up a fork and screamed, running straight at the Altoriae.

Waiting until the last moment, Shari shifted outside the castle before the metal came into contact with her shield.

She laughed, mildly incredulous.

Liz Ribeck, who was doing up her shoe, looked at her. "Well met, Shari. What has you laughing this morning?"

"Grace tried to stab me with a fork," Shari laughed again.

Giving her a concerned look, Liz rose. "That's funny?"

"I'm trying to decide if it's a step up or down from the dagger," Shari said.

Shaking her head, Liz said, "I'm not sure. But it makes me feel better that I didn't start my day off avoiding cutlery."

Shari grinned. "Better than some of the other things I've had to avoid." She gave Liz another grin and started her morning jog, keeping an eye on the shadows in case her cousin decided to ambush her with a spoon.

Arilla put Alan's plate on his table with a smile before moving back to the counter of the tavern.

Tania gave her a grin as she leaned back, elbows on the counter, her gaze on the crowd. Arilla was glad that everyone was behaving for once. The mainlanders leaving had helped to seep some of the tension away, but she was sure it wouldn't take too long before something else set off the residents again. Tensions were running too high with the upcoming convergence.

"Well met! What can I get for you?" she asked as she drew closer.

"Well met. Mum put in an order. She asked me to pick it up on the way home," Tania said.

"Right, let me grab that for you." Arilla smiled at the young Linked and disappeared out the back to get the order.

Calem was diligently working on a pie for Shari. The vallan had been simmering all day, and now it was time to assemble everything. He was carefully preparing the base when Arilla grabbed the stack of containers for the Hollingsworth order.

"Almost done?" she asked, giving him a peck on the cheek.

"Not long now."

"Brilliant." She flashed a smile and slipped back through the door.

Tania was looking at the weapons scattered amongst the bookshelves, brows drawn. "You still keep those sharp, don't you?" She nodded towards the nearest sword.

"Absolutely," Arilla said, handing over the bundle.

"I'm glad," Tania replied. "I think we're going to need them."

Arilla kept her smile firmly fixed, but inside, her stomach dropped. If Ronah's Linked was worried, then they should be too.

Shari breathed in deep, prepared to shift into the next part of the air motus, when a familiar scent tickled her nose. She stepped out of the move and crossed the room to the doorway.

"Don't think you escape training that easily," Samuel grumbled. He stood too, shaking his limbs out, his dark hair tousled for a change. Sneeze, who was permanently attached to Samuel, peered at her from the mess.

"I hope we're not disturbing you?" Arilla said.

"I hope we are," Calem grumbled, glaring at Samuel.

Samuel glared back, but he wasn't as menacing as normal with a tiny draci resting on his head.

"If you're hiding what I think you are, then not at all," Shari said, trying not to bounce on her toes. She felt the weight of Samuel's gaze settling heavily between her shoulder blades but ignored him in favour of the smell wafting out of the basket her father carried.

"Thought you might like a slice of home," Calem said, wrapping an arm around her for a hug.

"Absolutely!" Shari gratefully took the basket. "Will you join me?" She hated how needy she sounded.

"Not tonight," Arilla said softly and stepped up to wrap an arm around Shari on the other side. "We're moving."

Shari bowed her head and tugged her parents closer. "Oh," she said. Then the second part hit her. "Moving where?" She tried to soften her voice, but by Samuel's raised brow, she'd missed the mark.

"Back home," Calem said, resting his head against hers.

"To Ronah?"

"Yes," Arilla beamed at her.

Biting the inside of her cheek so she didn't shriek, Shari grinned back. "I'm glad," she said.

"We'd best be going, actually. Wolf and Belfar are very excited to have more space to themselves." Calem rolled his eyes but couldn't hide his grin.

"You love it." Shari nudged him with her hip.

"I love that Wolf finally woke up," he corrected.

"Me too. I'll see you tomorrow?"

Arilla kissed her cheek. "Of course you will. Try and get some sleep, okay?"

"I'll try," Shari said, blinking back sudden tears.

With one last squeeze, Arilla and Calem left.

Holding the handle of the basket, Shari stared at the empty doorway. After releasing a shuddering breath, she turned and almost shrieked.

Samuel was right behind her. Sneeze was craning his neck, trying to peer into the basket.

"Don't you have hatchlings to wrangle?" she asked.

He lazily looked her up and down and smirked.

"I'm not one of them!" Huffing, Shari pushed past him, heading for the small table they'd moved to the side.

"When it acts like a hatchling and huffs like a hatchling..." Samuel said.

"When it teases, it doesn't get pie," Shari threw over her shoulder.

"Pie?" Samuel asked.

"At least once a month, when I was a kid, Dad would slave for days, making vallan pie," Shari said as she pulled out the plates and cutlery from the basket. "The preparation for it is so fiddly, and it was years before Dad told me that vallan wasn't actually a vegetable."

In the act of conjuring water into the glasses he'd produced from nothing, Samuel froze. "It's meat? I thought you didn't..."

"Vallan is pretty much my only exception," Shari admitted. "It became my go-to, especially after a rough patrol. Although Dad didn't realise why I'd ask for it for years."

"And now?" Samuel asked, his eyes glued to the basket.

Shari had the idle thought of waving the basket to and fro to see if the Guardian's Apprentice and the elder of his race would follow the path with his eyes like Zoomer would.

"Now it's a comfort food that no one cooks as well as my Dad does." Shari reverently took the pie out and placed it between the two plates. "Would you like a slice?"

Samuel glanced at her, eyes wide. "I would be honoured," he said, throat bobbing.

"Is this a cultural thing? Did I just ask you to marry me or something?" Shari frowned as she sat.

"What? No!" Samuel sighed, slouching into the seat across from her. "It's odd. The strongest in the room eats first. Always. Whatever is left goes to the rest."

"So when Oalark ate the ambassadors, that's why you told Jetonyx to only take the tiniest morsel?"

Samuel nodded. "It was that or death. Which usually involved a similar, if not prolonged end like that of the fallen ambassadors."

"If that's the case, shouldn't you be eating first?" Shari grinned at him, placing a healthy serve on his plate.

'I *strong*,' Sneeze sent.

Sighing, Samuel snagged a crumb for the draci and placed it on his shoulder. Sneeze grabbed it with both claws and shoved it in his mouth, his eyes crossing in pleasure.

Draci taken care of, Samuel caught her gaze, and it felt like the Realm came to a standstill as he stared into her soul. "You are so much stronger than me," he said, his voice hoarse.

Shari found she didn't know what to do, and after a long moment, she dropped her gaze. "Samuel," she started.

"You fight me on everything else, Shari. You aren't going to win this one," he said. Gesturing with his fork to her plate, he said, "Eat."

"Only if you do," she shot back. Loading up her fork, she raised her brows and waited.

Sighing, Samuel did the same.

Lifting their forks at the same time, they both took a bite.

Moaning, Samuel dissolved backwards into his seat, eyes closed as he enjoyed the morsel.

Shari grinned. "Good?"

"Almost as good as rutenberries," he admitted.

'*Better*,' Sneeze said, holding out his claws. Samuel gave him another crumb. He'd learned better than setting a miniature plate on the table and expecting the draci to be civilised. The tiny creature much preferred to use him as a place to eat.

"You have such a sweet tooth–you're like my mum," Shari laughed.

"You actually like your parents, don't you?" Samuel asked.

Bite halfway to her mouth, Shari froze and looked at him for a long moment. "If anyone else had phrased it like that, I'd be getting all defensive. But seeing how your egg donor treated you, I can understand why you'd word it that way," Shari said. "Yes, I do." She glanced towards the doorway, as if her parents were still there and not moving back into her childhood home. "My parents are amazing. They mean more than the Realm to me."

The sound of a light bell filled the air, and Samuel's fork clattered to his plate. "Is that so?" he asked hoarsely.

"Of course. There's a handful of people I would sacrifice Lissae for, and they are at the top of that list." Shari stabbed at her slice of pie viciously.

"Who else is on the list?" he asked, lifting a finger to scratch his draci under the chin.

"You, Jonathan, the hatchlings, Zoomer, Sneeze," Shari said. "Mitch," she whispered, tears blurring the plate in front of her. A heavy weight leaned against her legs, and she reached down, burying her fingers in Zoomer's thick fur.

Gaze fixed firmly on his plate, Samuel said, "We all have someone we'd burn the Realms down to save."

Shari gave him a shaky smile as Samuel raised his eyes to meet hers. Somehow, she knew he was talking about razing everything to bring her back. "I know you tried. I know you wanted to do more," she said. "The thought of coming back, of getting the hatchlings to you, that's what kept me going."

Samuel nodded solemnly. "No wonder this pie is your comfort food. It's healing in more ways than one."

"It really is." After picking up her fork, she dug in once more.

Anika brushed her skirt, removing the wrinkles. She looked around the open space of the lounge room of *her* house. Seventeen and living alone. With a boy about to come over.

Despite the number of boyfriends she'd had, her parents had never left her alone with any of them.

Raven had made it clear that nothing inappropriate would be happening—they were going to practise attacks and defence—but Anika was trying not to worry about what it might mean.

A knock on the door made her jump. After swiping sweat-damp hands over her skirt again, Anika opened the door. "Well met, Raven."

"Well met." He tousled his hair, unable to meet her eyes. "I, uh, thought we could train outside today?"

"Afraid I'll corrupt you?" she asked, fluttering her eyelashes.

He gave her an easy grin. "Something like that."

"The backyard will be big enough, provided we're working with daggers and not swords."

"Daggers are why we're here," he said, gesturing for her to lead the way.

Slipping past him, Anika took the path down the side of the house and through to the back garden. She'd started a tiny patch for vegetables, leaving tools stacked to the side. Gardening had never been something Anika had enjoyed, but she'd have to get used to it if she wanted to eat.

Raven gave her that easy grin again. "All right, the first thing that we need to talk about is your posture. Those heels throw off your centre of gravity, and they might look good, but it means you need to learn to compensate."

Anika licked her lower lip. "I can do that. Show me how?"

Stepping up to her, Raven helped adjust her stance, and Anika had to admit that she felt more secure.

"Now, how about you try and stab me?" he said.

Although she'd known it was coming, Anika couldn't contain the shiver that ran through her.

"You don't want to?" he asked.

"It's just, after that assassin, I'm worried that if someone sneaks up on me, I'll hurt them." Anika blinked as her eyes welled up, but it failed to stop the tears from falling.

"I promise I'll never sneak up on you," Raven said. "And I promise I'll teach you how to go for less fatal measures for the first blow."

"Thank you," Anika whispered. On an island were beings trained to lead with fatality first, she had been worried he'd think her weak. Instead, Raven took the rest of the afternoon to show her less deadly measures for incapacitating her opponent.

And if it led to them laying in the leaf litter, limbs entwined more than once, well, Anika wasn't going to complain about that at all.

"You're late," Dealon said.

Shari's head snapped up, looking at Raven as he slumped into his seat. Broken leaves covered his back, and his hair was a mess. She glanced at the others around the table, who were all staring unabashed at him.

"I had somewhere else to be," Raven said, using his Innarn to lift a bowl and ladle the soup into it. He snagged a couple of pieces of fresh bread and set about eating like he hadn't seen food in years.

"Boys," Talofa said, rolling her eye and patting her lips daintily with a napkin before she pointedly placed it back in her lap.

Shari tried not to giggle. Dinner with her guild was always amusing.

"Some*where* or some*one*?" Lira asked.

Without missing a blink, Raven threw a hunk of bread at her head.

Grace popped up out of nowhere and snagged the slice midair before disappearing again.

"We sit on our seats to eat, Grace," Skye said.

Patience of a parent, Shari thought.

Reluctantly, Grace took her seat.

"Someone." Ashlen pointed at Raven. "I saw him rolling on the ground with the seamstress."

"Anika?" Elani wrinkled her nose.

"Yep."

"Buzzard-guts," she muttered.

Raven laughed. "Aww, don't be mad she prefers my company to yours."

Elani flicked a spoonful of soup in his direction.

It syphoned towards Grace's bowl without a drop making it to Raven.

"It is so hard to have a food fight with you at the table," Elani grumbled.

Grace grinned at them around a mouthful of bread.

Shari groaned and shook her head. *Maybe amusing was the wrong word.*

'*Shari, we need you to check something out,*' Jonathan sent.

"Gotta run." Shari stood up. Half the guild got to their feet as well. "You can stay here, it's fine."

Shovelling the last of his soup into his mouth, Raven shrugged. "Or we could go with you," he said, putting the empty bowl on the table.

'*Guild is coming with me,*' Shari warned him.

'*The more the merrier.*'

Nothing good ever started with that sentence.

With dread in her heart, Shari shifted the standing guild members to the museum.

CHAPTER FIFTEEN

These late-night sessions are truly getting to me. Tania rubbed her eyes and covered another yawn.

"Keeping you up, are we?" Cyrus asked, nudging her.

"*Some* of us have school through the day."

"Or work, or other duties to attend to?"

"How many of those duties involve exams which will affect the direction your life takes?" Tania snipped.

Oakley looked at her, head to the side. "You know your life's path has already been decided."

Tania blinked. With a headmaster and a teacher in the house, it sure felt like exams were the beginning of everything that led to a proper life. "That does take some of the pressure off."

"Now that's sorted, perhaps we can get back to the joining?" Zana asked. She appeared as serene as always, but something was off.

"What are you worried about?" Tania asked.

"The Realm keeps going silent," Domic blurted. "The elders are worried. There are old, half-forgotten stories about something hiding in the silence, and, well." He shrugged.

Zana shivered and rubbed her arms. "Change is coming."

"Change doesn't have to be bad," Fenix said.

Biting her lip, Tania found she didn't know what to say.

"I was going to invite Vannali's Linked to our next session to make sure that the joining is as smooth as possible," Zana announced, the subject effectively changed.

Domic groaned, but Fenix grinned and clapped. "Brilliant! I haven't seen Brinley in years."

With the two vastly differing opinions, Tania was interested to see what Vannali's Linked was actually like.

Shari glanced around the room at the museum, taking in the crowd.

Jonathan was talking to her father in low tones. A few Satyrs stood chatting to two Ilutri from Wolf and Belfar's team. Terrance Thorne stood awkwardly next to Samuel, who looked like he'd prefer to rip the limbs off the other man than strike up a conversation with him. Sneeze, who had liked everyone so far, was blowing little bursts of fire towards Terrance with a frown on his tiny draci face.

Shari tried not to laugh.

Raven, Elani, Lira, and Mu stepped up next to her, weapons bristling.

"We've had a report from Riomache that an invading force stormed their gateway in the early hours of yesterday morning. They've attempted to hold the invaders off but are having little luck by themselves and have requested aid," Jonathan said.

Terrance looked a little too happy with the news.

"A scout has corroborated the Riomachen story. I need you to aid them. They're the Realm below ours in the portal. If something unfriendly gains a foothold there—" Jonathan shook his head.

"We're on it," Shari said. The guild around her nodded.

"You have a few extras as well." Jonathan gestured to the crowd.

Clenching her jaw, she sent to him, '*I am not working with Terrance Thorne.*'

Jonathan raised a brow in her direction. '*We don't always get to pick who we fight alongside. Maybe he'll surprise you.*'

'*I'll keep an eye on the tuzar's guts. And the Guardian will ensure the safety of my hatchlings.*' Samuel's send was a rumble that seemed to be connected directly with her heart.

'*He puts a toe out of line, and you...*' Shari sent.

'*...send him back here.*' Jonathan overwrote her. He stared at her, hard. '*Perhaps the hatchings will be hungry by then.*'

There was an unspoken message in the send, and Shari didn't have to try very hard to parse it out.

"Let's go," she said aloud. With one last glare at her Guardian, Shari shifted the lot of them to the other side of Riomache's gateway.

Terrance sucked in a breath, looking vaguely green.

"You alright?" one of the Satyrs asked.

"Thought we were going to walk," Terrance said.

"Why waste time when lives are on the line?" Shari asked sweetly.

Samuel chuckled and clapped Terrance on the back, causing him to stumble forwards. "Let's see what we're dealing with."

Domic knocked his glass against Brayden's.

The Wandering Serpent was quiet at this time of night, the other Wisara having left the tavern for their beds. Perfect for a casual meet up.

"Any news?" Brayden asked. He had bags under his eyes that the lotus roots did little to hide.

"Well, I suppose it's more of the same." Domic stared at the blue liquid in his glass, watching the condensation slide down the outside. "We're aiming to get to Vannali as quickly as we can but—" His voice faded, and the sound was sucked out of the room in a rush.

Glass slipping from his hand, Domic waited for the crash that never happened.

Brayden threw his glass down and sprinted from the room, hitting the water without shedding his roots. Domic scrambled after him.

The two Wisara made it to the surface in time to be deafened by the waves crashing against the mountain of Ronah's beach.

Turning in a circle, his eyes wide and chest heaving, Brayden looked terrified. "Whatever is hiding in the silence is getting stronger," he said.

Domic took another look at the shore. He had the dreadful sensation that whatever it was, it wouldn't be hiding for much longer.

Riomache

The gateway of Riomache opened out onto a rough stone path which offered a view of the city square under it.

Shari had visited before, in disguise. The square was always bustling, the twin pools of water holding people who were seeking refuge from the sun. The city walls surrounded the square, providing shade for most of the day.

Despite it being the middle of the night on Lissae, it was closer to midafternoon for Riomache. The busiest time of the day was when the heat waned and various wares were peddled to travellers.

But the square was deserted.

There were no beings peering out of the windows of the rough stone buildings or hiding behind the few trees dotted around.

Shari frowned. *'Be on your guard,'* she sent.

Terrance rolled his eyes, but the rest of the group got their weapons ready.

Calem, Raven, Elani, and Samuel stood in a loose ring around her. The two Satyrs, Max and Yvonne, joined Varlee, Charin, Lira, Mu, and

Terrance to form an outer ring. Shari found it mildly amusing that even the newcomers worked to keep Terrance in front of the pack, rather than at her back.

'*What are you thinking?*' Calem sent.

'*There's nothing to...*' Terrance started to send.

And copped a blast of fire to his shoulder.

'*Looks like someone is hiding in the buildings,*' Varlee sent.

Mu doused Terrance with water. '*Put your shield up,*' he sneered. '*It's patrolling basics.*'

Shari refrained from commenting, but she desperately wanted to send the whimpering fizzpot away.

'*Better where we can see him,*' Samuel sent. '*There's a reason he wanted to be here tonight. Let him have it.*'

Flicking a shield around the entire group, Shari pushed her Innarn out and counted the others in the area. '*At least forty around the square. None are friendly.*'

'*Where are the locals?*' Varlee asked.

The lined face of the old woman who'd offered her chewy cheesy puffs flickered behind Shari's eyes. She felt the phantom hints of the last of the smiling lady's Innarn in the building to their right and knew they would find her body there.

'*Gone.*' Shari's send was short. The others got the hint. '*Split into two. Outer ring, take the left path. We'll take the right.*'

'*Good luck,*' Samuel sent, clapping a hand on the tuzar's injured shoulder.

Terrance flinched.

Turning before she could add insult to his injury, Shari led the way. '*Quiet and low.*'

The group crouched as they ran up the stairs, reaching a thicket of trees at the top.

Movement flickered in the archway opposite, and Shari tucked herself behind the trunk of a tree, strengthening the shield around them.

"What in the name of Lissae?" Elani breathed.

Cautiously peering around her tree, Shari's breath caught in her throat.

The invaders were trying to be stealthy, but there were so many of them it was hard.

'Forty?' Mu's send was a tad on the frantic side.

Way more than forty bodies were pounding across the balconies on the far side.

'Portal?' Calem asked.

Sending her Innarn out again, Shari nodded. *'Darker than expected.'* Tampering with the portal was the work of a few seconds. She felt the thing shut off as the new wave of bodies were halfway through. Bits of beings slid to the floor. Those closest to the mess didn't make a peep at the gory scene.

'Crack troops,' Shari warned. Innarnians on the opposite balcony were setting up in groups. Earth Innarn was a good call for the front lines. Air and Fire intermingled meant things were about to get hot.

'Incoming,' Lira warned.

Air and Fire shot off the first volley, which Shari slapped aside like a pesky bug.

'Try again,' she broadcasted. *'You want the rest of Riomache? You're going to have to go through us.'*

Samuel yawned and climbed the steps to the next level, muscles flexing as he prepared to change. *'Don't play with your food, Altoriae. It's bad manners.'* The golden Q'Aralide stared down at the trees. *'Light it up,'* he sent then took to the air, a single flap of his massive wings bringing him within firing range of the enemy.

Green gas spewed from his maw, and Shari fed it a flicker of flame.

Beings screamed and writhed.

"Feels like cheating," Shari muttered.

'Better than dying,' Calem said.

Shari turned to respond and felt something pierce her side. *'What?'*

She'd missed the archers.

Standing on the flat rooftops, well above the hoard on the balcony, a dozen archers were now meeting the jaws of the golden priest.

"Eww," Elani said. "That's…"

"Effective." Raven was nodding as he took in Samuel's snack, shooting an arrow at one far enough away from the Q'Aralide to be a menace.

Glancing over at the other team, Shari sighed. Terrance was down, acting as if he was hit. A quick scan showed little more than a scratch.

And lots of pretty colours.

Swaying slightly, Shari grunted as she pulled the arrow from her side, the blue coating so pretty she wanted to lick it.

She raised it towards her mouth, tongue out to lick the pretty when it was snatched from her hand.

'The Altoriae's hit,' Calem broadcasted.

A golden shadow was by her side in an instant. 'Destroy the others,' Samuel sent.

Giving in to temptation, Shari petted the scales of his chest. "Soft," she whispered, her eyes wide.

Scales turned to skin. "What was she hit with?"

Calem handed Samuel the arrow.

He groaned. "Wish I could say this wouldn't hurt," he said, brushing the hair off her face. "But I promised not to lie to you."

"Don' wanna 'urt," Shari slurred, standing by pure force of will. Looking up, she realised she was still petting Samuel's chest. "Oooh."

Someone giggled.

"Not a word," Samuel bit out. He twisted, and the wound on Shari's side screamed.

Or maybe it was her.

The sound bounced off the bricks, and she staggered, falling into Samuel's arms.

"Could you maybe try not to get hit?" he said, holding her steady.

'*All down. I repeat, the enemy is all down,*' Yvonne sent.

"Missed it." Shari pouted up at him.

"They didn't miss you. How did they get through your shield anyway?" Raven asked.

Shari stepped away from Samuel. Now the poison was out of her system, she was feeling more herself, although a little light-headed, which was possibly just from blood loss.

The other group was walking back towards them, Terrance in the lead, his shoulder miraculously uninjured.

Samuel narrowed his eyes, tracking the movements of the group. "I wonder."

Lissae

The second Shari shifted off Lissae, the Realm went silent. Jonathan's heart was beating so fast in his chest that he ought to have heard it.

Except he couldn't.

The Guardian reached out to the plinth beside him and staggered when his fingers went straight through it.

"What in the name of Lissae?" The sudden rush of returning sound drowned out his words.

Portal

Samuel gripped her arm on one side, her father on the other.

'*I'm perfectly capable of walking,*' Shari groused.

'*Then do it,*' Samuel snarled.

'*Don't argue,*' Calem added.

'*I think I preferred it when you two didn't get along,*' Shari sent.

Terrance's group was ahead of them, Raven and Elani bringing up the rear. Shari had never felt so crowded walking through the portal before.

A cloaked figure raised a hand and wiggled ze's fingers at the group, glowing eyes sliding behind zir.

'*Wait!*' Shari had to use her Innarn to get the men by her side to stop.

'No.' Samuel tugged her forward.

Craning her neck, Shari searched for the glowing eyes but couldn't spot them again. '*I think the Ducibus is in danger.*'

'*You're going to be in danger if you don't get your hide through the doors,*' Samuel rumbled.

Her father nodded.

The double doors appeared, and Samuel's grip tightened. He increased his pace, forcing the others into a jog.

Pala, still holding a stick, opened Lissae's gateway.

Their group stormed through, coming to a hurried stop to avoid squashing the Guardian.

'*All in one piece?*' Jonathan asked.

'*More or less,*' Shari replied, hissing as the wound on her side knitted back together.

Samuel flicked his gaze to the doors, which slammed shut. He let go of her arm and sent a wave of healing Innarn dark enough to make her stagger. '*You call being poisoned "in one piece"?*'

Calem made sure she had her feet before he let her go. "Any other injuries?" he asked.

'*You got it all out,*' Shari protested.

Terrance was doing his best to look wounded, his hand clamped over the wrong shoulder.

Shaking her head, Shari shifted him to the Healing Centre with Elani. She'd make sure he stayed out of the way.

Jonathan pinched the bridge of his nose. "So, a normal patrol then?"

CHAPTER SIXTEEN

Lissae

Zoeday

Seventh day of the second week of Nightcrest

alem settled the bags of swords against the wall of the training ground. "Anything else, love?"

Arilla smiled at him like he'd painted each of the stars that lit the night sky. "We've got it from here. I'll borrow you later, though," After giving him a cheeky wink, she turned to greet the first students coming in.

Crossing to the stand, Calem felt the impending shift before the being appeared. "Well met, Grace," he said.

His niece grunted at him, twirling a dagger in her hand. She scanned the grounds, and a tad of the tightness eased out of Grace's frame when Arilla came into view.

"Well met, Grace. Are you joining in today?" Arilla asked.

Grace shook her head and pointed the tip of her dagger towards Calem.

"You can't stab Calem either. I'm going to need him later." The dissonance between the cheerful tone and the words made Calem's eyebrows climb.

Growling, Grace settled into a seat a few chairs away from his.

Other students came in, picking their weapon and moving to practise their swings. His niece would grumble if anyone came too close to Arilla with the pointy end of a blade.

An Innarn barb struck his side.

Calem's head snapped around and he stared at Grace, who appeared enthralled with the warm-up exercises.

No stabbing, but Innarn is alright? Calem flung a barb back.

Grunting, Grace turned, eyes wide.

"Your shield could use some work,"

Grace snarled and fired another little barb.

Calem caught it and lobbed it back. He grinned when Grace used it to strengthen her shield.

Arilla's voice rang out, distracting them as she guided her students through the next lot of moves she wanted them to learn.

"How did you meet?" Grace asked, voice still raspy from disuse.

Calem batted away another of her barbs. "She was on the run. Literally." He laughed, but his brows drew together at the same time. "I was patrolling near some cliffs, and she ran right off them. By the look on her face, I knew it wasn't intentional." He flicked his fingers, calling forth the image of Arilla's face from all those years ago. For a moment, the air before them wavered like heat above stone on the hottest of days but did little to generate a picture. He flicked his hands again, and she appeared, face fraught as the ground fell away from beneath her feet.

Grace growled and surged forward as if to catch her falling aunt.

In the image, two powerful arms caught her, wings wrapping around Arilla for a moment before disappearing again. She looked up at him in awe, and the image faded away. "Arilla looked at me like I could catch the Realm and keep it safe."

Turning, Grace gave him an indecipherable look. "Can you?"

Before Calem had the chance to answer, Arilla was calling him from the ground.

"Come help demonstrate!" she yelled up at them.

"Coming, love," Calem called easily. "When someone looks at you like that, you do everything in your power to live up to their expectations."

He vaulted the seats and landed on the ground as light as a feather, the sword in his hand flashing out to be blocked by his wife.

Weary beyond what his bones could stand, Samuel collapsed onto the lounge, only to groan when something sharp poked at the delicate skin of his rump.

Slumping to the side, Samuel dug into the cushions and pulled out the sharp object. He glanced at it and froze, staring dumbly at his hand.

When he looked up, Jetonyx was sitting before him, tail neatly wrapped around his claws, wingtips quivering.

"What's this?" Samuel asked, holding the black object aloft.

'*One of my scales.*' The hatchling's thoughts were fairly vibrating.

Samuel swallowed heavily. "When did it happen?"

'*Last night, while you were away.*'

"You're moulting." Samuel's thoughts were thick, cold syrup. Moulting was normally something to be celebrated, heralding the arrival of colours and the start of a hatchling's true training. The acid pools of Altum were a vital part of the process to soothe the new scales and ensure they grew in correctly.

Impossible. With Altum on the wrong side of extinct, there was nowhere else in the Realms to ensure the safety of his hatchlings.

Kemanyr already had her colours, so only two to go.

Holding the scale up to the light, Samuel sucked in a breath.

It was tinged with gold.

Wolf tightened the strap of his quiver and shook his head at his gossiping team. "You lot know better," he said, voice like tumbling rocks. "Get ready."

"You don't want to know how patrolling went with the Altoriae?" Varlee asked innocently.

Wolf's head snapped around.

"I'm pretty sure Wolf wants us out on patrol as soon as we can," Belfar teased.

Sometimes, my mate can be so obtuse. "You can send and fly, can't you?"

The smile fell off Belfar's face, and Wolf wanted to punch himself.

Varlee looked up, as if hoping something from above would strike him.

Wolf found himself hoping to take the hit.

"The Altoriae was poisoned," Charin blurted.

Thank Vebnah he couldn't keep a secret.

Wait.

"Poisoned?" Wolf and Belfar asked at the same time.

"The Guardian's Apprentice fixed her up," Varlee soothed. "She was barely affected."

'*Calem?*' Wolf sent.

'*She's fine, brother.*' Calem sounded tired.

Furrowing his brow, Wolf racked his memory. '*You were on patrol, too?*'

Calem sent a lazy sort of affirmative, and his send drifted like a feather in the wind. He must have been tired; it was an age since Calem had been out on patrol.

"Anything else happen?"

Varlee frowned. "One of the flightless pretended an injury."

"Coward," Charin spat.

"Where was he from?"

"Ronah."

Asterion gently guided a curious toddler away from the water. For the third time in as many minutes.

He'd come to help the refugees settling in on Akoren in the Guardian's absence and couldn't figure out if they needed more of a babysitter than a defender.

The adults in the encampment all seemed to struggle to stay awake. One of the men stripped down to his pants and waded into the freezing stream at the base of the glacier, throwing the aqua water over his head. Large bumps broke out over his skin, but he still struggled to keep his eyes open.

Was he going to end up getting wet after all? The man waded out of the water before Asterion had to go after him and collapsed high enough on the bank that Asterion didn't have to worry too much.

The refugees were settling in well, for all they refused to talk to him. Which he understood. He was an outsider at the best of times. The children loved him, their sticky fingerprints all over his jacket.

His decidedly not-warm-enough jacket. Shivering, he hefted another child who thought a dip in the stream was a good idea and tried, again, to place a ward around the area.

No luck.

Breath steaming in the cold air, Asterion grabbed another child and wondered who was the best to call. The sleepiness affecting the refugees could just be due to their rambunctious offspring, but the Guardian, who was nowhere near, was similarly plagued.

'Shari, would you know of how to keep children away from water?'

The Altoriae popped in next to his side and waved a negligent hand, a ward springing into existence without even a word.

"Thank you," he said.

"Welcome."

She didn't ask the obvious question, and he didn't need to answer it. Whatever was draining their Innarn had caught him as well.

"Riomache wasn't that bad," Shari argued. "I only got a little bit stabbed."

"And poisoned," Samuel grumbled.

Jonathan sighed. "You need to rest, Shari. Even Holli said so."

Shari huffed and paced around the castle office. "Holli said that if I felt ready to patrol, I could. And I do. Feel ready, that is."

"I don't," Samuel said. He stared down at something in his hand and tightened his fist around it.

"What's that?" For a moment, Shari thought he was going to brush her off.

"Jetonyx is moulting," he said, slumping into a seat.

"Is that a bad thing?" Jonathan asked.

"When your only source of comfort is gone, yes," Samuel snapped then shot Jonathan an apologetic look.

"What can we do to make it better?" Shari asked.

"Find some acid pools for me."

The defeated tone made Shari want to wrap her arms around him.

"Rataeo has acid pools," Jonathan said.

Samuel's head snapped up. "Rataeo?" He scrubbed at the back of his neck. "Not a great idea."

"Too dark?" Shari asked.

"Rataeo was the last Realm borne of Lissae." Samuel rose to his feet, pacing the room. "I don't think it's a good idea to go for a visit at the moment."

"What if, instead of patrolling *outside* Lissae, you joined the others in a sweep of our borders? Give them a chance to rest," Jonathan suggested.

Shari wanted to grumble, but agreed instead.

CHAPTER SEVENTEEN

Adonday

First day of the third week of Nightcrest

In the early hours of the morning, Shari and Jonathan stumbled back towards the castle. They had grabbed the U'sala and done a lap of the joined Shifting Islands by foot.

Shari had blisters on her blisters. The cushioning Innarn she usually placed on her boot had worn off some time around Talhan and was barely a memory by the time they reached Akoren.

Of course it was when Shari was most tired that Grace lunged out from behind a large crystal pillar and tried to stab her.

Heart pounding, Shari blocked her mad cousin and cursed her. "I'm all for a decent stabbing, but can I at least get some sleep first?" Shari yelled.

Grace chuckled and left Shari screaming at empty air and holding the dagger Grace had left behind.

"Sometimes," Shari muttered, "I wonder what is going on in her head!"

"All the time," Skye said.

Whirling, Shari gripped the dagger, prepared to be the one to do the stabbing for a change.

A body appeared between her and Skye.

"No," Grace frowned at her, plucked the dagger from her hand, and disappeared again.

"Is she actually as infuriating as I think she is?" Shari spat through gritted teeth.

"Yep," Skye said, popping the 'p'. "But she'd also risk her life to save someone she'd barely met, so it kind of evens out."

"I'm not so sure," Shari said, stalking the rest of the way back to the castle. To her bed.

If Grace tries to stab me before I get some sleep, I will not be held accountable for my actions.

Joana sucked in a harsh breath, trying desperately to be quiet but failing.

The last of the guards of Chamele's quarters had either fallen or left. Her son, the only reason she'd stepped away from Ronah, gurgled as he breathed. Whatever the thrice-damned elder had injected him with would see him dead by morning.

Unless they could get back to Ronah.

Peering around the corner, Joana nodded. Halfair hefted Tobias, and the trio scurried forward.

In the eery calm of the early morning, the Travel Innarnian's post was unguarded. If they could make it to the crystal, Joana could amplify her Innarn enough to make sure they reached Ronah.

Where's Collis when you need him? Innarn came to that boy easier than breathing. Never thought she'd even think it, but Joana missed the stupid pocket-Realm where you knew death waited outside the walls, and you knew the face it would wear.

Pausing behind another corner, Joana took Tobias's weight and let Halfair shake out his hands.

"I'm sorry," Tobias whispered, breath rattling in his chest. "Thought... the... mainland... was... safe." Every word needed a new, sucking breath before the next.

Tears prickled and threatened to fall. "You just hang in there," Joana hissed. She knew as well as he did that he wouldn't make it to Ronah. But she had to *try*.

"Come on." Halfair motioned them forward, and together, they stumbled to the tiny hut on the edge of the cliff.

Joana left Halfair holding Tobias's weight, and she made to open the door.

Locked.

A scream bubbled in her throat, but Joana poured her frustration into a kick that sent the lock splintering away from the wooden door.

Voices raised down the path, and torchlight could be seen bobbing in their direction.

"Get the crystal," Halfair hissed.

Rocketing forward, Joana gathered her Innarn and took what Halfair sent her way. She touched the crystal, and it was like standing on the opposite side of a battlefield to Collis.

"I don't think it's going to be enough." She looked at Halfair, despair in her gaze.

"It has to be."

Nodding, Joana closed her eyes and pictured home. She let her Innarn wrap around them all, trying to ignore the voices getting closer.

Extra Innarn joined in, one Joana knew as well as her own. "Toby, no," she moaned.

"*Now*, Jo." Halfair's voice was closer, worry leeching from his very pores.

Fire lanced her arm and with a scream, she shifted them away.

Tania snapped upright, Ronah's wards ringing in her head.

'*Collis!*' The being felt like her soul-match, but not.

Ronah warbled in her mind. '*Came home. Help! Hurry. They're hurt!*'

'*Shift me,*' Tania demanded.

She arrived on the beach moments before Collis did, her blanket snugly wrapped around her.

Three beings were tangled in a pile of limbs at the base of the mountain. It looked like they'd shifted in but not known about the extra layer of security and taken a tumble.

"Joana?" Collis exclaimed.

The woman moaned.

Tania gasped. She knew her—she was one of the Returned.

"Collis, help. It's Tobias, he..." Joana extricated herself from the tangle and looked down.

One of the men lay still, eyes unseeing. The larger man was gently laying him on the sand. He reached out to close Tobias's eyes.

Joana wailed.

Tania shoved her fist against her mouth to stifle the sobs that rose at the sound.

Bodies filled the surrounding space, as the Returned shifted in from all over the island, weapons and Innarn bristling.

The net dropped over them. Stuck in the middle of the commotion, Tania was caught in it, too.

'*What happened?*' Collis's words were factual, cold almost. A different sensation to the healing he was pouring at the two newcomers.

'*Chamele, that rabid three-toed cedore, injected us with—*'

The word was lost to Tania, but she knew the feeling behind it.

Death.

'*Toby, he... we were at the Traveller's Crystal. About to escape. I didn't have enough left in me, and Tobias. He... My boy.*' Joana fell to her knees beside the body of her son.

Tania, caught in the emotion, did the same.

Collis's voice rose, loud enough that everyone could hear. "Although you have faded," he started.

Hundreds of voices joined in, speaking as one. "Your memory remains. Forever in our minds."

"Tobias," Joana whispered.

Then she let the tears fall.

Jonathan turned over, the wards of Ronah roiling like a boat in a storm.

"What's going on?" Zac asked.

'Tobias.'

The word whispered through his mind, layered with grief and pain.

Scrubbing at his face, Jonathan pushed back the covers and rose. "One of the Returned has passed into the Spirit Realm."

"I've never understood the Spirit Realm," Zac said around a yawn. "How does it run alongside Lissac but have a totally different system?"

"When the physical ceases to matter, things change," Jonathan said. He made a mental note to visit Joshua soon. It had been too long since he'd spoken with the spirit of his mentor. "Care for a cup of azehal?"

"I'll make it," Zac said. He paused for a quick kiss and made his way into the kitchen.

They stayed up late, talking about everything from Realm-wide defences to favourite foods. At some point, the heating charms had failed and they'd crawled under the covers, still talking but fully clothed.

Jonathan hadn't felt so rested in weeks.

A buzz filled the air and the Innarnians around him. An expectation that whatever was brewing was about to blow, and Jonathan didn't know if they were ready.

In fact, he was sure they weren't.

"It feels wrong," Tania said to her mother. "Someone died this morning, and now we're going to have a party?"

Liza hummed, her fingers weaving through Tania's hair. "Natal days are rarely perfect. If we expect them to be, we're bound for disappointment. There is always something that falls outside of what we plan. To be fair, it's not usually as bad as what you experienced this morning."

Tania blinked and tried to wipe Joana's wail from her mind. She'd never thought about a parent losing a child before. Even if the child was an adult. She spun, wrapping her arms around her mother's waist.

"Hey!" Liza dropped handfuls of hair to hug her back. "Come on now," she said, voice thick with tears. "We need to get you ready. Can't let all of Collis's hard work go to waste."

Tania nodded and let Liza finish the complicated style she'd decided on for Tania's hair.

An hour later, and she was set to go. Her family slipped out the door, leaving for the mysterious party. Collis was due to pick her up once 'everything was ready'.

Whatever that meant.

A knock on the door sounded loud in the quiet of the house.

"Collis, I thought you'd..." Tania pulled the door open and looked up.

Blue skin and purple eyes greeted her.

"Temira!" Tania beamed.

The technomancer shoved a wrapped parcel in her direction. "Happy natal day. I was invited, but crowds are..." She shook her head. "Know that your soul-match intended I stand with your family. I appreciate the honour."

Gripping the parcel tight, Tania nodded. "Of course you're family, Temira," she said. A certain vibrance was gone from the technomancer, and Tania heart sank. Before she was ready, she'd be the one wailing by Temira's body.

"Open it later," Temira ordered and was gone between one blink and the next.

Collis was walking up the path towards her. "Did I just see Temira?"

"Yes, she was, uh, called away," Tania said. With Temira, you never knew if she'd given her excuses or just assumed the other person already knew.

"I thought she might be." Collis smiled at her. "Are you ready?"

"For the mystery party? Sure!" Tania shifted Temira's gift to her room and took the arm Collis offered.

Collis paused for a moment and wrapped his Innarn around her. With one final look into her eyes, he shifted them.

"The training grounds?" Tania grinned.

"It was the only place big enough to hold everyone," he said.

A flick of his hand, and the doors opened. Her family was standing to the left of the doors, the Linked on the right, greeting each guest as they entered the space. Purple Plasma lights twinkled above them. Greenery was everywhere, and the multi-coloured shade cloths Collis had helped her with had been recreated to keep the worst of the snow at bay.

The grounds were thrumming with people. She could see Shari and Jonathan off to one side, talking to someone through a doorway. A giant scaled face told Tania it led to Samuel's house.

Elders from all the Shifting Islands gathered in the centre, their voices loud and merry. The politicians were rotating around the room, making connections and keeping people happy. Students from Ridden Hall descended upon Tania as soon as she arrived, keen to play upon their familiarity. Others watched in envy as Maeve shoved a drink into her hand, manoeuvring her away from Collis.

Tania looked over her shoulder. Even while Collis was standing amongst some of the Returned, he couldn't keep his gaze off her. Smiling at him through crowd, Tania was ripped away from the moment when Maeve tutted at her.

"There'll be plenty of time for you to make eyes at each other later. Right now, we need to party!" Maeve exclaimed.

This was the girl who barely spoke to her at school, who was cruel to Anika because she was a blank, and who scorned others on a daily basis. Tania took a sip of her drink to cover up her smirk. "Why?"

Maeve gave her an odd look. "What do you mean, why? It's your natal day."

Channelling her best version of Temira, Tania nodded as if it were a serious matter. "Another day upon which our Realm revolves around the sun. What makes it special?"

"Uh, because you were born on this day, seventeen years ago?" Maeve rolled her eyes and laughed, glancing at the others in her posse for reassurance.

"Why celebrate, though? I had no say upon the day I was born," Tania said, keeping her expression as blank as she could.

'*Laying it on a bit thick,*' Shari warned.

Tania felt the Altoriae move to stand beside her.

"Natal day celebrations can be *so* tedious," Anika said, coming up next to her. "But, you make that dress look amazing!" Anika motioned for her to twirl, and Tania did so with a laugh, the purple dress making her feel like a princess of old.

"I mean, the designer is pretty talented, so it's easy to make it look good," Tania said.

Anika blushed.

Shari jumped in. "That purple really is the perfect colour on you." She laced her arm through Tania's and gently tugged.

Floating her drink over to a nearby table, Tania grabbed Anika's hand so she wouldn't be left behind. "Great talking to you," Tania threw over her shoulder as Shari led them away.

"You need to make like Grace and stab them," Shari muttered. "Vultures, the lot."

Tania laughed and felt mildly guilty for it. "I'm sure they don't mean anything by it."

"Of course they do," Anika sniffed. "They know that their only claim to fame is going to the same school as the Altoriae. Every action at events like this will be to capitalise on that."

A woman with pale blonde hair and pointed ears popped up next to them, crystal slab in hand. "Can I quote you on that?"

Shari immediately went on guard. "Who would you be?"

"Ginna, reporter from *The Shifting Island Sentinel*. And I wouldn't actually quote a private conversation, but I couldn't think of a better way to come introduce myself to three of the most amazing beings on Lissae."

Tania wanted to say that Ginna was laying it on thick, but the reporter seemed genuinely excited to meet them. "Well met, Ginna. I'm Tania, this is Shari, and Anika."

"Oh, well met! You three are all stunning. I assume Anika designed today's gowns for you all?" Ginna was sketching something on the slab, and Tania was curious as to what she was doing.

"Of course," Tania said. The others seemed to be struck mute. "Anika does all our outfits for big events."

"Brilliant. Well, I'll leave you all to it. And happiest of natal days, Tania." Ginna slipped away into the crowd before anything else could be said.

"I see you've met our friendly reporter," Jonathan said, coming up beside them.

Shari blinked. "She is something else."

Anika's mouth was moving, but no sound was coming out. Tania squeezed her arm. "Do... do you know who that was? Ginna is *the* foremost lifestyle reporter for the Sentinel. And she thinks my dresses are *stunning*."

There was a buzz of sending over Tania's head, and Raven appeared on Anika's other side as if summoned. She looked at Shari, who tipped her head to hide a grin.

"Ginna thinks my dresses are stunning," Anika repeated.

As if he'd been doing it for years, Raven gently removed Anika's hands from Tania and held them in his own. "That's because they are," Raven said easily. "Why don't we get you something to celebrate the occasion?" He guided her away.

"Thank Lissae for Raven," Shari said.

Tania laughed.

Collis came up beside her and kissed the back of her hand. No matter what else happened, this would certainly be a natal day to remember.

CHAPTER EIGHTEEN

Inthday

Second day of the third week of Nightcrest

Shari tugged at the bottom of her shirt. She may have been done with school, but she still needed to teach. If she ever had time to rewrite her duties, she definitely would. Who wanted to teach after all night protecting the Realm?

Entering the classroom, Shari bit back a groan. It was full of older kids, those barely a few years younger than her. These classes were always the worst.

"Well met, all," she said, pasting a smile onto her face.

"Well met, Altoriae," the kids chorused back.

"I'm afraid it's just me today. Samuel will return in a while." Shari ignored the groans but made a note to tell Samuel about it. Preferably while Jonathan was around. "Today we're working on shields."

"We're *always* working on shields," groaned a kid in the back row.

Shari threw a dagger at him, nicking his ear. It *thunked* into the wall behind him.

A few kids around him screamed, and one looked green as the complainer raised a trembling hand to check his ear was still attached.

"And yet you don't use what you've been taught," she said coldly.

"Shields can't defend against physical attacks," a girl in the front row said.

"Can't they?" Shari asked. She spread her arms out. "Why don't you try?"

The boy next to her picked up a pencil and threw it at Shari. It bounced off her shield and hit him in the middle of his forehead. "Ouch!"

"Anyone else?" Shari asked.

Projectiles from all over the room started raining down on her. Shari made sure they all bounced back to the original owner. One kid got a bit too eager and used Air Innarn to lift her desk. Shari caught it and set it down at the front of the room instead of sending it back. She didn't want to have to explain why several kids got flattened.

"So, now you've seen it's possible, why don't you try to recreate it?" she asked. "You have five minutes to talk amongst yourselves and see what ideas you can come up with."

Alistair raised his hand. "Why do you never just tell us?"

"When I was learning, I had no one to ask. No one to talk to about it. And some of the hardest Innarn I figured out, others had never even thought of. By giving you the answer, I'm taking away the spark that could turn your Innarn into so much more."

Most kids rolled their eyes, but several were nodding slowly. Shari ushered those kids to work together and left them to it.

When the time was up, she clapped her hands. "Let's see what you came up with. Shields. Now."

Shari started throwing bits of detritus at the kids. Nothing that could cause permanent damage, but no one wanted to walk around for the rest of the day with rutenberry skin in their hair.

By the end of the lesson, every kid in the class could produce a viable shield to protect against physical objects.

"Brilliant! Now you just need to practise until it becomes as easy as breathing." Shari turned her head and tried not to laugh at the chorus of groans.

The smile slid from her face.

Glowing eyes in the middle of a white wispy form stared at her.

The day after her natal day was like any other. Tania was in the middle of a class and talking to the other Linked simultaneously.

'*Have you heard from Brinley?*' Tania asked.

'*Yes. Ze is going to join us in a few days. The convergence is coming faster than we anticipated,*' Zana sent.

'*And the issue with the mainlanders is doing little to help,*' Cyrus added.

Tania took down the notes from the board. '*We need to speak with Joana, if she's ready, and find out what happened.*'

'*Getting Innarnians away from the mainland should be our priority,*' Oakley sent. There was a bitter twinge to his words, no doubt due to his time spent as one of Chamele's 'guests'.

'*Can we do a scan? See how many are left?*' Tania asked.

'*That type of power... With Innarn being unreliable, I'm not sure who is capable of such a feat.*' Zana's send felt tired.

'*I bet the Returned could,*' Fenix sent.

'*I'll ask Collis and get him to check on Joana as well,*' Tania sent and turned back to the lesson. Admittedly, the thirteen uses of aquaphonics were interesting, but less so than saving those who might be trapped.

After class was let out, Tania hurried to catch Collis. She bumped into his arm. "Well met."

"Well met."

'*I was wondering if you'd mind scanning Lissae and seeing how many Innarnians are left on the mainland. Particularly where Joana came from?*' Tania sent in a rush.

'There are none left. We did one last night. Joana wanted to make sure.'

'What if there are more captives?' Tania wrung her hands.

'Joana took care of it.'

'Who was holding her?'

'Chamele.' Collis looked away from her, his jaw clenched.

Tania got the feeling that Chamele had met a particularly horrid end. She couldn't stop the rush of satisfaction that someone who had ceaselessly caused others so much grief was gone from this Realm. *'Perhaps Joana would share the memory with Grace?'* Tania suggested.

Collis gave her a considering look. *'Perhaps.'*

A little worried her sudden bloodlust startled him, Tania looked away.

Putting a finger under her chin, Collis tugged her face back around and gave her a swift kiss.

The bell rang, and Collis grinned at her before rushing off.

Tania felt rooted to the spot. Only the jostling of the other students got her moving again. The rest of the day passed in a fog.

Shari moved through the last motus, the sounds of fabric rustling as the rest of the guild followed along. She was leading this session alone, as Samuel was still stressed about Jetonyx's moult.

Joana was sitting off to the side, arms wrapped around her middle.

"So, who wants to spar?" Shari asked.

Hands went up all across the training ground. On the side, Joana's hand was up as well.

Shari pointed at her. "Go on then."

Joana rose, dusting off her skirts, and when her hands were back in view, she held a dagger in each one.

Falling easily into a defensive position, Shari let Joana circle her, moving to keep the other woman in her sights.

Despite everything she'd been through, Joana seemed steady on her feet. She carried the daggers with ease, and when she lunged, the movement was so fluid, Shari almost didn't react in time.

Steel clanged against her shield, and Shari grinned, showing more teeth than was needed. "You can do better than that."

Snarling, Joana lunged again, pushing forward with Innarn and dagger as one.

Shari's glove snapped into being, and she parried, the twin blades screaming across the edge of the dagger.

Snapping her leg up, Joana kicked Shari in the ribs, sending her spiralling away.

Chest throbbing under the buckling of her shield, Shari strengthened her Innarn and whirled back to the fight, glove lashing out and catching Joana's sleeve.

A thin streak of red appeared under the gaping material, and Joana surged forward, snapping daggers far closer to Shari's skin than she was comfortable with.

Ducking out of the way, Shari twisted around Joana and smacked her arm, sending a dagger sliding to the other side of the grounds.

Joana snarled and rounded on Shari, another dagger pulled from the pockets of her skirt. She threw one then another and another, a never-ending stream of steel.

Shari twisted and turned to avoid the blades. The constant hammering was draining her shield at a rate she hadn't experienced before.

Then she dodged when she should have ducked, and metal pierced the meat of her arm.

Although she felt a scream leave her lips, no sound emerged.

The Realm was silent once more.

After pulling the dagger from her arm, Shari roughly cleaned the blade on her pants leg and gave it back to Joana, handle first, who was mouthing wordless apologies.

"Great session," Shari said as the sound rushed in. "I might go get cleaned up. Continue to spar if you're up for it!" She flashed a smile as blood dripped between the white knuckles of her fingers and down her arm.

Asterion stepped through the door to Jonathan's study, the diary he'd been studying burning a hole in his pocket.

"Guardian," he started.

"Asterion, please. Call me Jonathan."

"Unless we are talking about Realm-saving business. Then Guardian is acceptable, is it not?" Asterion said.

"Are we talking about Realm-saving business?"

"Yes, I think I have..." Asterion continued to speak, but no words came out of his mouth. A body shot out of a door that hadn't been there a moment ago, and Asterion was shocked to find his hand wrapped around the apprentice's throat.

As Asterion hastily let go, Samuel dropped to his feet, and the two stared at each other as the sound rushed back into the room.

"Let's never speak of this," Samuel said.

Too stunned to do anything other than nod, Asterion retreated to the desk outside the office and stared at the fingers he was surprised were still attached.

The diary in his pocket was all but forgotten.

CHAPTER NINETEEN

Kerday

Third day of the third week of Nightcrest

A shriek had Arilla vaulting over the counter and storming into the backroom, sword at the ready.

Calem, backed up against the bench, was leaning away from what looked like the biggest bug in the Realms hovering in front of his face.

He shrieked again.

Arilla put the sword down and grabbed a jar instead.

The bug darted closer and backed away just as quick. Sneaking up behind it, Arilla eased the jar over the top and slid a plate across the opening.

"I'll take it outside, love," she said gently.

Nodding, Calem didn't release his white-knuckled grip on the counter until she was back inside.

"All gone," she said. "How did it get in?"

"I, uh–" Calem cleared his throat. "The wards around the shop must be failing. I'll give them a bit of a boost. Later."

Wrapping her arms around his middle, Arilla held Calem. When they'd been boys, Wolf had tormented Calem with a bug that had stung him so badly, he'd ended up in the Healers Centre for a week.

It had been tricky, when Arilla had seen him face down an insect for the first time. A fully grown man, able to decimate armies and rip limbs off, shrieking and flailing at a creature not even a hundredth of his size. Still, if Calem could hold back armies for her, she'd slay all the bugs on the island for him.

Once the adrenaline had bled off and he'd stopped shaking, Arilla gave Calem a last squeeze and let him go.

"Maybe ask Shari to help? It'd be nice to see her again," Arilla suggested.

Calem nodded and dusted his apron off.

Arilla left him to his thoughts. Picking up her sword, she went to open the tavern for the day.

Samuel sat back in the chair behind the Guardian's desk, paging through the book Jonathan had handed him. "What's this?"

"Part of your duty as my apprentice is to keep the handbook updated," Jonathan said.

"The handbook?" Samuel raised a brow.

Jonathan looked away. "*The Altoriae's Handbook.*"

"I'm hearing about this just now because?" Samuel's voice dropped an octave.

"Honestly, I meant to tell you sooner—when you'd come back from the conclave—but with everything that happened, I thought it better to wait." Jonathan was an open book, doing nothing to hide his mistake.

Staring at the Guardian hard enough to see his soul, Samuel gave a single, sharp nod. "What is the purpose of the handbook?"

"It contains the writings of knowledge of the Altoriaes and their Guardians who have come before us. We use it to keep track of happenings on the Realms, of beings or creatures just discovered, of allies and foes, and new things that may make saving Lissae easier."

"And you're giving it to me because?" Samuel wanted him to spell it out.

"Because I trust you. I know you will do everything in your considerable power to ensure Shari's safety, and this will help you with that quest."

Samuel nodded slowly. "Do you mind if I read through it?"

Jonathan tipped his head. "That's your copy. What you do with it is up to you. I just ask that you keep it safe. It's linked to the ones Shari and I hold. If anything were to happen to it..."

"They would all suffer the same fate," Samuel finished.

Rising from his seat, Jonathan said, "I'll ask Lizbeth to watch the hatchlings for you, give you a bit of time to digest some of the things in there."

Feeling the heft of the tome in his hand, Samuel hummed in agreement. "Thank you." He hoped Jonathan realised the words were not just due to the hatchlings.

Pausing in the doorway, Jonathan nodded to him then slipped from the room, leaving Samuel to his thoughts.

And to the book.

What I wouldn't have done to get my claws on this a mere season ago.

Which was precisely why the Guardian had waited to hand it over.

Samuel didn't blame him.

Still, he had unprecedented access to a book thought to be myth, and he was going to take full advantage.

Hours later, a sound at the door had him looking up, eyes bleary from squinting at tiny text.

Tuzar-Terrance stood on the threshold, staring at the book in his hands. "I thought the Guardian would be in," he said.

No greeting. "He's not," Samuel said shortly, snapping the book closed.

Terrance eyed the cover and frowned. "Did the Guardian lend you that? Only, I saw him reading it the last time I was in. Was hoping to get a peek at some of the knots."

Samuel would be quite happy to get the hemmit-loving tuzar a knot around his neck. "Sorry, not for loan."

There was a movement behind Terrance, and Shari's distinctive black hair appeared over his shoulder. Before she could do anything, another dark head appeared, and Shari sighed.

"I swear you have more daggers than I do," Shari said to the girl beside her, pulling a dagger from who knows where to wave in Grace's face.

He didn't bother to hide his smirk when Terrance almost left his skin behind.

"Altoriae!" The basalt-chewing buzzard turned and caught Grace's next attempt with his shoulder.

"Oh dear," Shari and Grace said at the same time, their expressions both devoid of emotion.

A shiver ran through Samuel. An image of the two girls growing up together flashed through his mind.

The Realms wouldn't have stood a chance.

Sighing, Samuel roughly shifted the absolute blyknot to the Healers Centre. He was sure they were used to dealing with fools who didn't know how to avoid the pointy end of a blade.

Lizbeth puffed her cheeks out, trying to hold back the sigh that wanted to escape. When Samuel had asked her to watch the hatchlings, she hadn't expected to be dodging projectiles.

Jetonyx was scratching. Again. Scales were going everywhere, and they were *sharp*. The two smaller ones were shrieking and playing catch with the deadly projectiles.

Next time Samuel asks me to look after them, I'm demanding armour!

Chapter Twenty

Narday

Fourth day of the third week of Nightcrest

Creeping up behind a chicken felt like the most ridiculous thing she'd done today, but Tania was sure it could be worse.

Esse was on the run again, and nothing seemed to be working.

She'd tried worms, seeds, and wrangling the blue menace with Innarn, but, of course, Esse was one step ahead of them all and was happily clucking her way out of the garden.

"You're a terror of the highest regard," Tania hissed after her. "One day, someone is going to think you're meant for stew, and then you'll wish you'd picked the worms."

The potential stew ran straight at a pair of legs and flapped her way upwards, right into Collis's arms.

"Threatening chickens rarely goes well," Collis said, soothing Esse's ruffled feathers.

"What if the chicken threatened me first?" Tania asked, blowing a bit of hair out of her face.

Collis grinned and tucked the strand behind her ear. "Esse would never do that, would she?" He winked at her, and Tania felt her knees go weak.

"She has you wrapped around her little blue feathers," Tania grumbled but smiled up at him.

"Heading to school?"

"As soon as I can get this one in her pen." Tania nodded at Esse.

Collis carried her over and tucked the chicken back into the pen. Esse cooed softly up at him.

Tania rolled her eyes. "Pretending like she's all sweet, when really, she wants to run amuck and scare the neighbours' palon. Again."

Laughing, Collis linked arms with her and led the way to Ridden Hall.

Jonathan stared over non-existent glasses at the knock on the office door. "Yes?" If it was Terrance, he'd think about shifting the man straight to the dungeons. He was showing too much interest in the handbook.

"Lunch!" Zac called and nudged the door open, a large silver tray in his hands.

Shaking his head and grinning, Jonathan cleared his desk with a swipe of Innarn.

"Oh no, we're having an indoor picnic." Zac moved to the rug and started laying everything out. "I was going to suggest outside, but the snow said no."

Unable to wipe the grin from his face, Jonathan joined Zac, marvelling at the spread he'd brought.

"Thank you."

"You're more than welcome. Now—" Zac picked up a roll and started buttering it. "Tell me what troubles you."

Barking a laugh, Jonathan shook his head. "I don't even know where to start. I can't decide if the convergence needs to hurry up or never happen, I don't know how to handle a moulting Q'Aralide, and one of Ronah's own residents is behaving in a very suspicious manner."

"Who?"

"Terrance."

A nasty look came over Zac's face.

Pointing with a forkful of rice, Jonathan asked, "What was that?"

"Terrance Thorne is a menace who deserves to stand still while Ronah rides through the waves."

"Leaving him behind? That was not quite the reaction I was expecting," Jonathan said.

"He was always bragging in school about how he'd be the next Guardian. When you showed up, he wasn't happy. Especially because you're younger than him. There have been things he's done through the years that make me wonder if they were as accidental as he claims."

Jonathan paused, fork halfway to his mouth. "You think the trip wire on Zelbon was on purpose?"

Zac nodded. "Things don't add up. But I wouldn't trust the guy as far as I could kick him."

Shari almost stabbed Domic when he appeared next to her. As it was, she had to calm her racing pulse.

"Well met, Akoren's Linked," Shari said.

Domic smirked at her. "Actually well met, or do the words just drip off your tongue by default?"

"The second," Shari admitted.

Laughing, Domic held out his hand. Shari looked at it but didn't move to take it.

"Well, now I'm stealing you away to show you more of my isle. While you've seen the under city where we live, there's more that you've missed out on."

The smirk and the tone did little to change Shari's mind about jabbing him with something pointy. "I think Grace is rubbing off on me," she muttered. "You expect me to drop everything and accompany you on a tour around Akoren on a whim?"

Domic had a way of tilting his head that made his whole body go on an angle, much like a fish. "When you put it like that..."

Sighing, Shari got to her feet. "Fine." She looked at her discarded lesson plan, lying on top of the handbook. "I wasn't doing much, anyway."

"Excellent." Domic beamed at her and tucked his hand away.

She still hadn't taken it.

The Innarn of Akoren's Linked wrapped around her, and they were standing on the highest peak, surrounded by clouds.

Sucking in a deep breath, Shari reached out with her Innarn. *On Lissae. Still on Lissae. It's fine. I'm safe. Where's Samuel?*

At just the thought of his name, Samuel appeared next to her, mid-change. Shari put her hand on his arm, smoothing away the scales. He stared into her eyes for a moment and nodded then shivered.

Shari conjured them both coats and gave Domic a smile. "Looks like the Guardian's Apprentice wants a tour as well."

Domic's gaze fell to where her hand laid, and he smiled. "Well, of course he does." He turned back to the cloud and breathed out, the vapour fading but not vanishing all together. "Welcome to Fog City, the zenith of the Shifting Islands."

Stretched out around them was a bustling city drenched in cloud and so high up few would think it would be there. Beings wrapped in whites and greys moved around, at ease in the altitude and the moisture in a way that Shari didn't think she'd ever be again.

"Fog City is our best defence against attackers, simply because of the cloud cover and the fact that most beings don't look up. There is a tale about how the first Ilutri who visited Akoren flew through the fog, thinking they would be able to pass, and found themselves plastered against the side of a mountain. They fell in love with the place and made it their own." Domic was smirking slightly, but Shari couldn't blame him. The idea that her staid uncle would smack into a wall of rock was ridiculous but amusing.

"Many of the refugees on the island still aren't aware the city is here," Domic continued. "Shall we shift below?" He flicked an image to Shari's mind, and she nodded.

Hand still on Samuel's arm, she shifted the three of them close to the bay where the allegiance ceremony had taken place.

"If we go just around the bend, you'll see Osithys, the rainy plane city, where most of the refugees have settled," Domic said, leading the way.

The sight of an entire city nestled behind a grove of trees took Shari aback. While the residents of Fog City were wrapped to the point that it was hard to tell they were beings, those in Osithys were comfortable wearing shorts and shirts, only their boots protecting them from the falling snow.

Shari stopped, watching as beings went about their day, laughing and playing. A few still held the remnants of wounds from their conflict with the mainlanders' army, but even they seemed happy.

"How are they cities?" Shari asked.

"Our population is roughly fifty thousand per city. We live closer together and depend on pooled resources rather than individual farms and trade. Plus, we have Merthin, our under city, as well," Domic said.

Something about the way he said it raised Shari's hackles. "I didn't know that was the name. We aren't visiting today?" She tried to keep her tone light but failed.

Domic kept his face turned away, appearing for all the Realms to be fascinated by an older lady dusting snow off her porch. "No, not today."

"Tomorrow then," Samuel said, voice harder than it needed to be.

"Probably not tomorrow either," Domic said. He turned to face them, resigned. "The Lore Keepers don't want you in the water. They're terrified."

For a moment, Shari was tempted to jump into the waters of the bay and see what Domic would do to stop her. Responsibility won out, and Shari nodded. "I see."

"I don't," Samuel said. "What if Shari going into the water was coincidence?"

"And what if it wasn't?" Domic shot back. "Whatever is hiding in the silence is bigger than I care to find out. And if you had any sense at all, you'd be trying everything in your power to make sure that it doesn't win."

A forgotten conversation tickled at the back of Shari's brain. She glanced around the room, seeing a scene she'd all but forgotten. *Globes of Innarn zooming around her, and Lissae's voice echoing through her mind. 'Change is coming. Soon.'*

Sucking in a breath, Shari looked away from Domic. "I don't think we have a choice."

Tania stroked a careful finger down the delicate crystal leaves of the sculpture. Temira's gift had been so thoughtful, and so unlike the technomancer, that Tania was worried.

Flutter twittered at her, and Tania nodded.

"You're right. I really should go and say thank you," she said.

It turned out that tracking Temira down was easier said than done. The technomancer was not in her usual office nor in the chambers she used for healing, or anywhere in the Techno Centre.

Standing on the pavement outside the centre, Tania huffed out a breath. Temira was usually easy to find.

'Talhan?' Tania asked. Would an island that wasn't hers answer her?

The ground under her rumbled softly.

It was enough of an answer that Tania thought it worth a shot asking, *'Do you know where Temira is?'*

Her feet started to be sucked down, and Tania had enough presence of mind to close her eyes as the ground swallowed her whole.

Every one of the particles in her body seemed to be bouncing when she was spat out somewhere near the edge of the farmland on Talhan. Glancing around, Tania spotted the distinct bald blue head through the trees and set off.

Temira was staring out at the crashing waves of the ocean, the oranges and purples of the setting sun painting fire across her skin.

"Temira?" Tania called.

The technomancer sniffed and turned.

"I came to say thank you for your gift." Tania walked closer and stared out over the sea with her friend.

"You don't know what it is, do you?" Temira said flatly.

"No idea," Tania admitted. "Apart from it being so beautiful it almost hurts, and that it must mean a lot to have come from you."

"It's a memory holder. Each leaf holds a memory of something good for you. I've added a few—you can see the different colours. The purples are from me. Others can add to it as well, once you figure out how."

"Will you tell me?" Tania asked.

"No. As a Crystal Innarnian, you must figure it out yourself."

Tania nodded. She'd suspected as much. "You gave me a test as a present," she said, grinning.

"I gave you a lesson as a present," Temira corrected.

That's more like what I expected from Temira. Still grinning, they sat side by side and watched as the sun slipped away.

CHAPTER TWENTY-ONE

Rasshday
Fifth day of the third week of Nightcrest

The guard wrinkled his nose and tried to avoid inhaling deeply. The cloying scent of days-old death permeated the air.

Making his way down blood-slicked ziom stairs, he froze.

There was something in the cell.

Moving.

He crept closer to the closed door and immediately regretted it.

Rats were feasting on the fallen body of a prisoner, ripping away chunks of skin instead of scurrying from the light of his torch.

Gagging, he turned away, only to snap his head back around when a glint caught his eye.

Heavy silver rings lay amongst the bones of the hand.

Rings like the ones Elder Chamele wore.

The elder who was missing.

A rat turned and hissed at the bright light, eyes glowing ominously.

The guard backed away.

He had to let his superior know he'd found the remains of the elder.

Dead.

In her own dungeon.

Might be best to leave the rats out of the report.

Kilgaroth
Rasshday

Raven peered around the tower wall and swore.

The Guardian had sent them out on patrol to Kilgaroth, where the town closest to the gateway had been plagued by a tuostinet. The creature was as tall as three men, with claws as long as his torso tipping each finger. Long, curved horns sat on either side of the cat-like head. Fur covered the four limbs and powerful body. Only the three toes at the end of each leg seemed to be skin, although another quick glance showed that one toe was at an odd angle.

Leather-clad soldiers with pointed metal helmets faced off against the roaring creature. The way they waved their weapons made it seem like they were more interested in fighting each other than the creature they claimed was plaguing their Realm.

Looking back at the guild members, Raven jerked his head. They were here to stop the tuostinet, not get involved in the local squabble.

'*How in the name of Lissae are we meant to take that out?*' Mu's voice echoed in his brain. The others hummed in agreement.

He couldn't blame them. With one sweep of an arm, the tuostinet wiped out half a dozen soldiers, one catching the point of another's helmet in a rather unfortunate place.

Then the tuostinet turned and saw them.

"Oh no," Raven muttered.

Lira and Mu leaned around him and swore.

"Keep him distracted," Lira said and darted forward.

"Wait!"

Too late. Lira was weaving between the soldiers then ducking under the bulk of the tuostinet's body before Raven had the chance to stop her.

'If you die, I'm going to kill you!' he sent to her.

Lira laughed.

Mu flicked his hands, creating a fog that settled low to the ground, enough to disguise Lira's presence, even though a few soldiers had obviously seen her.

Elani heaved a sigh and flicked her bow over her shoulder. Using the rough stones of the tower, she climbed upwards. *'Taking high.'*

'Taking low,' Raven replied, getting on the ground and keeping tight up against the wall.

'Mid ground,' Mu sent.

'Toe,' Lira replied.

'Toe?' the others repeated.

There was a mighty grunt, followed by a bellow, and the tuostinet's body swayed, the anger falling from the beasts' face. He sat down heavily, the ground shaking from his fall.

How am I going to explain that Lira was flattened by a tuostinet's arse? Raven thought wildly. Hasty steps pounded next to his head, and Lira was there, back against the stonework and breathing hard.

'What in the name of Lissae was that?' Elani sent as she dropped beside them.

'He had a broken toe.'

The tuostinet was lifting his leg at an odd angle, tongue lapping at the now straight digit.

The soldiers were slowly lowering their weapons.

Was the suddenly docile beast enough of a reason to lay down their arms?

When hostile faces turned their way, Raven shifted them back to the gate before anyone could argue.

'Never, ever do that again,' Raven sent.

The tuostinet's horns could still be seen from their vantage point, bobbing as the beast continued to clean.

"Let's get back before something else breaks," he said, and ushered them through the gateway. *Or before the soldiers come up with a common enemy to fight.*

Lissae

Rasshday

"Are you sure you want to patrol?" Shari glanced at Yessna.

"Afraid, little healer?" Yessna's purr sounded dangerous.

Rolling her eyes, Shari gestured to the double doors.

Right as they sprang open.

Members of the guild wandered through.

"I can't believe you did that!" Mu was saying.

"I grew up around animals. If something is broken, they're going to lash out." Lira looked quite pleased with herself.

Raven, last through the doors, closed them firmly. "You need to warn us before you decide to play healer to a... Oh, Altoriae."

"To a what?" Shari asked, struggling to keep a straight face.

The patrollers looked at one another, uneasy.

"To a tuostinet," Elani said, bumping her shoulder against Lira's.

"Elani!" Lira hissed.

"What was broken?" Shari asked. Beside her, Drah's shoulders were shaking. She tried desperately to ignore him.

"His toe," Lira said.

Shari clamped her jaw shut so it wouldn't drop. She could almost picture the scene. Tiny Lira struggling to straighten a toe as long as her own leg. "Well, that's one way to end a patrol."

"Is that where you're heading now?" Raven asked.

It took considerable effort not to swear. Shari was *technically* not meant to leave Lissae without Samuel or Jonathan. But both seemed like they needed a rest, and when the U'sala had caught up with her outside the museum, it seemed fortuitous. Plus, she was pretty sure Yessna was one of the few Samuel trusted.

"Yes," she said shortly.

Raven raised his brows but gestured to the doors. "All yours."

Shari lifted her chin and walked through. How long it would be before Jonathan realised she'd left Lissae?

By the startled look Raven was giving her and the way he wriggled his finger in his ear, Shari figured it would not be long. He beckoned her back to the doors.

The moment Shari poked her head through, sound ceased to exist.

Wide-eyed, she stared at Raven, who looked paler than she'd ever seen him before.

Heart pounding in her chest, Shari snapped forwards and slammed the doors closed, the sound returning in a rush.

She turned to Yessna. "Change of plans," she said. "I think... I think we need to stay on Lissae."

The Ferah nodded, gaze darting back to the doors. "Viorath can wait," she said.

Drah glanced at the closed gateway. "Don't think the portal has ever felt like that before," he rumbled.

"Like what?" Mu asked.

The guild was watching them with various horrified expressions.

"Oppressive."

Calem was cursing in the kitchen.

Arilla poked her head in to see if he was alright. "What's going on, love?"

Looking at her shamefaced, he said, "No matter what I do, I can't get the crystal hot enough."

She glanced out to the tavern full of hungry beings. "What about fire-cooked food? And I'll get started on some Wisara fish."

Throwing one last scowl at the crystal which usually heated all their food, Calem nodded. "Best change the menu, love."

"Already on it," Arilla sang.

"So, the final joining is coming up, and you need a gown."

Shari stared at Anika like she was speaking a different language. After the non-patrol, she'd stalked the streets of Ronah, trying to make sense of the silence and what it might mean. Before the Xanderri, she would have said clouds were benign, fluffy things in the sky. But if they could be menacing, whatever was hiding in the silence could be worse.

"Right." Everyone else was worried about the convergence, and the only thing Anika was concerned about was what form of fabric to cover her in.

"Like you don't need a distraction," Anika huffed, guiding her past the empty outdoor tables of the cafe. Everyone was avoiding the cold tonight.

"Ouch!" Shari pulled her leg away, and two eyes glared at her from under a table. "Grace?"

"Shield better!" Grace snarled and disappeared with a *crack*.

Anika looked at the empty spot. "I didn't know shifting could sound angry."

"I didn't know dinner forks could go through leather," Shari countered, "let alone my shield."

Glancing at Shari, Anika shook her head. "Maybe I need to add reinforcements to your dress?"

Shari nodded. With Grace around, reinforcements were a good idea.

Chapter Twenty-Two

Vebaday

Sixth day of the third week of Nightcrest

Time seemed to crawl, and if Shari wasn't one of only a handful of Lissaens with the ability to stop or speed through the pace of living, she would have sworn someone was slowing the progression of the day.

The students were filing into the classroom at a regular pace. Despite the itch under her skin to speed the lesson up, Shari straightened and refused to give into the urge.

"Samuel tells me you've all come a long way since our last lesson," Shari said. "Show me what you've got!"

There was a flurry of movement as the students pushed their desks away, and Shari grinned. After the last lesson, she knew their shields would be closer to protecting them when the mainlanders came knocking.

Alistair was up first. He gave her a shy grin and pushed his hands forward, flaring his fingers out.

Nothing happened.

The grin fell, and he tried again.

Nothing.

Reaching out, Shari froze.

From the moment Alistair's Innarn had awoken, it had wrapped so thickly around him it was almost overwhelming to be in his presence. Now she felt only the faintest of sparks, hardly enough to make a shield.

"It worked yesterday," Alistair said, trying the motus again.

Shari stilled his hands. "I believe you." She looked around the room. Expressions were ranging from worried to smug. The same look she'd suffered through every time an instructor gave lessons in Innarn. "Everyone try," she snapped.

The students looked at her, startled, but did as commanded.

Smug looks faded as the rest of the class tried and failed to produce even a flicker.

Refusing to let them see how worried she was, Shari got them to put their desks back. "Looks like we're studying instead." She was half tempted to get them to practise their weapons movements instead but thought it safer to keep frustrated teens away from sharp objects for the time being.

Tania smiled at Brinley and passed another plate her way.

Domic was hosting them again, this time in his underwater home. The table before them was covered with food preferred on Akoren. Lots of heavy, savoury dishes in tiny pots, perfect for enjoying in cold weather dotted the sandy coloured table, with most of them containing some sort of fish. Green and blue crackers lined small platters of tiny, delicate orange orbs. Clear, round bowls the size of a large teacup had been placed before each of them. Dark blues and purples gave way to lighter tones at the tops of the bowls, which were decorated with a swirl of cream, red berries, and slices of citrus.

"What's this?" Tania asked, picking up the decadent concoction.

"Well, it's iccecot sorbet—the perfect treat for a winter's night," Domic said.

Lifting the cold bowl, Tania raised her brows at Domic. He nodded and picked his own up before taking a big spoonful of the dessert.

Hesitantly, Tania took a bite. Tart, sweet flavour burst over her tongue. Another bite, and the sweet richness of rutenberries perfectly complimented the tart iccecot. There was a burn somewhere under the sweetness, and Ronah rumbled a warning. "This is amazing," Tania said.

"Delicious!" Cyrus agreed.

Brinley laughed from under her hood. "Don't have too much, or you won't make it home."

"You are no fun," Domic grumbled but grinned at her.

"We have very different definitions of fun." Brinley sniffed, a smile on her lips.

"What won't be fun," Zana said, "is the convergence."

Spoon halfway to her mouth, Tania nodded before she even thought. Fenix and Oakley looked as troubled as she felt.

"Is there anything we can do to make it less... daunting?" Brinley asked.

Zana nibbled on a piece of fish stew. "I don't believe so. There are reports from all over the islands that Innarn is becoming unstable. We must be prepared for whatever Lissae has in store for us."

"Surely there are records?" Brinley asked. "I've searched Vannali's hold but couldn't find a thing."

Tania looked away. For a selfish moment, she wanted to be normal, a teenager without the fate of an island and an entire Realm on her shoulders. Tears prickled at her eyes.

Ronah reached out to her, rubbing along the edges of her consciousness, reminding Tania that she wasn't alone. A shuddering breath later, Tania allowed herself to become distracted. Fish of all shapes and sizes swam past the window, and all she wanted to do was dive into the water and swim with them.

Cyrus lent against her shoulder, nudging her back to the present conversation.

"Without records, how are we to know what to expect?" Brinley's voice was entering the upper octaves of what was comfortable.

"Unexpected comes with being a Linked," Zana said. "We may not be able to control what is about to happen, but we can control how we react to it."

The conversation moved on, but Tania's mind stayed on Zana's words. She didn't know what the future held, but she would choose her reaction well.

"How's my favourite niece?" Terrance beamed at Anika.

She scowled at him. "If by favourite, you mean the one you got kicked out of home, then fine." Anika made to flounce away, but Terrance grabbed her arm.

"Honestly, I did it for you," he said. "Rany wanted to stifle your creativity, and I wanted to set it free. Look at how much you've changed."

Anika pulled her arm away from him and huffed but didn't leave.

"And since I did you a favour, I wondered if you could do one for me?"

She narrowed her eyes at him. "What sort of favour?"

"I've been trying to find time to get to the castle. The Guardian said I could borrow a book from him, but I haven't been able to pick it up."

"You want me to bring you a book?"

"Yes." Terrance had to tread carefully. He couldn't appear too eager. "*The Sea Tailor's Handbook.*"

The girl glared at him. "Since when have you been interested in sailors?"

"Oh, no. There's just a particular knot I was hoping to learn. The Guardian said it was in there last time we spoke." Terrance waved her concerns off. *Nosy chit.*

"Why didn't you get the book off him then?" Anika asked.

"He was still using it." Sweat was beading along his hairline. It took everything inside Terrance to not grab his niece and shake her into submission.

"I'll ask," she said. "But he might not be finished with it yet."

The way she spoke, it was clear Anika would never bring the book up with the man who called himself Guardian. "Thanks, Anika."

Anika glared at him one last time and left.

'Guardian, I wondered if I might have a moment?' Asterion sent.

"Join us," Jonathan called out.

Stepping into the room, Asterion stood to the side as the Guardian finished his meeting with the elders of the Shifting Islands. As they left, the elders shared pleasantries with him, and Asterion felt the stirrings of hope warring with the feeling of dread in his chest.

"You wanted to see me?" Jonathan asked.

"Yes, Guardian, I..." Asterion started.

"You'll never believe what the little tuzar did!" Samuel burst into the room.

The book in Asterion's pocket was once again forgotten.

"Your precious Altoriae tried to go on patrol. Alone!"

The Guardian shared an amused glance with Asterion. "Did she?"

"Why are you not more upset?" the apprentice snarled.

Asterion's hackles rose.

"Because I told her she could. A shackled Shari is far from pleasant," Jonathan said.

"And why did I have to find out from Yessna?"

"Perhaps because you two gossip more than the elders?" Jonathan suggested.

Asterion took a good look at the Guardian, trying to sear the man's measurements into his mind, sure he'd be digging a grave soon enough.

Samuel, however, scowled, then slumped in a chair. "Do not."

"And you pout worse than our charge."

The apprentice signed something in Veti Cant that must have been rude, if the Guardian's blush and startled laugh was anything to go by.

"Sorry, Asterion, you were trying to say something?" Jonathan said, turning back to him.

Shaking his great bull head, Asterion said, "I'll come back later." Hand wrapped around the book in his pocket, Asterion just hoped there would be a later in which he could come back.

Tania rested her head against Collis's shoulder. He'd organised a picnic under the stars, and she was determined to enjoy every moment.

Collis seemed fascinated by the pinpricks of light in the sky. "I missed this, while we were away."

'Away' was such a tiny word for what happened to him. To all the Returned.

"The sky was different?" Tania asked.

"Very. It was an eternal twilight. A pink sky that never ended. But if you walked for more than a few hours, you ended up right where you started." Collis kept his gaze on the stars.

Tania focused on him. "Do you want to talk about it?"

A dark shape, bigger than any creature had the right to be, flew overhead, blocking out the stars for a moment.

Underneath her cheek, Collis stiffened. "We had Q'Aralide there. In the pocket-Realm. Until it arrived, we were mostly safe. But they don't kill for food; they kill for fun. More than once, I was dragged away, feet dangling until it decided to drop me."

Shuddering, Tania wrapped her arms around Collis, who suddenly seemed very far away.

"Sanithane and his hatchlings are different. There is a certain, unmissable menace to him, but the way he looks after those under his care is admirable." Collis returned her embrace, holding her close for a moment.

"The way you look after others is admirable too," Tania said. She felt entirely safe, nestled up against his chest.

Then Ronah started to cry.

CHAPTER TWENTY-THREE

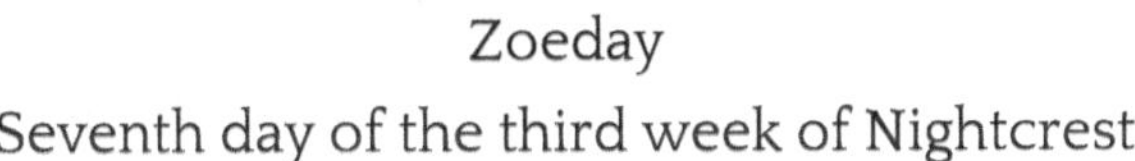

Zoeday

Seventh day of the third week of Nightcrest

Ronah was sobbing, crying out for Vannali. On the periphery of her thoughts, Shari could feel the other Shifting Islands joining in.

Closing her eyes, Shari sought out Tania and shifted to her side. The Linked, arms wrapped around Collis, looked overwhelmed.

"Talk to Ronah," Shari begged.

"What do I say?" Tania asked, tears streaming down her face.

"How long until we join with Vannali?"

"A month, maybe more," Tania said.

Ronah wailed, the sound cutting through to Shari's very soul.

"Can it be less?" she asked through gritted teeth.

"Yes," Tania hiccupped.

The wail subsided enough that Shari could hear her own thoughts again. "When?"

"Without being able to shield, it's hard to say. Fourteen days?"

The sobs filling her mind quietened.

"Fourteen days," Shari nodded, smiling at Tania.

There would be time to be terrified later.

Jetonyx sneezed, and Samuel stepped to the side, avoiding the scale that flew from the hatchling's face.

The not-so-black Q'Aralide laughed. '*Whoops,*' he sent.

"Mind your scales," Samuel said.

'*Wish they'd all come off,*' Jetonyx replied. '*They're itchy!*'

"I know," Samuel soothed. He reached for the jar Lizbeth had left and held it aloft.

Jetonyx bared his fangs in a grin and lowered his snout. Samuel liberally applied the paste designed to calm the itching.

'*Can we get back to our lesson now?*' Tormorylth whined.

'*Just you wait until you moult,*' Jetonyx warned, his voice dark.

Tormorylth poked her tongue out at him.

Off to the side, Kemanyr rolled her eyes, sitting primly as she waited for him to continue.

Another sneeze, and Samuel wished he could remove the rest of the loose scales before they impaled him.

"There was a way, once, to remove them quicker, but it requires two Dark Innarnians, and..." He broke off at the knock on the door. Innarn reaching, he called out, "Enter!"

Shari came in, and Tormorylth all but bowled her over.

'*You came!*'

"Samuel said you'd been wanting to see me," Shari laughed, hands rubbing against the smaller Q'Aralide's sides.

'*What took you so long?*' Tormorylth pouted.

Samuel shook his head and glanced away. He was sure he'd never been that dramatic when he'd been young.

"I've had a bit to do, lately," Shari said.

He could feel the weight of her gaze on his face, but Samuel found he couldn't meet it. The hatchlings had regaled him with tales from their time in Zuefie and the Realm growing ever smaller around them. Between that and the destruction of Altum, he had no desire to mention that their time on Lissae may end sooner than any of them wanted.

"But I'm here now," Shari added.

"So am I," a rusty voice said from behind Shari.

For the space of a heartbeat, Samuel thought the shapeshifter was back and taking Shari's form once more. But no, it was her cousin, arm wrapped around Shari's throat with a blade in hand, ready to spill blood.

Shari shifted her weight, and Grace went flying over her shoulder to land with her back against the floor. Before Shari could move to pin the other girl, Tormorylth was there, front claws digging into soft flesh, acid dripping menacingly from her maw.

Leaning down, Tormorylth opened her mouth, ready to bite Grace's head off, when something in the shadows rumbled.

Q'Aralide and Lissaen alike froze and turned to look.

Glowing eyes blinked at them, and wisps of white gathered into the form of a canine. One happy rumble later, and the Shadow Bringer was gone.

"Tormorylth, no. You can't eat Grace," Shari said, pushing ineffectively at the hatchling's side.

'Glowy eyes said yes.' Tormorylth scowled.

"We should be doing the opposite of what the Shadow Bringer wants until we know who sent it and why," Samuel said. Personally, he was quite happy for Tormorylth to eat the girl, but prudence must prevail.

Grumbling, Tormorylth got off Grace, digging her claws in more than necessary as she did so.

Grace sprang to her feet, growled at them all, and shifted away.

"Is no one else concerned that Grace keeps trying to stab me?" Shari asked.

"If you can't defend yourself against one slightly murderous relative, then how are you going to defend the rest of the Realm?" Samuel asked.

Shari sighed. "I thought you would say something like that."

"Perhaps you could give me a hand?" Samuel said.

"Sure," Shari replied.

Part of him wanted to caution her about agreeing so easily to things, but Samuel stopped. Shari trusted only a handful of beings enough to be so accommodating, and he should consider himself fortunate to be among them.

"I've thought of a way to speed up Jetonyx's moult," he said.

The hatchling across the room stopped gnawing at his side and twisted around to face them. 'Really?'

Kemanyr, in all her golden glory, sidled up to Jetonyx to nibble on another scale for him.

"It needs both of us, though," Samuel said. He started second-guessing himself the moment the words left his mouth.

"What do you need me to do?" Shari asked.

Samuel pushed an image into her mind of using Innarn to scrape the scales off Jetonyx's hide.

"Like sunburn?" she asked with a frown.

"Similar. But with the Darkest Innarn you have."

Shari chewed on her lip for a moment. "Okay, but the moment it starts to hurt, you have to let us know," she said to Jetonyx.

The hatchling nodded frantically and wriggled closer, knocking Tormorylth to the side. She hissed at him and flew upwards to perch above their heads.

Raising his hands, Samuel gathered his Innarn, sending the dark force spiralling around Jetonyx. He could feel Shari thinking of Altum, how Innarn had felt different in the darkest of Realms, before she pushed her Innarn towards him.

Before them, Jetonyx was starting to glow. Golden scales were being revealed, and the black ones were breaking away, thudding into the wooden walls at the far end of the room.

Grinning triumphantly at Shari, Samuel almost missed when Tormorylth slipped from her perch, falling straight into the maelstrom of Innarn that had stripped Jetonyx of his old scales. Her eyes were glowing, much like the Shadow Bringer's were prone to do.

Shari's grin fell.

Tormorylth shrieked as scales were forcibly stripped from her hide.

Eyes wild, Samuel frantically tried to call the Innarn back, but it seemed to have taken a life of its own. It didn't stop until Tormorylth was a sobbing mess on the floor.

"Tormorylth?" Shari asked, tentatively stepping forward.

The hatchling moaned from under the pile of discarded black scales. She lifted her head, and Samuel shielded his eyes from the glare.

Three golden hatchlings were catching the sunlight, refracting it around the room until one of them thought to draw the blinds.

Samuel looked at the trio of golden Q'Aralide hatchlings, dumbfounded.

Arilla was finishing the last of the sweeping, humming to the music coming from the direction of the kitchen, when strong arms wrapped around her middle.

"Care to dance?" Calem asked.

The moment Arilla turned in his embrace, the lights flickered and went out.

"What happened?" Arilla asked, glancing up at his silhouette.

"Innarn's still acting up," Calem growled.

The street outside was dark, bathed only in the glow of the half-full moons and the light of the stars.

"Romantic." Arilla leaned up and kissed his jaw.

Calem huffed a laugh. "I suppose we can still have that dance."

The music had stopped when the lights went out.

Arilla started to hum, and Calem danced her through the tables until she was laughing.

Elder Ben from Kenorvia stared slack-jawed as the guard repeated himself.

"I found Elder Chamele's remains." The man was pale and shaking. Sweat beaded his brow, and he looked like he'd seen a particularly gruesome ghost.

Elder Gywn from Vendalbara sighed. "Good riddance. Her ridiculous plans always caused unnecessary loss of life."

Ben frowned. When was loss of life considered necessary?

"You will let us avenge her?" the guard asked.

As Jinkor's largest neighbour, Kenorvia had the right to rule over them until another elder could be found and appointed. Although, with the number of deaths occurring, soon there wouldn't be anyone over the age of forty left on the isle.

"You want to avenge Chamele?" Gywn asked.

Despite his pallor, the guard wore a thunderous expression. "*Elder* Chamele deserves no less."

"The loss of Chamele truly is devastating." Gywn wiped away an imaginary tear. "If you want to avenge her, fine. Make sure to send your finest men." Gywn's smile was predatory. "Just do it quietly. We don't need to start a war."

Ben sighed into his teacup. It looked like Kenorvia was about to expand past their borders, and the Shifting Islands were about to meet what was left of Jinkor's army.

He didn't know what was worse.

While Gywn's focus was elsewhere, Ben palmed the cheese knife. If Vendalbara was going to make a move to establish rule on Jinkor, he'd put an end to it himself.

Temira held out her hand and felt the solid *thwack* of a handle landing in her palm.

She adjusted the screw a minute amount and sighed, stepping back.

"Do you think you've got it?" Cyrus asked in hushed tones.

Given another century or so, and the Lissaen might be as in tune with her as Xani had been. Stilling the trembling of her hand by placing it on the bench beside their latest creation, Temira knew she didn't have that long left.

"We will know after testing." Something inside her bones said that this prototype would be just like all the others.

Useless.

"Being phase one," she said anyway.

Cyrus opened the valve on the B.I.T., allowing a skerrick of Innarn to eke out.

The device, instead of gathering and amplifying the Innarn, lay dormant.

In a fit of temper, Temira picked it up and hurled the whole thing across the room, where it smashed against the wall in the most satisfying manner.

"I'd say that's a no then," Cyrus said, his voice loud in the sudden stillness.

"Again," Temira demanded. With what little time she had left, she would ensure her last remaining friends had a future to look forward to.

CHAPTER TWENTY-FOUR

Adonday

First day of the fourth week of Nightcrest

Anika hung behind after the early-morning training session, helping Arilla gather the spare swords.

The sessions were becoming bigger than she'd ever imagined. Beings from all over the Shifting Islands were joining in, and the training ground rang with the sound of sword strikes more often than not.

A few of the Satyrian army took over after Arilla left for the tavern each day, teaching different weapon skills to those who stayed. Whenever Anika thought she could get away with skipping a lesson, at school she'd linger, letting her headmaster leave first and staying back to train even harder.

Today saw her lingering for another reason.

"Arilla, can I ask you a question?" Anika packed the final sword into the bag and turned to the trainer.

"Always," Arilla said with a smile.

"Someone has asked me to get something from the Guardian, and I'm not sure I should," she said.

"Why do you feel like it's inappropriate?" Arilla asked.

Anika squirmed and looked away.

Grace was in the stands, glaring at her.

"Something feels *off*. The Guardian is generous to a fault. Why wouldn't he share a book unless there was a good reason? He has a *bookstore*, for Lissae's sake, and employees who could take packages to Terrance at a moment's notice."

"Terrance?" Arilla sounded a bit like Grace, growling her uncle's name.

"Yes," Anika confirmed miserably.

"Honestly, I'd do the opposite of whatever that steaming pile of dung asked just on principle."

Anika had never heard the normally calm Arilla speak like that about anyone before and had to close her gaping jaw. "You really think so little of him?"

Arilla nodded. "All beings have intrinsic worth. His is just less than a sandfly and twice as useless."

Snickering, Anika nodded.

If Terrance wanted the book, he'd have to get it another way.

Samuel kept sneaking glances at the shiny new hides of his hatchlings.

Shari really couldn't blame him. All the gold was distracting. Zoomer huffed at her as he trotted past, stopping for a quick pat before he went to Samuel.

The eldest Q'Aralide looked on the verge of hyperventilating.

As soon as Zoomer leaned against him, Samuel buried his hands in the palon's thick fur. Slowly, his breathing evened out.

Smiling at Zoomer, Shari forcefully blinked tears away and tried to concentrate on what Jetonyx was sending. It was no use though. Her thoughts were a mess. Shari had come back from patrolling the border last night, alone, and eaten a solo meal she'd thrown together in haste, barely able to stand. Even her bones felt tired. And when she'd woken in the morning, everyone else had already left. Now, in the home of another, Shari felt out of place. Separate from the Q'Aralides, who were rapidly sending about *acid baths* and *trips to the caustic falls* and other things not meant for her fleshy hide.

To make matters worse, someone else needed her biggest source of comfort.

"I should go," Shari said abruptly, rising, only to freeze as glowing eyes appeared in her path.

"Freeze," Samuel said.

Shari glared at him, having already come to that conclusion.

Wisps of white were gathering around the eyes, and the shape was becoming more solid than Shari could remember seeing.

Samuel made a movement, and the Shadow Bringer growled low in its forming throat.

"I don't think you should move," Shari said. Would there be enough time to summon her blade before it ripped out her throat?

The hackles on the beast went down, and it lowered its head before nudging her belly with it. Shari fell back into her seat with an *oof*.

The beast climbed up onto her lap, curling around like a cat before decisively licking her from chin to temple.

"Ew," Shari laughed. "No licking!"

Samuel made a choking sound. "I thought it was going to rip your head off," he said.

"Somehow, I don't think that's part of its plan."

The beast gave her one more lick and disappeared.

Shari grinned at Samuel, feeling lighter than she had in days.

She wasn't alone anymore.

Jonathan took his glass from Zac with a smile and a shake of his head. "You know I can..." The rest of the words were lost as sound was sucked out of the room.

Everything was painfully silent. Zac was looking at him with eyes as wide as saucers.

The silence dragged on. Jonathan grabbed a fork from the table and gently tapped it on the side of his glass every time his heart took a beat.

Probably shouldn't be that fast, he thought, and tried to calm the blood racing through his veins.

Twenty beats later—*or was it more?*—sound rushed back in with such force, Jonathan's ears were ringing.

"It's getting longer," Zac said.

"Don't worry," Jonathan said automatically, and felt like a fool as soon as the words slipped from his mouth.

Zac raised his eyebrows at him. "When should I worry, if not now?"

"When it becomes more frequent," Jonathan shot back. *Please don't let it happen.*

He had a feeling that particular plea was going to go unanswered.

The last thing Temira was expecting when she exited the Techno Centre was a mid-sized golden Q'Aralide sitting neatly in front of the doors.

"You," Temira said and attempted to sweep past the hatchling, who stood and kept pace with her.

Temira refused to indulge in her curiosity. She would *not* ask why the creature was now golden instead of black. It was, of course, the same one who had declared them friends. She could tell by the blue eyes.

'I *thought I should visit*,' the gold nuisance sent. '*That's what friends do.*'

'We *are not friends*,' Temira shot back.

'But I *want to eat you! To help you honour your traditions!*'

Growling, Temira turned abruptly into an alley too small for an adolescent Q'Aralide.

The nuisance slid in behind her, wings raised to keep from knocking into anything.

Temira refused to acknowledge the jolt of her heart. *What happened to make this one so small?*

But she couldn't ask. To ask was to open the proverbial gate to the friendship the nuisance desired, and unless that came in the form of a lumbering crystal chair and grey skin, Temira wasn't sure she wanted it.

Samuel knew he must look as pathetic as he felt when Lizbeth all but thrust her tray of cookies at his chest.

"Eat and tell me what's wrong," she demanded.

"You're quite bossy for a guest," he said but took a cookie and shoved it whole into his mouth.

Lizbeth laughed and pushed passed him, a thin stick held in one hand. She used it to knock against the floor, and when it struck the couch, she smiled. "I doubt bossy guests are your problem."

Chewing, he stalked to the couch and slumped. "I don't know how to be the eldest of my kind."

"Is it better to be the eldest than the last?"

Jolting, he turned his head to look at her. "You knew that's what I feared?"

"Subtle you are not, my friend." Lizbeth stole a cookie from the tin.

Samuel growled at her.

As usual, Lizbeth ignored him. "You know who *is* the last of their kind? Temira. You should talk to her."

"Temira of Ulnan would prefer to eviscerate me slowly rather than entertain a conversation." Samuel stole another cookie.

Lizbeth's sightless eyes stared through his soul. "Temira will want to talk to you, sooner than you expect."

"I expect 'never', so anything before that would count," he grumbled around the sweet mouthful.

"Despite rumours to the contrary, Temira is not immortal."

Frowning, Samuel looked away, searching for another treat. Thinking about the mortality of the last Ulnan was not on his agenda today. Not when he was still coming to grips with being the sole adult in charge of a clutch of golden hatchlings.

Jonathan was startled by the frantic call and shifted to Viorath before he was fully aware of what he was doing.

Rubbing sleep out of his eyes, he tried to make sense of the situation. Mu was holding a rapidly reddening cloth to Lira's side. Raven was snarling and stomping around, and Elani looked, as always, faintly amused.

Dealon lent up against the wall on the portal side of the double doors, writing in a small notebook. "Well met, Guardian."

"What seems to be the matter?"

"Lira caught an arrow with her gut, and we can't seem to get the doors open," Dealon summed up.

Raising a brow, Jonathan crossed to the door and pulled.

Nothing happened.

Looking at the young guild members, Jonathan heaved a breath. If he couldn't open the doors from this side, then he'd shift them all back. Gathering his Innarn, Jonathan was startled to find there was barely enough there to move a thimble, let alone a patrol group.

'Pala?' The sound inside his mind was so muted, he wasn't sure it actually sent.

CHAPTER TWENTY-FIVE

The doors to the museum were still stuck. Jonathan pulled on them harder, and they rattled for a moment before coming free.

'*Pala, what's going on?*'

The Ducibus, still clutching his staff, appeared by the Guardian's side. '*It's almost time.*'

'*Time for what?*'

Pala's hood moved, as if he was glancing behind Jonathan. Sucking in a wheezing breath, the Ducibus shifted again, and the Guardian of Lissae was unceremoniously thrust through the doors, the rest of the patrol group tumbling in behind him.

'*No more patrols. Shift everyone back. Now!*' Pala sent then slammed the gateway closed.

"No more...? Pala!"

The *now* echoed through his skull, and Jonathan reached out to Shari. '*We need to pull the patrols back—now.*'

In between one heartbeat and the next, Shari was by his side, decked out in full leathers. "Why?"

"Pala's orders," Jonathan said grimly.

Shari's blinked twice, then her mouth set in a grim line and patrollers started to shift in all around them.

Rolling up his metaphorical sleeves, Jonathan started helping her. Innarn seemed to be returning in pulses, and he was going to take what he could grab. The way Pala had sent, he had the feeling they had only a short amount of time, and with the number of beings from Lissae scattered all over the Realms, he didn't have enough Innarn left to slow Time down and give them some more.

'*Samuel. A little help?*' Jonathan sent.

Samuel instantly appeared by Shari's side, his skin covered in the outline of scales, as if he were halfway through changing form.

'*We need to get everyone home. Now. Pala's shutting down the gateway.*'

'*Tuzar's arse.*'

The swearing seemed loud in his head, and when Jonathan sent a quick probe, he could feel that, in the far corner of Samuel's mind, he was chittering with fear.

Shari was shifting in body after body, a fine sheen of sweat the only indicator of the strain.

Glowing eyes watched her from the corner of the room. They could deal with the Shadow Bringer *after* every Lissaen was home.

"How many more?" Samuel asked.

Jonathan took a quick glance around. "Three dozen."

"That's not so bad," Samuel said.

"Groups," Jonathan clarified.

Between shifting beings in, Samuel glared at him.

"Faster!" Shari ordered. "It's closing."

Reaching out to grab the next lot, Jonathan could sense what she meant. There was a narrow field which they could shift beings through, and it was pulling tighter. If they couldn't get everyone back, they'd be stuck outside Lissae.

Redoubling his efforts, Jonathan shifted in groups between one heartbeat and the next. Sweat dripped down his brow at the excessive expenditure of Innarn. He wasn't even going to question where the reserves had come from, but by Lissae, he was going to use every last bit.

"Three groups left," Shari panted beside him.

Samuel grunted.

They each grabbed one group and shifted. As the last being hit the ground beside him, Jonathan felt the doorway to Lissae close for good.

A gong sounded. Beings all around him clapped hands to ears, and in the middle of them all, Shari stood with her hand on the seam of the doors, devastation clear through the slump of her spine.

Suddenly, Shari pounded on the doors. "Pala? Pala. You open up right now! Pala!"

Shari sank to her knees.

Her father rushed through the crowd to her side. "What's wrong?"

The Altoriae lifted a tear-stained face. "I wasn't quick enough. The U'sala..." She broke off.

A cough sounded by Jonathan's side. "You didn't have to, Altoriae," Collis said. "As soon as you shifted us in, I grabbed them, too."

She turned and stared at him, her jaw dropping in astonishment.

"Like you could get rid of me that easily, little healer," Yessna said.

Shari burst into tears, setting everyone in the room off. The museum filled with shocked laughter and sobs as voices raised in confusion, beings trying to figure out why they had been recalled so abruptly. Jonathan found he wasn't sure which was the most appropriate reaction, so he settled for doing both.

He made rounds of the room, checking on everyone. Some smart soul, probably Calem, had called for the healers at some point. Lira's wound was recovering nicely, although Jonathan did his best not to gawp at the dressing the healers insisted on. They were moving through the crowds, making sure the slightest scrape was attended to.

Asterion arrived with Arilla and started handing out clay mugs of soup and warm slices of thick-cut bread.

Shari holed up in the corner of the room, her fingers tangled in the white fur of the Shadow Bringer.

"Does he have a name yet?" Jonathan asked, nodding his head at the creature.

Shari looked down and contemplated the big canine. "Wisp."

Jonathan nodded. A mere wisp of thought had saved them, and the name seemed more than appropriate.

"Have the doors ever been closed before?" Shari asked. Her voice was still hoarse from her earlier crying.

"Not in my lifetime. There's mention in the handbook of Muran requesting it during Anriluka's first attack. Despite his pleading, the Ducibus denied him."

Shari shot a glance at the closed doors. "I wonder what made them seal the doors now?"

Jonathan shrugged. "I'm not sure I want to know."

But they'd find out.

Well before they were ready.

The castle was nearly empty of the usual occupants. Terrance sucked in a harried breath and slid through the door to the Guardian's office.

Laying on the desk for anyone to take was *The Sea Tailor's Handbook*.

"Such a shame if it were to go missing," Terrance muttered. Swiftly, he crossed the room and paused before the troublesome book. From the way the Guardian carried on, this tome had to have the answers as to why his Innarn was failing.

Reaching out, Terrance was barely a breath away from lifting the pages when a blade flashed.

His fingers slid away from the rest of his hand before Terrance had a chance to process what had happened.

Pain kicked in, and he screamed, clutching his fingerless hand to his chest in shock.

Green eyes glared at him from across the desk. "Run," the Altoriae's duplicate snarled.

Terrance did as he was bid, leaving his still-twitching digits behind.

Chapter Twenty-Six

Inthday

Second day of the fourth week of Nightcrest

Jonathan walked into his office at the castle and paused. Dark drops dotted the wooden floor. The scent of fresh blood coated the back of his nose.

Crossbow snapping into being, the Guardian cautiously continued into the room, following the trail.

Someone had left in a rush—that much was clear. The droplets were far enough apart that they must have been running but still bleeding enough for him to notice.

Footsteps sounded behind him. Jonathan held a hand up in warning. A swift glance over his shoulder and he spotted Zac, frozen in the doorway.

When Zac saw the crossbow, he reached into his vest and pulled out a device before snapping it onto his wrist and pointing it towards the area not already covered by Jonathan.

The pair crept forward, Zac circling the room, so he was aiming at the doorway, while Jonathan followed the trail of semi-dried blood right to his desk.

The handbook sat there, innocuous cover still in place. But on the top of it lay four fingers in a pool of blood.

Jonathan frowned and poked at one with a crossbow bolt.

"Why is the book not wet?" a raspy voice asked.

Raising his weapon on instinct, the Guardian wasn't surprised when it flew out of his hand. "Grace. What happened?"

The chair behind the desk turned around. Grace, legs curled beneath her, looked up at him with eyes that were so much like Shari's. "Bad man tried to steal your book. I stopped him."

"He's gone?" Zac asked, lowering his arm.

Grace nodded.

"But you made sure he left a few things behind," Jonathan noted.

She nodded again.

"Do you know his name?" Zac asked.

Shrugging, Grace poked at one of the abandoned digits.

"Someone missing their fingers should be pretty easy to find," Jonathan said.

"Before Ronah joined with the other islands, maybe. Now there are plenty of places to hide," Zac said.

"Next time I'll stab him better," Grace said.

Jonathan compressed his lips so he wouldn't laugh at her earnest tone. He made a non-committal hum of agreement.

She poked at the book again, and the cover shimmered.

All three of them froze.

"Is it meant to do that?" Zac asked.

The Guardian's gaze snapped to Grace. "Only for a select few."

Grace nonchalantly poked it again, pushing it closer to the pool of blood. "Still not wet," she muttered.

"It's warded," Jonathan said, carefully picking the tome up. It felt heavier than ever. Giving the book a sharp look, Jonathan frowned. Additional weight like this usually meant that another copy was about to be created.

For a new Guardian, a new Apprentice...

Or a new Altoriae.

"Fingers. On your desk," Samuel said. He was half-glad the hatchlings had decided to go for a fly, rather than be home for this particular conversation. Sneeze, curled up on his shoulder, was softly snoring, entirely unconcerned with the topic of conversation.

Jonathan took a healthy drink of his azehal. "Yes."

"And you don't know who they belong to?" Shari asked.

"Asterion checked with Holly, and Zac checked with Cyrus, but no one has reported to any of the healing centres with missing digits." Jonathan was having trouble meeting his gaze.

"What else happened?" Samuel asked.

Jonathan's head snapped up, but his gaze still landed somewhere over Samuel's left shoulder. "What makes you think something else happened?"

"Weak, Jon," Shari said, her tone flat.

The Guardian winced. Shari hadn't called him by the diminutive of his name for quite a while. "The handbook. It's replicating."

"What?" Samuel asked.

"Protective feature?" Shari suggested.

"Maybe," Jonathan's words said. His face screamed *doubtful.*

Samuel looked at Shari. She'd gone from lounging on the floor, slumped against the wall, cup held loosely in her hand, to sitting upright, her white-knuckled grip giving more away than the Guardian's words.

"You think something is going to happen to one of us," Samuel said.

"Exactly," Shari blurted before Jonathan could answer.

His first instinct was to cover Shari with a shield. His second was to see if he could get closer. Wisely, Samuel froze before he acted on impulse. "You need a guard."

Sneeze huffed a warning breath onto his cheek.

"Who says it's me?" Shari said.

"You and Jonathan are notorious for not being able to protect yourselves on Ronah. And with the portal closed, it's impossible for you to go anywhere else." Samuel looked away. "If I was still under Oalark's command, this would be the time to strike." There was a tense moment while Samuel waited for the Guardian to strike him down, or the Altoriae to pull his heart from his chest, but nothing happened. Shari rolled her eyes, as if the thought of him turning on them was impossible.

It was now, but he wondered if she realised it hadn't always been that way.

"Why doesn't Jonathan need a guard?"

"Zac wouldn't let anything happen to me," Jonathan said, cheeks flushing.

"Then I'll guard you," Samuel said.

"Are the hatchlings going to fend for themselves?"

Snarky Shari is annoying. "Hardly."

"Then how?"

'*Ronah? Can you create a door between here and the castle?*' Samuel sent.

The island didn't reply. Samuel thought that perhaps the request was too bold, that the island wasn't happy with him—*although how did one annoy a sentient hunk of dirt?* Before he could send again, a frame of wood, smaller than what he expected, appeared on the wall next to where Shari was sitting.

It was almost painful, watching the door eke into existence. The frame, the hinges, the handle. The smooth panel of the door itself filled the gap with a groan.

'*Ready*,' Ronah sounded like she had been running.

Could islands run?

'*My thanks,*' Samuel said.

Shari got to her feet with a groan that rivalled the door. "Come on."

"What?"

"We'd better test it," Shari said. She opened the door and walked through.

After scrambling to his feet, Samuel was on Shari's heels, ducking his head low and stepping through half a heartbeat behind her, a hand raised to keep Sneeze in place.

A black sucking hole surrounded him, sound falling away until not even his pulse ricocheted through his ears.

Shari, eyes wide, was the first thing he saw.

Sound rushed in as the Realm was set to rights. Glancing around, he noted the bed, the pile of discarded clothing, and the stack of neatly oiled weapons on the table.

He was in Shari's bedroom.

"Not quite what I expected," he said. Shari blushed, and Samuel paused. Should he be more worried about having direct access to the Altoriae's bed chamber or the increasing bouts of silence?

Arilla smiled at the last student leaving the training ground and waited until they were well out of sight before she sagged.

Despite not using Innarn, she was discovering just how much she relied on it. The burners in the tavern weren't working, so it meant gathering enough wood for the fire. And because the islands were a carefully balanced ecosystem, you couldn't just chop down a tree the way those on the mainland might. Early mornings were now spent scouring Ginorti's forest for fallen logs amongst all the others who were hoping to find fuel for their fires as well.

Not having the warming charms working at home was also a cause for concern. More than once, she'd thought about setting up a cot in the tavern and heating just the one area for a multitude of people.

After stamping her feet to get the feeling back in her toes, Arilla straightened her spine and finished gathering up the bags of weapons.

As she moved towards the exit, Calem appeared, a gently steaming container in his hands.

Years of looking after the blades she carried was the only thing stopping her from dumping the lot and rushing to her husband. Arilla couldn't remember the last time she'd eaten. She was pretty sure she'd forgotten lunch, and breakfast had been a cold bowl of oats eaten in haste. *Or was that yesterday?*

"Here you go, love. Got to keep your strength up," Calem said, easily taking the bags and passing the container into her hands.

"Have I told you how much I love you lately?" Arilla popped open the lid and inhaled. Richly scented steam made her moan. "So much," she muttered, digging in with the fork Calem presented her with.

Calem laughed. Arilla fairly inhaled the spiced fish, rice, and seaweed dish. It was only when she came to the end of the meal and was contemplating the etiquette of licking the bowl that she realised she hadn't seen Grace all day.

Wary of saying her name in case it summoned her, Arilla took a stack of bags from Calem and twined their free arms together. "Let's go home."

Shari watched Grace from the shadows. Her cousin had yet to notice, and instead was fixated on her parents.

A bitter part of Shari wished that Grace would leave, that she could have her parents back, all to herself. The more responsible part of her kept whispering about *how hard Grace's life had been so far* and *how she was capable of compassion and sharing.* Still didn't mean she wanted to.

Her foot scuffed against the ground as Arilla and Calem left.

Grace whirled; a movement almost too fast to track.

Shari waved at her. "Pretty sure this is where you try and stab me again."

The noise Grace made was meant to be a chuckle, or she'd been gargling with razor blades. Then Grace was moving, spinning through the air, blades flying from her person like leaves falling from autumn trees.

Ducking and dodging, Shari twisted away, heading for the middle of the grounds. With that much flying steel, she was going to need all the space she could get.

Then a white blur passed between them, and the blades stopped.

Low growling filled the air, and Shari couldn't say with any certainty if the noise had come from Grace or Wisp.

Grace grinned, and Shari almost fell over.

"About time," she rasped.

"Time for what?" Shari snapped.

A negligent wave of her hand, and the plethora of daggers disappeared into the folds of Grace's skirts. Her cousin smiled at Wisp, glared at Shari, and vanished.

"If this is what having extended family is like, I'm not sure I'm cut out for it," Shari said. Wisp trotted over to her, licked her hand, and faded away, leaving Shari alone on the training grounds.

A single dagger from Grace remained at her feet, dripping with white ichor and lying next to the imprint of paw pads.

CHAPTER TWENTY-SEVEN

Kerday

Third day of the fourth week of Nightcrest

The castle was in an uproar.

Shari had decided that the guild still needed to train, and she wasn't sure if she was a glutton for punishment, or a genius.

With the unseasonable cold outside, Asterion had suggested a different type of training. One where they tried to find Shari's old mask. Something small enough to be easily hidden, but so deeply layered with Innarn that it would still prove to be a challenge.

It also gave them the perfect opportunity to see if anyone was missing any fingers.

The castle was tightly warded, preventing anyone from shifting. A hundred guild members were scouring the rooms, looking for the scrap of cloth hidden in Shari's pocket.

Shari was racing through the halls, aiming to get to the highest room in the castle before anyone could capture her and the prize. Lungs heaving and legs pumping, Shari rounded a corner and froze. At the other end of the long hall, Elani lay in wait, an arrow pointed directly at Shari's heart.

'*Going to hand it over?*' Elani sent.

'*I'm searching, just like you should be,*' Shari lied.

Elani drew the bow back. '*Try again.*'

Gathering her Innarn, and hoping it would work, Shari jumped and grabbed hold of a wall hanging just as Elani let the arrow fly.

'*Rude!*' Shari sent.

Great, flying leaps took her from one hanging to another, crossing the length of the hall before the archer could blink. Shari twisted and landed on Elani's shoulders.

"Dead," she whispered, tapping a finger on Elani's forehead.

"Rude," Elani echoed.

Shari laughed. Her head snapped up as muffled voices drew closer. After scrambling to her feet, she took off, taking the stairs two at a time.

Reaching the top, she peered around the corner.

Joana was guarding the final staircase.

Her pursuers had spotted Elani, if the raised voices were anything to go by. They would be on her any moment.

'*Are you waiting for an invitation?*' Joana sent.

Shari peeked around the corner again, and the other woman was beckoning her closer.

Taking a risk, Shari bolted.

The rug under her feet undulated, trying to throw her off course. Years of racing through the waves made it easy to keep her feet. Shari launched herself at Joana, only to crash through empty air.

A *mirage.*

A heavy body fell onto hers, the breath forced from her lungs. Groaning, Shari shoved the being off. For a moment, she was face to face with grey skin and sightless eyes. Shari swung, hard, and the solid *thwack* of flesh striking skin snapped her out of it.

Warm blood poured out of Remmy's nose as he appeared before her.

"Sorry," she gasped, and pushed him away. After bolting up the last set of stairs, Shari slapped the mask down on the assigned table.

A bell rang out, signalling the end of the exercise.

Bending at the waist, Shari fought to regain her breath as her chest heaved.

"Preddy sure dere wasd't mend to be any bloodshed," Remmy said, pinching the bridge of his nose.

Shari sent a jolt of green Innarn his way. A single resounding *crack*, and Remmy's nose looked the same as it always had.

He touched it gingerly. "Thanks."

"Sorry," she said again.

"What did you see? When I fell on you?"

"A dead body."

Remmy nodded, as if this was an everyday occurrence. "Understandable then, lashing out."

Pounding footsteps were coming closer.

He syphoned the blood off his shirt and winked at her. "Our secret," he said.

Shari dipped her head at him and grinned. It felt nice to have someone else to share secrets with again.

Tania cleared her throat. Sure she already knew the answer to the question, she desperately wanted to be wrong. "Is it normal for the islands to sound tired?" Tania asked.

Zana froze in the act of pouring tea. "No," the older Linked said. "The islands are eternal. They shouldn't sound nor feel tired."

Wrapping the blanket she was using as a cloak tighter, Tania wavered. She had to know. "Does... does Rakemyst sound tired?"

"Yes." Zana sounded as worn as her island.

"Talhan does too," Cyrus confirmed.

Fenix lifted their head from the table. "And Cantash."

"Ginorti is exhausted," Oakley confirmed. "I thought it was just from the Innarn dampeners, but it sounds like it's more widespread."

"Has anyone heard from Domic or Brinley?" Zana asked.

The door to Fenix's home opened, and the dripping form of Domic was revealed.

Domic's teeth were chattering so hard, it was difficult to understand him. "Sorry I'm late. Got a bit flooded."

"Don't you live under the water?" Tania asked, wrapping freezing hands around the warm cup Zana passed to her.

Oakley draped a blanket around Domic to still the shivering and guided him to the prime spot in front of the fire.

"Yes, but it's not meant to be *wet*."

Zana shared a look with Cyrus. "Then our Innarn is fading too," she said, words barely a whisper.

Tania shuddered again, but this time it wasn't from the cold.

Shari laughed as Kemanyr dropped from the ceiling to attach herself to Jetonyx's back. She played at biting his wings, the older Q'Aralide rolling on the floor in pretend pain.

It felt like an age since she'd laughed.

Tormorylth was curled up next to Shari, the underside of her jaw resting on the Altoriae's shoulder as Shari tried to write in the handbook. The hatchlings were sufficiently distracting her from the task.

Samuel had claimed he needed to stretch his wings but wanted her safe. She'd agreed to watch his brood, mostly to see the look on his face, then shooed him out the door.

A knock had the book replaced by her sword before she stood.

'It's *me*,' Jonathan sent.

Shari crossed the room to unbolt the door. When, exactly had she ceased relying on her Innarn?

Jonathan stepped inside, stomping the snow from his boots and unravelling his scarf. "Well met, Altoriae," he grinned at her.

"Does this mean you come bearing good news?" she asked.

"Even better." Jonathan grinned at her and pulled a box out from under his coat.

"What's this?" Shari asked.

Kemanyr bounded over, shoving her head between them and sniffing at the box intently. She backed away, frowning, her mouth open slightly as if to rid herself of the smell.

"Blue mushroom soup," Jonathan said.

'Meat?' Kemanyr asked.

"Mushrooms are a fungus. Like a vegetable, but different," Shari said.

The tiny hatchling—who was much bigger now than when she'd attempted escaping—grumbled and backed away. 'Meat.' The send was forlorn.

Jonathan suppressed his smile, the corners of his mouth twitching.

All three of Kemanyr's eyes narrowed. The muscles of her shoulders bunched and shifted, but she caught Shari looking and didn't move.

Frowning thoughtfully, Shari plonked herself on the floor before opening up the container of soup. After blowing on it, she looked up at Jonathan. "Any news on what's waiting in the silence?"

He shook his head. "I've scoured the handbook, and the older parts of the library, but haven't found a thing. Asterion mentioned something a while ago. I need to get back to him on that."

"If he knows something that could help, you really should," Shari said.

Jonathan hummed in agreement. "How do you feel about not going off-Realm?"

"Trapped." The word fled her mouth before she could think it through.

"Me too," he admitted.

Shari tried for a smile but caught sight of the not-so-sneaky hatchling creeping towards Jonathan.

Seemed like Kemanyr had decided to practise pouncing on the Guardian.

Not wanting to give the game away, Shari hunted for another topic of conversation. "Did you find the owner of the fingers?"

"Not yet—hey!" Jonathan shot to his feet, shaking his hand out.

The golden hatchling grinned when the Guardian inspected the row of perfect fang marks imprinted into his palm.

"I'm not meat either!"

"Well, technically," Samuel drawled, leaning against the doorframe and letting the snow in. He gently rubbed the top of Kemanyr's head. Sneeze climbed down his arm like it was a bridge and nestled on top of the tiny hatchling's skull.

Jonathan scowled at them both.

Samuel heaved a sigh. "We don't eat friends," he reminded the hatchling. He closed the door, leaving most of the cold outside.

Kemanyr blinked at him. *'Friends bring meat.'* She looked mildly absurd with the tiny black draci perched like a winged hat.

"Indeed, they do." Samuel stared at Jonathan.

Shari shoved another spoonful of soup into her mouth, flicking her gaze back and forward between the four Q'Aralides' expectant faces and the Guardian.

"Insatiable," Jonathan muttered. From under his coat, he pulled a massive hunk of meat and placed it on the table.

A rumbling purr escaped from Kemanyr, who pounced on the morsel like she hadn't been fed in days. Sneeze, jostled from his perch, flew to the table and shot a jet of flames her way.

"You can purr?" Shari spluttered, looking at Samuel.

He scowled at her. "Eat your fungus."

The ships had been loaded with enough supplies that even if the Shifting Islands were in the very middle of the Deep Sea, they would be able to get there and back.

This time, they were going to teach those aberrations who was really in control and show them that if they messed with the mainlanders, they'd see the bottom of the ocean before long.

They had to. It was the only way to avenge the Elder Chamele.

Blinking away the image of her torn body, the guard faced the sea, hoping the spray could wipe the memory from his mind.

If it wasn't, maybe the blood of an Innarnian would be.

Samuel gathered his courage and knocked on the doorframe of the technomancer's lair.

"Enter!"

Taking a steadying breath, he strode into the room. Sneeze had been reluctantly left with the hatchlings for this delicate venture.

A bald blue head was bent over the open carcass of a sleek metal machine as Temira fiddled with something on the inside.

Waiting was not his strong suit, but if anyone deserved his patience it was the last Ulnan.

Letting his eyes wander over her desk, Samuel found that he was unable to name most of the things there. A glint of gold called him closer, and a shiver of Dark Innarn reached out to caress him.

He'd felt that before.

Stepping closer to the gold, Samuel startled.

Soul-seeker arrow.

"It's a replica." Temira sounded bored.

"This is no replica," Samuel said.

Temira's head snapped up, and she winced, a hand coming up to rub her neck.

"But you knew that already," Samuel said slowly, glancing between the arrow and the technomancer.

"It is my end," Temira said. "And you are the one who is going to deliver it."

Samuel shook his head, backing away from the arrow. "I was complicit with the destruction of the rest of your race, I will not..."

"You *owe* me," Temira hissed, stepping closer to him. "You destroyed my Realm, my people. And now, when I ask it of the golden priest, you will end me too."

Bile was rising in his throat, and his vision was going black around the edges. "I'm not that being anymore," he gasped.

"But you can be."

"And if I don't want to?" All he could see was Temira, looming over him. The edges of the room were fuzzy and pulsing with each beat of his heart.

"That doesn't concern me." Temira turned away, as if they were done discussing how he would murder her.

Nauseated, Samuel fled.

CHAPTER TWENTY-EIGHT

Narday
Fourth day of the fourth week of Nightcrest

Shari glanced over her shoulder and slipped into the museum. It was almost like being a kid again, sneaking in after the patrollers, but the halls were empty tonight.

Creeping through the various rooms, Shari felt as if she were an intruder for the first time. Running her gaze over the displays, she wondered what it would be like to look after their history, instead of being the one to create it.

Reaching the double doors at last, Shari grasped the handles and pulled.

The Realm went silent as the Altoriae's jaw dropped.

On the other side of the doors, there was no Ducibus to greet her, no endless corridors or branching hallways.

Just a smooth, unblemished wall.

"What in the name of Nar'eh is going on?" Shari mouthed, the words lost as the silence gathered around her.

There was no sudden rush of sound this time. Insects took up their call again, but they were outside, muted.

The emptiness of the museum only intensified the sound of Shari's heavy, harsh breaths.

Asterion held the diary in his hand, determined that he would speak to the Guardian about it this time.

Opening the door to the office, Asterion faltered, the book falling as he backed away before shutting the door quickly.

That was a side of the Guardian he didn't need to see.

All thoughts of the diary flew out of his head as the minotaur scrubbed at his eyes, willing the image out of his head.

Arms full of material, Anika froze.

Behind Shari was a huge white canine. The beast's head looked at her over the Altoriae's bed. It stood, tail wagging as Shari rubbed under its chin.

"Who's this?" Anika asked.

"Wisp," Shari said.

Never did a creature look less like a wisp than this one.

"Right. Tell Wisp not to shed on these gowns. I'll be devastated," Anika said drily.

The canine rolled its eyes at her and huffed but went to settle in the corner.

Cautiously, Anika entered the room and laid her packages out on the bed. "You have a choice. Dresses, of course, formal robes, or pants." The benefits of living alone came in the form of material spread out over every flat surface and sewing at 3am until her eyes blurred too much to see the thread anymore. "They're mix and match. Wear the dress or pants with the robes over the top. Gives you more options."

Shari ran her fingers over the fabric, the spiral scars on her hands reminding Anika of her own. She pulled her sleeves down as Shari lifted the dress up. "Does the skirt detach?"

Anika made a rude noise. "Did I start designing for you yesterday? Of course it does. Here." She pulled Shari's hand up until the bodice was in the right place. In the process, Anika's sleeves slipped down, showing the silvery lines she tried not to look at.

The Altoriae didn't react.

Ignoring the scars, Anika showed Shari how to rip the skirt away, and how easy it was to reattach.

"You're determined to get me into a skirt."

"I have already. Just wear your leathers underneath, and when the fighting starts, pull the skirt off." Anika rolled her eyes like it was no big deal and hadn't required a feat of design brilliance.

Shari's gaze fell to her hidden scars. "You're sure there will be fighting?"

"We're six for six. If there isn't, I'll eat my daggers."

"Is that why you're practicing so much?" Shari asked, the tips of her fingers running over the silvery lines on her own arm.

"Yes," Anika said shortly. She picked up the pants and held them to Shari's waist.

"If anyone can protect themselves, it's you," Shari said.

"Go try something on already," Anika said around the lump in her throat. It was gratifying to hear the Realm's foremost expert in fighting thought she would be able to defend herself.

Shari returned and twirled, the skirt flaring out around her.

"Amazing." Anika grinned. "As expected." She'd veered away from grey this time, and Shari wore navy blue. The corset top mimicked the leathers she normally wore, but instead of buckles, she'd used embroidered stars.

There were a lot of stars.

Floaty sleeves with a spiralling silver pattern which emphasised the scars of Shari's failed transformation completed the look. The skirt was a work of art, with the constellations from Lissae's sky created from hemibise beads painstakingly sewn into place.

Anika ran her finger over the Pomacanth Cluster. "These will glow as soon as it gets dark."

"You recreated the sky," Shari gasped.

Anika startled when she chanced a glance up and saw tears spilling down Shari's cheeks. "We all need light in the dark. You might be ours, but if I can give you a bit to hold on to, I will."

Shari reached down and enveloped her in a hug. Anika returned it, and they stood like that for some time.

Shari was glad that Anika was as good with makeup as she was with fabric. Attending the guild dinner prior to the last joining with a face puffy from crying was not ideal—at least not when her parents were there as well.

Jonathan and Samuel were either side of her. Anika sat farther down the table with Raven. Her parents were on Jonathan's side, and the others were laughing at something Dealon had done. Grace was across from her, next to Skye, and as predictable as the rising sun, she was scowling viciously at Shari.

She just knew she was going to get stabbed.

Wisp pressed into her side, growling low enough that she could only feel the vibration against her leg.

Dropping a hand to his head, she stroked him absently. *Maybe if I added more power into my shields?*

Grace sprang, directly across the table.

Shari had a moment to be thankful that everyone had finished eating, then Grace was on her, knife flashing. Wisp barked and jumped to stop her, but was thwarted when Samuel slapped the knife out of Grace's hand. A tiny shower of sparks landed on her unprotected skin, and Grace shot Sneeze a withering look.

A chair shrieked as it was pushed backwards.

"Girls!" Arilla said.

Grace froze, hand wrapped around Shari's throat.

Shari tried to pry the steel bands away from her throat whilst Grace looked at her mother, to no avail.

"That is enough. No more stabbing, choking, or fighting of any kind! You are on the same side. Now act like it."

Withdrawing her hand as if it was burning, Grace fell back onto her haunches, turning doe eyes on Arilla.

"No, Grace. Every time you try to hurt Shari, it hurts me."

'*And me,*' Samuel sent to Shari.

Below the table, Wisp whimpered and gave Grace the biggest puppy eyes Shari had ever seen. It was slightly disconcerting.

"Fine." Grace retreated across the table.

Wisp huffed, his breath hot on Shari's arm, and she felt him vibrate. He huffed again, and the muddy thought of *solid* slipped into Shari's mind.

"You can't phase?" she asked.

Wisp nodded.

Samuel looked concerned, eyeing the knife on the table as if it would protect him from the Shadow Bringer. Sneeze licked the side of his face, distracting him.

"No more, Grace," her mother was saying.

"No more."

Shari sagged. She might not have to worry about semi-regular stabbings, but what was Samuel thinking? Could she trust Wisp as much as she thought?

Asterion stumbled into the room, great clouds of steam billowing from his nose.

"Mainland ships have been sighted."

Arilla, still standing, swore.

CHAPTER TWENTY-NINE

Rasshday

Fifth day of the fourth week of Nightcrest

Last night's guild dinner seemed like a lifetime ago. Tension thickened the air.

By now, everyone knew the mainlanders were getting closer.

Beings snapped at each other, and weapons were carried by everyone. Children had been taken to the lower level of Cantash, with all the schools being combined into one in preparation for the attack. Lizbeth and a few of the other vulnerable adults were watching over them, along with groups of guards.

Patrols were being regularly swapped out. The islands spun slowly, trying to keep the only opening away from the ever-closer ships.

Vannali was a low undertone in every movement Shari and the Linked made. A constant whisper of, '*Hurry, hurry, hurry,*' left her feeling unnerved and off-centre.

After climbing to the top of Ronah's beach-side mountain, Shari looked out and sighed. In the distance, smoke from the ships polluted the horizon.

By her side, Wisp rumbled a warning.

"I know," Shari whispered, one hand sinking into the fur at the top of his head even as her other gripped the hilt of her sword tighter.

Wolf and Belfar winged around the islands, their team flying higher. He'd offered to get closer to scope out the incoming ships, but Shari refused.

Flying just above the clouds, he scoffed. His team was more than capable of...

As Belfar yelled, the thought disappeared.

Just like his mate, who was sinking through the clouds, eyes wide and hand reaching.

Wolf paused, shocked.

Varlee was a bullet, tearing through the cloud beside him.

Shaking his head, Wolf took off after her.

Belfar was a tangle of wings and limbs as he flipped through the sky.

'*Withdraw the wing,*' Wolf sent, but the thought echoed in his mind. Of course sending wouldn't work. If Belfar's wing wasn't responding, the smaller Innarn tricks they relied on were unlikely to as well.

"Withdraw the wing!" he shouted, hoping the noise would reach his terrified mate.

Slapping at his chest, Belfar was doing as requested. After his last tumble through the sky, they'd visited the technomancer, who had shown him a freckle-like button that could be pressed to retract the wing in dangerous situations. Belfar had laughingly said he'd never need it, but Wolf begged him to remember.

Orange light flared bright, and the crystal wing on his mate's back disappeared. Belfar spread his limbs, trying to use his remaining wing to slow his descent.

Varlee tossed Wolf a bundle of fabric. He tucked his wings in tighter, willing the air to thin so he could get under Belfar.

Twisting, he tried to pull on his Innarn but found none. Wolf pulled again, reaching for the air of Lissae. There was the barest hint, but it would have to be enough.

Falling below Belfar, Wolf tried to ignore the whites of his mate's eyes.

Gathering the scrap of Innarn, he tossed half the sheet back to Varlee, who fumbled the catch.

"Come on," he growled. Wolf threw the fabric again, and she caught it. "Let go!" he roared at Belfar.

Others from the team had arrived and were grasping the emergency sheet, trying to prepare.

Belfar glanced down, and Wolf couldn't help but look too. Below them, the islands were turning. If their current trajectory continued, they'd pass above Talhan's borders and hit one of Cantash's smaller mountains when they fell.

Not the death he'd been planning on.

The team had practised this. Any closer, and they wouldn't be able to land safely. They'd all be injured, or worse.

"Now, Belfar!"

Tucking his limbs in, Belfar dropped. The sephina silk wrapped around his body. Wolf wasn't the only one who grunted at the extra weight.

Belfar dangled between them, safe in the cocoon.

The team worked together, flying carefully so their wings wouldn't tangle as they came in for landing.

The moment he was free of the silk, Belfar wrapped Wolf in his arms. "You saved me again," Belfar said.

"Always." Wolf rested his head on Belfar's shoulder.

"If you two make out, I'm going to fly home," Charin warned.

Varlee laughed, and the moment was broken.

Still, Wolf laced his fingers with Belfar's as they began the trek back to Rakemyst.

Terrance glanced around furtively. No one was in sight. Grinning, he slipped into the museum, heading for the forgotten statue of Frointh.

As a boy, he'd discovered the statue, and had often sought solace under the forgotten god's gaze, polishing the name plaque so much the letters had worn off. Now Frointh's sanctuary would be the perfect place to see if he could discover the secrets hidden in the book he had finally swiped from under the Guardian's nose.

Settling down by Frointh's knee, he paged through *The Sea Tailor's Handbook.*

Nothing.

Faint squiggles on otherwise blank pages, yet the Guardian poured over this for hours.

Maybe it had a password?

"Altoriae."

Nothing changed.

"Lissae."

Blank.

"Guardian."

Is it me, or were the squiggles getting fainter?

"Innarn," he said, desperate.

The page was blank.

He stared at the book for ages, mouth agape. How could he get so close to saving the Realm only to be thwarted by a tattooed tree that refused to reveal its secrets?

Standing, he shook the book, wishing something would change.

Of course, it remained the same.

Roaring, he grabbed the edge of a page with his good hand. Blood rushing in his ears, he ripped it clear of the binding.

Sound stopped.

He could feel himself screaming, lungs compressing, throat burning, but there was no sound. Furious, he ripped page after page out, decorating the floor with bits of torn paper.

Gasping filled his ears with a rush.

Glancing down at the mangled book, he shuddered. Now all hope was gone.

A shadow fell over the remaining pages. Looking up, he grasped the full weight of hopelessness.

Samuel stared down at the man with the handbook in his lap, hands clenched at his sides.

He had destroyed it.

Destroyed the book.

The one Jonathan had *just* entrusted him with. His own copy was burning a hole in his pocket, but this piece of tuzar dung had ensured it would never be readable again.

Reaching down, Samuel grabbed a fistful of the man's shirt and lifted him up. "That was a mistake."

"You're the mistake," the idiot spat at him. "An off-Realmer taking the role of apprentice? It was meant to be me."

"You were never even in the running," Samuel snarled.

"I'm too talented for a mere competition," he sneered. The acrid smell coming from his trousers took the edge off his attempt at a menacing look.

Samuel saw red. "Your talent lies in one place. Dying."

The little colour left in the basalt-chewing buzzard's face fled. "No, please," he whimpered.

Dropping the pathetic excuse, Samuel strode forward until the feseor's back hit the statue's knees. "Why don't you show me how good you are at it?" Samuel drew his hand back and swung his fist, hitting the coward right in his face.

Hissing, Samuel shook out his hand.

"Weakling," the trusnuck taunted, holding a palm to his streaming nose. A hand without fingers.

"Flesh might be weak, but scales aren't," Samuel said. Fist changing to claw, he then struck again, enjoying the sound of bones breaking beneath the skin of the thief.

He cried out, the noise turning to a wheeze when Samuel drove his other fist into the ketarr's gut.

Over and over, he struck, not even seeing the being dying before him. All he could picture was the devastated look on Shari's face the next time she opened the cover of the handbook and the pages were all but gone.

"Samuel!"

His thoughts had summoned her. Eyes wide, Samuel twisted his neck to seek Shari out, even as his fist fell, one, two, three, slamming into the mess that was below him.

"Samuel, stop!" Shari said. She was approaching him carefully, hands raised, the backs of them pointed to him.

He froze.

"Can you come here?" Shari asked.

Obediently, Samuel rose. He shook the gore off his claws and moved to Shari's side.

Another body moved past him, and his arm shot out, grabbing the material of a shirt.

Shari's hand grabbed his. "It's just Jonathan."

Jonathan.

Blinking, he looked at the sandy-haired man. It took a long moment to place him.

Jonathan. Guardian. Friend.

He let go.

"Can you tell me what happened?" Shari asked. She raised the hand not holding his, and a tiny black draci stared up at him like he could do no wrong.

Samuel bent and picked a page off the floor. Sneeze used the opportunity to fly onto his shoulder. "He did this." Samuel waved the tattered edge towards the bloody mess.

Shari gasped.

"Who was it?" Jonathan asked from behind Samuel.

The Altoriae's Innarn licked out, and she growled, "Terrance Thorne."

CHAPTER THIRTY

Temira felt every single one of her years.

She wanted to see if Tania had figured out her present yet, but she had forgotten that her young friend was still in school. Huffing, Temira shuffled her tired bones towards the main street. Something to eat and a warm drink were in order before returning to the Techno Centre.

Teeth chattering, Temira slowly walked towards the main street.

An impact of a landing body had her spinning, and almost falling.

It was the mid-sized hatchling.

'*Well met,*' ze sent. '*I am Tormorylth. I'm going to be your friend.*'

Every time they met, the hatchling insisted on reintroducing herself. Temira couldn't decide if she was glad someone had finally noticed her trouble remembering names, or annoyed that it was *this* someone who noticed.

'*Well met,*' Temira sent, and turned back towards the main street.

'*What are we doing today?*' Tormorylth sent as she waddled along beside her. Nothing that large could be graceful on the ground.

'*I am getting food.*'

'*Excellent! I am rather hungry.*'

Temira sighed. '*I eat alone.*'

The smile dropped from the hatchling's face. '*I've tried that. It's quite boring, isn't it?*'

Her gaze slid away. '*It is, rather.*'

'*Perhaps we could eat together today?*' Tormorylth suggested.

'*Fine.*' Temira didn't have the energy to snarl.

Tormorylth bounced as she waddled. And slowed, her three eyes trained on the trio making haste towards the Healing Centre, a bloody form hoisted between them.

'*Change of plans,*' Temira sent.

'*I mean, maybe we can still eat.*' Tormorylth was eyeing the trail of blood.

Temira smirked. There were few on Lissae who appreciated black humour. '*Maybe.*'

They hurried after the trio, entering the healing centre.

The first thing she saw was Samuel's dark hair, a stark contrast to his pale face.

'*What happened?*' Temira sent.

"Terrance Thorne happened. Then Samuel happened," Shari said.

Frowning, Temira tried to parse out the meaning.

'*That's a being?*' Tormorylth's send was on the shrieky side.

Professional curiosity caused Temira to peer at the form on the stretcher. '*Was,*' she corrected.

Samuel winced.

"Everyone out," the Guardian said. "The healers have him now. We'll wait to see what they say."

Mind whirling, Temira eyed Samuel. If he was capable of such violence, then surely he'd have no issue stabbing her? As they walked out of the centre, she reached into her jacket and pulled a narrow parcel out. "You'll have no difficulty, I'm certain," she said, pressing it into Samuel's hands.

The golden priest looked pale enough to pass out.

'*Lunch?*' She turned and headed once more for the main street, Tormorylth by her side.

Belfar looked around. It felt wrong to move into Shari's old room, but with one wing and a hunk of crystal on his back, it wasn't like he had much of a choice. He hadn't even been able to fly to their house to pack himself. Wolf had done it all.

Arilla and Calem were even taking the day off from the tavern to help them move in.

He didn't know if he should be grateful or angry.

"That's the last of it," Wolf said, alighting on the balcony.

Belfar twisted his lips into a smile. "Thank you."

"It's alright to be angry," Wolf rumbled.

"I think I've had enough of being angry for today." It was true. Even without the uneven weight tugging on his back, Belfar felt exhausted. "Could sleep for a week, though."

Wolf's eyes darkened.

Laughter rang out, surprising Belfar as he realised it was his own.

Tania kept tapping her nails on the table.

Oakley gently laid a hand over hers. "Stop," he said.

"Sorry." She winced and started bouncing her knee instead. They'd been going over the plans for the last part of the convergence for the better part of the afternoon, and something was not sitting right. It felt like a vital piece of the puzzle was missing, but it remained hidden, just out of sight.

"We will survive this," Zana said.

Tania's stomach clenched. A tiny feeling inside her said that they would not all walk out of this joining unscathed.

Jetonyx exhaled deeply and rested his head on top of his claws. Samuel had charged them with guarding the doors to the underground lair of the Daens.

It had been a long day. Lava, he'd found, was not an appropriate substitute for acid. It was, however, excellent for flinging at nest mates when they became too annoying.

Tormorylth had tired of the game and disappeared a while ago, and Kemanyr had dozed, curled up next to a stream of magma, for most of the day.

Jetonyx had never thought he'd miss the heat of the desert, but he did. The constant cold snow brought was something he would gladly trade for scorching sands any time.

'*We are the last ones standing,*' he sent to Sneeze and Kemanyr.

Neither responded.

He huffed.

Smoke caught his attention, lying thick across the water.

Squinting, Jetonyx could just make out the metal hull hiding in the roiling darkness.

'*Mainlanders.*'

Every bite tasted like sawdust.

He'd beaten a man bloody today, had probably ended his life because of it. Beings all around were laughing and joking, a nervous tension pulling tempers tight and forcing smiles when there was nothing to grin about.

Jetonyx burst into the room. '*They're here!*'

Shari's chair scraped against the floor as she stood, alighting every nerve in his fragile mortal form.

"Who?"

'The mainlanders.'

"They can wait," another voice said. "Guardian, you might want to return to the Healers Centre. Ter... The victim won't last much longer."

The healer, Samuel realised.

"Guild, man the borders. Find out how far away Vannali is," Jonathan said. "Shari, Samuel, with me. We will join you shortly."

Unless the Guardian kills me first.

CHAPTER THIRTY-ONE

Vebaday

Sixth day of the fourth week of Nightcrest

Jonathan dragged him to the waiting room but left him outside. Samuel didn't know what was worse—having the option to enter or being told he wasn't welcome.

Terrance Thorne was dying a slower death than Samuel had initially considered was appropriate. Now he thought of the pages of the handbook, strewn on the floor.

Did they pick them up?

The healers were scurrying around, carrying packets and preparing beds. With Innarn now unreliable, it seemed they were trying to prepare to heal the old way.

Such a shame they were all busy, and there was no one to stop him from returning to the museum.

The moment Samuel stepped outside, Ronah rumbled under his feet.

'*You made a promise,*'–the island sounded out of breath–'*to not hurt anyone. And yet you did.*'

Samuel's body froze, but his mind whirled. Slowly, he lifted Sneeze off his shoulder and prepared to throw him to safety.

'*Samuel Caragnton of the Q'Aralide, you are lucky your chosen victim was going to do worse than he did. We are lucky you stopped him. You have our thanks.*'

Before him, in a neat stack, the pages of the handbook appeared.

After gently placing Sneeze back on his shoulder, Samuel accepted the bite on his ear as penance for disturbing the draci's rest.

'*Ronah, I swear, I never meant to do any harm.*'

'*Brains are for thinking; fists are for fighting. Choose which one you use wisely,*' Ronah sent, and fell silent once more.

Arilla turned around and gasped.

Grace was right behind her, a slightly feral look in her eyes and a dagger held firmly in her hand.

"Grace?"

"Not stabbing. Keeping safe," Grace said, gaze darting all around the room.

"I can keep myself safe," Arilla said gently.

"Helping."

"Come help gather the weapons at the tavern then. We need to distribute them to the fighters."

Some of the wildness retreated, and Grace nodded. The dagger disappeared, but it wouldn't take much for Grace to retrieve it.

"Hope you've been carrying more than just daggers around. Swords are heavy."

"Helping," Grace repeated firmly.

"I know," Arilla said. She just hoped that Grace would be helping their side this time, and that her niece would not fall under Chamele's thrall again.

Shari and Jonathan eased into the room, Wisp slinking in after them.

What was left of Terrance Thorne barely looked able to form noise, let alone answer the questions she wanted to throw at him.

"How are we meant to find anything out?" Shari whispered. Despite the grief Terrance had given her over the years, it felt wrong to talk normally during his last moments.

Jonathan clenched his jaw. "Like this." He approached the bed and peeled away the bandages around Terrance's head. Grimacing, he placed his fingers against crushed temples.

An unearthly moan sounded from the living corpse on the bed.

"What do you want to know?" Jonathan asked.

"Why did he do it?"

Closing his eyes, Jonathan hovered over the dying man, and pulled back, wiping wet fingers on the white cloth covering Terrance's chest. "Pride. Hope turned ugly. And the worst kind of stubbornness."

"They're not even good reasons," Shari said. "You caused so much grief because you're *stubborn*?"

Terrance's eyes opened the tiniest bit. He glanced at her and rasped something unintelligible.

Shari stepped closer.

The light left his eyes.

The rattling death knell she expected never sounded.

It would remain lost to the depth of silence.

A fitting end for a horrid being.

By her side, Shari could feel the rumble of Wisp's chest. Sure enough, the first sound she heard rushing back in was the Shadow Bringer growling.

"Who do we fight for?" the guard screamed.

"Chamele!" the soldiers called back.

"Who do we fight for?" the guard yelled again.

"Chamele!" the soldiers repeated, thousands of voices layered on top of each other.

Shivers ran down his spine. He knew his superiors didn't expect him to return, but there was no way he was letting the aberrations get away with killing someone like that.

"Charge!" he ordered.

Wave after wave of soldiers swarmed off the boats, wading through the icy water towards the mountainous shore.

It was time to teach the aberrations a lesson.

Tania rubbed her arms. They were getting closer to Vannali, but so were the mainlanders. All the Linked had been at the dinner in the castle when Asterion burst in with the news, and they had retreated for one final meeting.

"What if they come between the two islands?" Tania blurted. "They'll be crushed."

Zana smoothed her gown. "Let them be. Ships are far easier to stop than islands."

"They're *people*, Zana. Surely we can't..." Tania started.

"No one who kills to take over their victim's land is a *person*." Zana was as serene as if she were discussing the weather. The only indicator of her tension was the whitening of the knuckles as she wrapped her hand around the banister. "If they come between our islands, let them be crushed."

Asterion was waiting for them as they left Terrance's room. "They've entered our bay and are scaling the mountains."

Asterion's gaze flicked to Shari. "Don't... don't leave her side."

"It kind of happens on the battlefield," Shari said, moving to push past the minotaur.

Asterion grabbed her arm, careful of his strength. "Please. There's something waiting for you. Hiding in the Silence. I think... I've done some research, and I think it's going to take you."

"Research?" Jonathan asked.

"Trust you to focus on that," Zac said. He was leaning against the wall behind Asterion.

"Altoriae, please. You are more than capable of defending yourself, but we need you to be safe. If we lost you..." Asterion gulped.

Jonathan ran a hand over his face. "Perhaps it's best that you sit this one out, Shari."

She spun, eyebrows raised and fire in her gaze.

"I mean it." Gathering every last scrap of Innarn he could find, Jonathan sent Shari to Samuel's house and mentally flicked the switch for the lockdown wards.

"She's safe?" Asterion asked.

"As safe as the Altoriae can be," Jonathan replied grimly.

CHAPTER THIRTY-TWO

Zoeday
Seventh day of the fourth week of Nightcrest

Arilla stood at the base of the ramp that led to the defensive positions along the top of Collis's mountain, passing weapons to each grim face streaming past, the early morning light painting them in macabre shadows.

Grace, beside her, was surprisingly growl free. She worked alongside Arilla's students, creating more blades from nothingness.

Arilla almost wanted to ask her how she was doing it but had learned long ago those sorts of questions were not answered when a blank was present.

The last of the defenders started the trek to the top, and Arilla turned to her students. "Shall we join them?"

"Wait!" Ronah's Linked was running towards them, the hem of her fine robes held in fists. "Vannali, she's coming!"

Arilla shivered as bumps broke out all over her skin.

The convergence was about to happen.

Right now.

Kemanyr threw her body against the door and bounced off. Again.

"Stop, little one," Shari said. "There's got to be another way."

The ground under her moaned, and Kemanyr froze.

'*Ronah?*' Shari sent.

'*My sister approaches.*' The island sounded excited, like a child who had had too much sugar.

'*I'd like to meet her,*' Shari sent.

Quietly, the door swung open.

The Altoriae grinned.

"Watch out!" someone called.

Ship-bound marksmen fired, and studded orange balls flew from the boats, crashing into the mountain wall.

Tania shrieked.

Collis stepped in front of her, staff gripped in one hand, sword in the other. He groaned and swayed.

"What is it?" she asked.

"Innarn dampeners."

On her other side, Cyrus swore.

"Can you call them back?" Tania asked.

Cyrus bobbed his head. "I can try."

'*Heading for their ships,*' Domic sent.

'*Wait! It's not safe yet.*' Tania could feel him frantically sending after her message.

'*On your command,*' he sent.

Tania looked at Zana, who merely nodded at her.

She gulped.

Cyrus was twisting his fingers through the air, as if he was pulling something from the earth. A blue hand appeared on his shoulder. Temira, lending her Innarn.

The orange glow on the side of the mountain faded.

"Got them all." Cyrus grinned.

'*Now!*' Tania gasped.

She could feel the power of Domic moving through the water, the Wisara a silent but deadly force, climbing up the outside of ships.

None of the mainlanders saw them coming.

The ones clambering up the mountain weren't looking at the water. Tania remained focused on what was behind them.

Far on the horizon, was a smudge of land.

Vannali.

Arilla stood next to Calem, twisting her wrist so her sword swung in a neat circle by her side.

Calem was holding a sword too, and had a bow slung over one shoulder, a quiver over the other. He saw her looking. "My Innarn isn't working at all."

Arilla noted that more beings were holding weapons than she expected. Only the Linked seemed to be without them.

"You aren't the only one."

Shari stepped outside and growled. As if summoned, Wisp appeared at her side.

She wanted to say, *Let's go stop the mainlanders*, but as she opened her mouth, silence descended once more.

Glancing down at Wisp, she nodded and shifted them to the fight.

Chapter Thirty-Three

Mainlanders were leaving their ships in droves. The Wisaran attack had caught them off guard.

Maybe they aren't as stupid as expected. The never-ending bodies heading their way made Asterion's gut clench. Still, Asterion felt better knowing Shari was locked away somewhere safe.

Of course, that's when the Altoriae appeared by the Guardian's side, and all the noise in the Realms fell away.

Shari snarled at Jonathan, ready to punch him for being so quick to isolate her.

She drew back her fist, but before she could strike, a bolt from one of the mainlander's ships smashed into the ground, knocking her off her feet. Shari and Jonathan fell in a tangle of limbs.

Strong hands gripped her arms, yanking her upright. Samuel raised a brow at her. By her side, Wisp was growling at the air.

"Incoming!" someone shouted, the sound deafening after the silence.

Shari slammed her hands outward, and the oversized bolt bounced off, clattering down the side of the mountain and taking out a few soldiers on the way.

She looked at her hands in awe. "My Innarn is back."

"Push the ships away," Tania said.

The Altoriae nodded, shoving her hands out again. The ships in the bay rocked but didn't do much beyond that.

"Anchors," Jonathan said.

"What?"

"They'll have anchors."

"Can the Wisara get rid of them?" Shari asked.

Tania nodded. "On it."

Wolf lined up his next shot.

Breathed in. On the exhale, he released the arrow and watched it land, right in the eye socket of another mainlander.

Beside him, Belfar aimed his longbow lower at the soldiers still in the water. It was running red now, eddies of blood staining the shore.

Wolf wanted to pause, wanted to stop time, and map out each perfect line of his mate's face.

Instead, he notched another arrow and took aim.

Tania gasped. "Domic says the anchors are too heavy." Tears laced her lashes as she looked at Shari.

"We need to stop them from swarming the shore. If too many more come, we're going to be overrun," Jonathan said, kicking a mainlander backwards just as he reached the top. The man fell, shrieking as he went.

Shari didn't wait to hear the thud. "You need to be safe," she said to Tania. "All the Linked do. Tell them to get back to their islands—now."

"Move the ships. Please, Shari?" Tania asked.

She nodded.

Tania shifted away, and the other Linked disappeared one by one.

Raising her hands again, Shari pushed with every ounce of Innarn she had.

Nothing.

It was as if Innarn had fled the battlefield when the Linked had.

"Together?" Jonathan asked.

"We have to try."

Shari could feel the very edges of the Guardian's Innarn, and the darker slick that was Samuel's. Gathering it, tried again.

A single ship edged towards the opening of the bay but stopped, swaying before the entrance.

Panting, Shari wiped the sweat from her brow. And froze. On the horizon, getting closer, was Vannali.

"Well, that's one way to fix the problem," she said.

"Crushed by an island? Interesting way to die," Samuel muttered, and slashed at a soldier who stepped too close.

"Is your breath Innarn-based?" Shari asked.

Samuel frowned at her.

"In your other form," Shari said impatiently.

"No. Completely biological."

"Well? Why don't you go use it?"

He glanced behind him, where three hatchlings were watching their conversation avidly.

'I *can help*,' Jetonyx sent.

'*Me too!*' Tormorylth added.

Kemanyr bounced on the tips of her claws, jostling Sneeze, who was perched on her head again.

"But I need your help here," Shari said, feeling like a fraud. If she had enough Innarn left, she would have sent all three back to Samuel's house.

"Oh, we do," Jonathan agreed.

Too *fast*.

Jetonyx narrowed his eyes. '*Doubtful.*' With one downward thrust, he was airborne and winging towards the ships.

In seconds, Samuel had joined him.

"Where are you going?" Jonathan yelled.

'*Saving your thick skull, as always,*' Samuel sent as he beat the hatchling to the ships.

"Tormorylth, wait!" Shari begged. She pointed to the platoon, who were clambering out of the water.

'*Stay with the Altoriae. Eat anyone who hurts her,*' Tormorylth ordered Kemanyr, and took to the sky.

Green gas enveloped the boats and any unfortunate souls who were too close. Another breath, and they all went up in flames, their dying screams ringing in her ears.

The Realm fell silent again as the tiny hatchling, barely as big as Wisp, took Samuel's place by her side. Kemanyr ripped the arm off the next mainlander to climb over the edge and shoved him backwards with her maw.

He screamed all the way down.

Arilla ignored the blood trickling from her temple and blocked the sloppy strike from another mainlander. It almost felt too easy.

Or it would have been, if Grace wasn't plastered against her back.

Calem was beside her, kicking arse and wielding the sword like he'd never stopped.

The next fool stepped up, and Arilla swung again.

Blocked.

Parried.

Stabbed.

She was starting to see why Shari fought so hard to be able to protect them. It was quite the rush.

Collis could feel the thrum of returning Innarn under his feet like the slowest of heartbeats.

Beat.

Gather the Innarn, swing the staff. Block the sword from taking off his head.

Beat.

Release Innarn in a brutal wave, pulling on the ground under the feet of every intruder.

Beat.

U'sala, Guild, and Returned all around him were taking notes, even as they fought the attackers off.

Beat.

He could feel the Returned net beginning. So long as they could hold it, they would be able to...

Beat.

He shoved the end of his staff into the mainlander's solar plexus, pushing the man backwards off the mountain.

Beat.

A little more. The Altoriae noticed. Was staring at him. She could feel the Innarn but wasn't as in tune with it as the Returned. As he was.

Beat.

Remmy's glaive smashed down on the skull of one foolish enough to get close to him.

Beat.

Mainlanders were streaming across the mountain top now, their black uniforms moving like an oily stain right along the border of the islands.

Beat.

Each time, it was a reminder of the old days, trapped in the infernal pocket-Realm.

Beat.

But now, they were home. And there was only one way he was going to leave it.

Beat.

Collis gathered all the Innarn from the net and wove it around the Shifting Island residents.

Then, on the next *beat*, he *pushed*.

CHAPTER THIRTY-FOUR

hari felt like her very essence was being ripped apart.

She opened her mouth to scream, but no sound came out. At some point, Shari must have closed her eyes, because when she opened them again, she was surrounded by Ronah's residents and they were standing in the town square.

Confused mainlanders were glancing around, the tips of their weapons dropping even as Ronah's residents raised theirs.

Collis roared and smashed the kneecaps of the closest soldier.

The landing Q'Aralides drowned the man's scream out, their feet crushing those in black uniforms who were stupid enough not to move out of the way.

The next moment, Samuel's back was pressed against her on one side, Jonathan's on the other.

"You stay with us," Samuel yelled over the clashing of blades.

Shari nodded, not wasting breath on talking. Blocking with her sword, she jabbed the blades of her glove into a soldier's belly.

Wisp, a blur of white teeth and flashing fangs, dragged the man away before he could make a noise.

Anika slashed down, splitting the skin. The man howled, and she flipped the dagger in her hand, point aimed up as she thrust it through the underside of his jaw. She'd designed the blades so they would be long enough to pierce a man's brain.

Turned out she'd been right.

Her father stood next to her, whimpering ineffectively at the sound of every blow. He didn't even see the mainlander prowling towards him.

Anika pushed Rany to the ground and parried the blow meant to take off his head. She slid the dagger along the mainlander's blade, fluttering her eyelashes as he leered down her cleavage.

Then she stabbed him in the throat.

"My eyes are up here," she snarled.

"Mainlanders everywhere," Rany whimpered.

Blowing her fringe out of her eyes, Anika wished she had the breath to sigh. Spinning, she countered another attack.

The only problem with being sent away was that Vannali was about to join with Ronah, Rakemyst, and Akoren.

'*Zana, what do we do?*' Tania sent.

'*We must create the bridges. It's the only way the islands will be safe,*' Zana sent back.

'*How?*' Tania cried.

'*Ask your soul-match for help.*' Zana's voice sounded faint.

'*Domic?*' Tania sent.

'*I'm ready. Vannali is approaching.*'

Settling down cross-legged on the covers of her bed, Tania took a deep breath. '*Collis. I need your help.*'

Bridges of pure Innarn arced across empty space, spanning the gap between the four Shifting Islands.

The Weavers, prepared for the last part of the convergence, reached out as one and completed the bridge as they slammed to a stop, land against land. Nothing but the crushed remains of mainland ships between the islands.

The sounds of the battle faded away as Ronah joined Vannali. Shari almost lost her footing at the jolt of the Shifting Islands colliding.

Swinging around to take out the mainlander who just wouldn't quit, Shari froze. Although she didn't fall, her jaw dropped.

Behind her mother, in the middle of Ronah's town square, was a glowing speck of light that was getting bigger by the second.

"Watch out!" she screamed.

A whirlwind of white streamed from the rooftops and across the cobblestones, making Shari flinch.

Cursing Grace's cloud-like attire, the Altoriae tried to shift.

Not even a molecule moved.

She tried again and felt the same sapping energy that reminded her of Xaviour, a Realm where Innarn didn't work. Whatever Innarn had been building was gone.

Stabbing her sword backwards, Shari screamed in frustration as she took off running.

The glowing light behind her mother was getting bigger.

"Shari. Shari!" Jonathan screamed at the retreating form of the Altoriae.

Samuel's head snapped up.

Jonathan was starting to go after her, but the surrounding soldiers cut him off.

"Help her!" the Guardian screamed at Samuel.

Before he could take a step, blue skin filled his vision. Temira met his gaze directly. "It's time."

CHAPTER THIRTY-FIVE

S winging her sword hard, Shari ignored the trickle of blood dripping from her brow. On her left, Arilla grunted as her blade connected with the weapon of another. To her right, Grace was a dervish, whirling and fighting like no one else.

Her cousin was the only one in the immediate vicinity still able to use Innarn.

Grace was rising higher above the crowd, floating in her white robes above them all. She was raining down Innarn bolts, which looked to be hitting indiscriminate targets, but from where Shari stood, they were dropping only those in mainlander uniforms.

There was a *bang* from behind Shari, but she dared not look back.

Not until three things happened at the same time.

Grace shrieked, her flushed face rapidly paling.

Arilla let out a soft, startled noise.

And Samuel, who she trusted with her mother's life, pulled a golden arrow out of Arilla's side.

The Realm went deathly quiet.

As Asterion charged towards her, Shari Dawn, the Altoriae of Lissae had time for one final thought.

It all ends with a trip through a portal and a charging Minotaur.

Find out what happens next in Vannali

books2read.com/u/vannali

lissae.com/vannali

GLOSSARY

A

Aberration – A slur used by mainlanders to refer to Innarnians.

Adonday – First day of the week on the Realm of Lissae. The other days are **Inthday, Kerday, Narday, Rasshday, Vebaday,** and **Zoeday.**

Akoren – One of the sentient Shifting Islands on Lissae. Originally home to Lissae's deities, she is inhabited by the **Wisara** and refugees from the mainland who required a place to stay after the civil war.

Altoriae – Protector of the Realm of Lissae. Traditionally a female role, although there has been one male Altoriae. Previous Altoriaes have included Kay'imi, Muran Curtis, Jali Thorne, and Fiona MacAde. Forces of nature cannot kill her. They must swear to uphold the seven duties of the Altoriae.

Altum – The home Realm of the Q'Aralide. Now destroyed.

Apprentice, The Guardian's – The Guardian's Apprentice is to take over the role of Guardian once the current holder of the title falls in battle or dies of old age.

Azehal – A drink favoured by the Guardian. A rutenberry-flavoured stimulant drink, typically served with sweetener and milk.

B

Beads – A form of currency on Lissae created out of **ziom**. The technical name is **ziom beads**.

Bereni trees – Trees that are grown to be used as buildings. The size and design of the tree can be controlled by an Innarnian or by one of the sentient islands.

B.I.R.D. – Stands for "Bio Instructor for Relative Distance." Designed by Xani of Talhan to ensure beings would stop bumping into things if they were absorbed in their crystal slab. The B.I.R.D. device acts as both a guide and a guard.

Blank – A person who can't use Innarn.

Blyknot – a curse used by Samuel. See **Curses**.

C

Cantash – One of the sentient Shifting Islands on Lissae. He is home to the Daens.

Castle, Ronah's – The centre point of Ronah and the traditional home of the Altoriae, the Guardian, and their respective families.

Cedore – a curse used by Samuel. See **Curses**.

Crystals – Hold energy which is turned into electricity. Often installed in clusters to gain more power and last longer. Different coloured Crystals do different things. White Crystals are used for communication. Black Crystals gather power and Orange Crystals connect currents to create fences. Crystal necklaces are given to young children and blanks for them to manipulate the Crystals.

Curses – Several curses are common on Lissae, including: Adeon's fire; By the Life of Lissae; Ke'ra's Flash; Zoemer's Rocks; Rasshnae's Floods; Vebnah's Breath; Na'reh's Ghosts. Other curses from the Realms include: ketarr; dathae; tuzar; tongue of a Ne'fora; whale's ass; basalt-chewing hemmit-loving buzzard; cestoray; slime vattar; hanotqe; slime-filled cedore; feseor; gozochas; thrice-damned; fizzpot; trusnuck, blyknot.

D

Deities – Lissae has six deities who are said to have lived on Akoren. See: **Beings and Creatures: Adeon**, **Ke'ra**, **Na'reh**, **Rasshnae**, **Vebnah,** and **Zoemer** for more details.

Ducibus' Hall – The place between Realms, guarded by the **Ducibus**. Also referred to as the **portal**.

E

Earra – A Grey Realm whose gateway comes out at the top of a cliff which overlooks a winding river fed from a glacier. Their major city sits on the opposite bank. A broad, paved platform indicates the inhabitants frequently travel across the Realms. Earra is aiming at taking Luerix over.

Elders – Those who have, through age and experience, managed to survive the Realms long enough to guide their people. They also act as advisors to the mayor.

Elements – Lissae has seven main elements that Innarnians can manipulate: earth, air, fire, water, plasma, spirit, and technology.

F

Fog City – Found in Akoren, this city is the highest point of all the Shifting Islands. It sits within the clouds. There is a tale about how the first Ilutri flew through the fog at the top of the mountain and crashed into it. After the accident, they decided to make the peak their home.

G

Ginorti – One of the sentient Shifting Islands on Lissae. He is home to the Satyrs.

Guardian – The rank for the person who is in charge of training and caring for the Altoriae, and for Lissae. In cases of emergency, the mayor and elders defer to the Guardian.

H

Hazelcrown – The second month of autumn on the Realm of Lissae.

Healers – Similar to Earth's doctors, they heal patients who are sick or injured, usually using Innarn, although they also use the old methods.

Healers Centre – Also called the **Hospital**. A place on Ronah or Rakemyst to go when sick or injured.

Hemibise – Iridescent stones which glow in the presence of star light.

Hemmit – a curse used by Samuel. See **Curses**.

I

I bid thee well – A traditional phrase when two or more people part ways.

Iccecot sorbet – A tart, sweet sorbet native to Akoren. Served in small glass bowls, and typically decorated with cream, berries and citrus slices, the sorbet has an alcoholic component. Strongly recommended to eat in moderation.

Innarn – Predominately elemental magic which is present in all Realms to varying strengths. Innarn is split into three main groups: Dark, Grey, and Light. Each variant of Innarn has its own specialties. See **Elements** for more information. There are also other disciplines of Innarn, including Animal, Crystal, Mental, Realm, and Time.

Innarnian – (said Inn-*ar*-ni-an) A person who can use Innarn.

Inthday – Second day of the week on the Realm of Lissae. The other days are **Adonday**, **Kerday**, **Narday**, **Rasshday**, **Vebaday**, and **Zoeday.**

J

Jinkor – A fixed island on Lissae.

K

Kenorvia – A continent on Lissae.

Kerday – Third day of the week on the Realm of Lissae. The other days are **Adonday**, **Inthday**, **Narday**, **Rasshday**, **Vebaday,** and **Zoeday.**

Kilgaroth – a Grey Realm.

L

Linked – A soul joined with that of one of Lissae's Shifting Islands. As the Shifting Islands are sentient, it was decided long ago that they should link with a being on their island to ensure that they remain in touch with the current needs of their population, and not remove themselves from the trials and tribulations of everyday beings.

Lissae – A Grey, sentient Realm who is defended by the Altoriae. Comprising six continents, seven sentient Shifting Islands, and multiple fixed islands, she is home to ten races. She is said to be a Mother Realm. There are two moons in her orbit.

Lissaen – A person who lives on Lissae.

Luerix – A Grey Realm slightly darker than Lissae. Monolithic standing stones ring the gateway. Home of the Sky Mother.

M

Mainlanders – A name for those residing on the mainlands or fixed islands of Lissae.

Maru – A Grey Realm, slightly darker than Lissae.

Merthin – Akoren's underwater city. Home to the **Wisara**.

Mother Realm – The only Realm capable of giving birth to new Realms. Highly guarded and sought after.

Motus – The movement used to create Innarn. One must have thought, intent, and movement correct for the Innarn to work. Motus can be an individual construct or a widely recognised form. Forms of motus used: Air; Sleep; Wind Blast; Wall of Stone.

N

Nanka – A Grey Realm. Home to billions of beings, this futuristic Realm has buildings that brush the sky and glowing neon lights.

Narday – Fourth day of the week on the Realm of Lissae. The other days are **Adonday, Inthday, Kerday, Rasshday, Vebaday,** and **Zoeday.**

Natal day – A day to celebrate a being's birth and another revolution around their sun. Known in other parts of the Realms as a birthday.

Nightcrest – The first month of winter on the Realm of Lissae.

Nine Hells – The name given to a particularly nasty set of nine Realms.

O

Osithys – Known as the rainy plane city, this is where most of the refugees have settled on Akoren.

P

Patrol – Any Innarnian resident over fifteen is required to help the Guardian and the Altoriae patrol the Realms to watch for any possible threats.

Pocket-Realm – A small Realm that is attached to a larger one.

Pomacanth Cluster – A constellation of stars found in the Lissaen sky depicting a fish.

Portal – The place between Realms, guarded by the **Ducibus**. Also referred to as the **Ducibus' Hall.**

Q

Quiver and Quill Tavern – The tavern run by the Altoriae's parents on Ronah.

R

Rakemyst – One of the sentient Shifting Islands on Lissae. He is home to the Ilutri.

Rasshday – Fifth day of the week on the Realm of Lissae. The other days are **Adonday, Inthday, Kerday, Narday, Vebaday,** and **Zoeday.**

Rataeo – A virtually uninhabited Dark ice Realm with a time speed double Lissae's. It is home to the **U'tan**. Most of the animals are relatively harmless, except for the **metsari**.

Realms – Planets which inhabit various parts of the multiverse on three main levels: Dark, Grey, and Light. There can be many sub-levels and a mix of Dark and Grey, or Grey and Light within the same level. Dark Realms are places with little to no natural sunlight. Most lights in these Realms are made by Innarn. Grey Realms are places with a similar amount of light to Lissae and Earth's equator. Light Realms are places where there is an abundance of natural light.

Returned – The name given to those from Ronah who survived being eaten by Anriluka.

Ridden Hall – The school on Ronah.

Riomache – A Grey Realm. A level below Lissae, their gateway opens out to a desert city square.

Ronah – One of the sentient Shifting Islands on Lissae. She is home to a variety of races and the traditional home of the Altoriae. Traditionally, Ronah selects a being to be her spokesperson. Ronah is one of the six gateways to the Realms.

Rutenberry – The frosted, dark-purple skin of the rutenberry hides the chocolate-like fruit inside. It can be eaten raw, although the skin can be bitter. Skinned, mashed, and cooked, it can be added into cakes, biscuits, and other sweets, including drinks.

S

Send/Sent – The word used for telepathic communication.

Sentient – Able to perceive or feel things, capable of thought and communication.

Sentinel, The Shifting Island – The major source of news for the Shifting Islands of Lissae. Available on your crystal slab with the low-cost subscription of 3 ziom beads a day!

Shifting – The Innarn art of mental teleportation from one space to another.

Shifting Islands – The name of the group of islands that travel around Lissae's seas, seemingly on a whim. They are sentient beings who care for the residents who make them their home. See: **Akoren**, **Cantash**, **Ginorti**, **Rakemyst**, **Ronah**, **Talhan**, and **Vannali.**

T

Techno Centre – Located on Talhan, it is the hub for all of Lissae's crystal and technological advances. The building also holds the Healing Centre and the labs of the technomancer and Talhan's Linked.

Technomancer – The head of the Techno Centre has been given the nickname of technomancer due to the number of times her advances have brought the seemingly deceased back to life.

U

Ulnan – Temira's home Realm. It was destroyed, and all that remains is a burned door in the Ducibus' Hall.

Ulnanian – A race from Ulnan. The only known surviving member is Temira.

V

Vannali – One of the sentient Shifting Islands on Lissae. She is home to the Weavers.

Vebaday – Sixth day of the week on the Realm of Lissae. The other days are **Adonday**, **Inthday**, **Kerday**, **Narday**, **Rasshday**, and **Zoeday**.

Veti Cant – Or Cant, is a sign language that uses hands and facial expressions to communicate. It is often helpful when overcoming language barriers. There are variations for beings with more limbs, but the essentials of the Cant remain the same.

Vendalbara – A continent on Lissae.

Viorath – A Dark Realm.

Vitreus Academy – The school on Talhan. Vren is the current head of the academy.

W

Wandering Serpent, The – A tavern in **Merthin**, favoured by **Domic Iabor** and **Brayden**.

Wards – Innarn shields designed to protect specific areas.

Well met – A traditional greeting throughout the Realms.

X

Xanderri – A cloud-like race relying on the bodies of their hosts to move around.

Z

Ze/Zir/Zim – A gender-neutral pronoun.

Zelbon – A Light realm whichh almost saw the untimely demise of the Guardian of Lissae, due to a tripwire placed at waist height.

Ziom – The hardest metal in the Realms, found on Lissae. Used for the creation of housing frames, precious jewellery, and weapons.

Ziom beads – A form of currency on Lissae. Also referred to as **Beads**.

Zoeday – Seventh day of the week on the Realm of Lissae. The other days are **Adonday, Inthday, Kerday, Narday, Rasshday,** and **Vebaday**.

BEINGS AND CREATURES

Annotated by the Guardian's Apprentice, Samuel.

A

Adeon – The God of the Element Fire and husband of Ke'ra.

Akoren – One of the sentient Shifting Islands on Lissae. Originally home to Lissae's deities, she is inhabited by the **Wisara**, and refugees from the mainland who required a place to stay after the civil war.

Alan Pratt – of Ronah. Mayor of Ronah.

Alistair Hollingsworth – of Ronah. Youngest son of Liza, stepson of Jordan. Brother of Caleb, Christopher, Tania and Jessica Hollingsworth. Former candidate for the Guardian's Apprentice.

Anika Thorne – of Ronah. Student at Ridden Hall. Blank. Stylist to the thirteenth Altoriae. *And the Guardian. And me. I feel like I've been branded.*

Anriluka – An U'tan from Rataeo who is older than Lissae's calendar. Defeated by Shari Dawn, the thirteenth Altoriae, in the spring of 4059. *Glad she's gone. Ugh.*

Arilla Dawn – of Ronah. Mother of Shari Dawn, wife of Calem Dawn. Owner of the Quiver and Quill Tavern.

Ashlen – One of the Returned, and a member of the Altoriae's Guild.

Asterion – formerly of Atlantis. A former professor who donated his mind to become myth embodied. Currently residing on Ronah.

His way of protecting Shari is even weirder than mine.

B

Belfar – of Rakemyst. Mate of Wolf Dawn. Second in command of Elder SilverCloud's guards.

Ben – of Kenorvia. Elder.

Brayden – of the Wisara. A spokesperson.

Briar – of the mainland. Tried to assassinate the Guardian.

Failed Miserably

Brinley – of Vannali. Vannali's Linked.

C

Caeli – of Akoren. Former candidate for the Guardian.

Caleb Hollingsworth – of Ronah. Eldest son of Jordan, stepson of Liza. Brother to Jessica, Christopher, Alistair, and Tania.

Calem Dawn – of Ronah. Father of Shari Dawn, husband of Arilla Dawn, son of SilverCloud, and brother of Wolf Dawn. Owner of the Quiver and Quill Tavern. *He thought I wanted to do what with his daughter?!*

Cantash – One of the sentient Shifting Islands on Lissae. He is home to the Daens.

Chamele – of Jinkor. Elder. *There are few who deserve her fate. But she was absolutely one of them.*

Charin – of Rakemyst. One of the patrol members in Wolf's group. Spouse of Varlee.

Collis Iuvo – of Ronah. Unofficial leader of the Returned. Sworn guardian and soul-match of Ronah's Linked. Member of the Altoriae's Guild.

Crystal Intelligence – ~~of Lissae and Atlantis.~~ *of trouble and mayhem. Never trust a talking crystal. And for the love of the Nine Hells, never take a machine from Atlantis!*

Cylanthar – The Q'Aralide deity of destiny. She makes her presence known by the ringing of bells when events which have the potential to change her disciples' lives occur. *Her bells are both a blessing and a curse.*

Cyrus Petram – of Talhan. Talhan's Linked.

D

Daen – A short, fierce, and loyal race with amazing control over the Fire Element.

Daivi – of Ronah. One of the Returned. Killed by the Crystal Intelligence.

Dealon – of Ronah. Formerly of the Wisara. Former candidate for the Guardian's Apprentice. New member of the Altoriae's Guild.

Domic Iabor – of Akoren. Akoren's Linked.

Draci – Tiny dragon-like creatures that grow no bigger than a human's palm. The draci are native to Cantash, and those who have not found a being to bond with live in the gardens.

Drah – of the U'sala. Twin brother to Kerk. *Currently missing a foot. And a brother.*

Ducibus – The Ducibus guard the gateways between the Realms. No one really knows what they look like, as they all wear dark cloaks. There is a theory that they come from different Realms and comprise many races. They ensure the safe travel between Realms and that those who aren't meant to get through, don't.

E

Edward Thorne – of Ronah. Husband of Harmony. Elder of Ronah. Grandfather of Anika Thorne.

Elani – of Ronah. Formerly of Ginorti. Member of the Altoriae's Guild.

Eobustus – Native to Cantash, the coal-black equines with manes of fire are a physical representation of energy and heat transference. They use heat from their surroundings to gather energy, then convert that energy into other things—movement, Innarn-boosting, running without rest. They are the fastest creature in all the Realms—provided they've had a good feed of magma or the sun is at full strength.

Esse – Tania's escape-artist chicken. *Snack with blue feathers.*

Eva – of Talhan. Orphaned. Now works at Books 'n' More.

F

Felton – of the U'sala. Explosives expert.

Fenix – of Cantash. Cantash's Linked.

Ferah – Humanoid beings with cat-like features, including fur, tail, whiskers, and claws.

Frointh – Forgotten Lissaen deity of Crystal. His statue can be found in Ronah's museum.

Fulni – An animal similar to Earth's buffalo but carnivorous and with two heads. The last fulni herd went extinct over two hundred years ago. Their tails are attached to a major artery, and if the tail is removed, they will bleed out in seven seconds.

G

Garayen – of the Wisara. An Elder.

General Morrow – of Ginorti. Head of the Satyrs army. Father of Liza Morrow. Grandfather of Tania Hollingsworth.

Ginna – of Lissae. Reporter for *The Shifting Island Sentinel.*

Ginorti – One of the sentient Shifting Islands on Lissae. He is home to the Satyrs.

Grace – of Jinkor. Former slave of Chamele. The Altoriae's cousin. Formally known as Lissa. *Likes stabbing family I can relate to that.*

Gwyn – of Vendalbara. Elder.

H

Halfair – of Ronah. One of the Returned.

Henot – of the U'sala. Gnome.

I

Ilutri – Winged humanoids from Lissae. They are usually found on Rakemyst and are high-level Innarnians. They include some of the finest archers on the Realm.

Indijo – of Ronah. Collis's childhood best friend.

J

Jetonyx – Kin to Samuel. of ~~Alteum~~ Ronah. *Golden Q'Aralide. Potential farmer.*

Joana – of Ronah. Mother of Tobias. One of the Returned.

Jonathan Buan – of Ronah. The Guardian to the thirteenth Altoriae. Owner of Books 'n' More. *The Realms may just freeze over. The Guardian trusts me. Think I may have betrayed that, inadvertently*

Joshua Izzaya Clemise – of the Spirit Realm. Formerly of Ronah. Former Guardian.

K

Kay'imi – The first Altoriae. She lived until she was 1217 years old when a lone Ahana archer killed her.

Kemanyr – newest Q'Aralide. *Recently hatched. With colours. And a penchant for escaping.*

Ke'ra – God of the Element Plasma and husband of Adeon.

Kerk – of the U'sala. Twin brother to Drah. *Deceased*

Kibon – of the U'sala. Long-range weapons expert.

Kieran – of Ronah. One of the Returned.

L

Lira – currently of Ronah. Formerly of Tevon. Former candidate for the Guardian's Apprentice. Member of the Altoriae's Guild.

Lissa – Sarina's daughter. Cousin to the Altoriae. More commonly known as **Grace**.

Liza Hollingsworth – of Ronah. Daughter of General Morrow. Wife of Jordan, mother of Caleb, Christopher, Alistair, Tania, and Jessica. Headmaster of Ridden Hall.

Liz Ribeck - of Ronah. Named after her aunt Lizbeth. Classmate of the 13th Altoriae.

Lizbeth Ribeck – of Ronah. *My friend. Hurt her, and I will peel your skin off, piece by piece, and make you watch while I rip your still-beating heart from your body*

M

Max – of Ginorti. Part of the Satyr's Army.

Milo – of Cantash. Self-appointed secretary to Cantash's Linked. *Deceased*

Mu – of Ronah. Formerly of Nindonia. Member of the Altoriae's Guild.

N

Na'reh – Goddess of the Element Spirit and wife of Vebnah.

Nerina – of the U'sala. Healer.

O

Oakley – of Ginorti. Ginorti's Linked.

Oalark – ~~Queen of the Q'Aralide.~~ *Could she not have mentioned her life force was tied with Altaun? A little warning would have been nice. Still not sad she's gone.*

P

Pala – Leader of the Ducibus and sentinel of Lissae's gateway.

Palon – Native to Lissae, the palon is a small, six-legged creature descended from wolves. They have soft fur and long tongues, with a preferred diet of insects.

Q

Q'Aralide (said Que-*ral*-die) – A vicious Dark race who wield Spirit, Earth, Plasma, and Air Innarn. Approximately thirty feet tall, their social status depends more on their colour and abilities than anything else. Apart from their Innarn, their breath is something to watch out for, as it can strip the flesh and the life from someone in just one exhalation.

R

Rakemyst – One of the sentient Shifting Islands on Lissae. He is home to the Ilutri.

Rany Thorne – of Ronah. Father of Anika Throne. *And a perfect example of how not to treat your hatchlings.*

Rasshnae – Goddess of the Element Water and wife of Zoemer.

Raven – of Ronah. Formerly of Freeson. Former candidate for the Guardian's Apprentice. New member of the Altoriae's Guild. Excellent tracker.

Remmy – of Ronah. One of the Returned.

Ronah – One of the sentient Shifting Islands on Lissae. She is home to a variety of races and the traditional home of the Altoriae. Ronah's current Linked is Tania Hollingsworth. Ronah is one of the six gateways to the Realms. *Crying islands are potentially more annoying than crying beings.*

Ruthford – of Earra. Tasked with guarding their side of the gateway.

S

Samuel Caragnton – currently of Ronah. Formerly of Altum. Golden Priest of the Q'Aralide. The Lissaen Guardian's Apprentice.

How did I become the patriarch of an entire race?

Sanithane – See **Samuel Caragnton**.

Sarina – Mother of Lissa. Aunt of the thirteenth Altoriae.

Satyrs – A humanoid race from Lissae with legs and tail similar to a horse. They are usually found on Ginorti. They include some of the finest crack troops on the Realm.

Shadow – of Ronah. The only creature to be one of the Returned. See ~~Zemmar~~ *Only answers to Shadow now.*

Shadow Bringer – sent to watch over others, sometimes to protect, often to kill. *Usually to kill. I do not trust this one.*

Shari Dawn – of Ronah. The thirteenth Altoriae of Lissae and creator of the Altoriae's Guild. *The most stubborn, infuriating being on all the realms.*

I would burn everything to ash for her.

SilverCloud, Elder – of Rakemyst. Father of Calem and Wolf Dawn. Grandfather to the thirteenth Altoriae. Deceased.

Sky Mother – of Luerix. A gigantic whale who rides currents of Plasma through the sky.

Skye – Former aide to Elder Suni. Current carer of **Grace**.

Sneeze – ~~One of Gwenith's draci.~~ *My draci. Can you train them out of chewing on ears?*

Suni – of Lawrgaea. Elder. Falsely accused of being an Innarnian and summarily executed whilst she slept.

T

Talhan – One of the sentient Shifting Islands on Lissae, and the only one to start with an all-human population. He now accepts immigrants from all races on Lissae.

Talofa – of Ronah. Formerly of Sulanta. Youngest member of the Altoriae's Guild.

Tania Hollingsworth – of Ronah. Ronah's Linked. Daughter of Liza, stepdaughter of Jordan. Sister to Caleb, Christopher, Alistair, and Jessica. Soul-matched to Collis Iuvo.

Temira – of Talhan. Formerly of **Ulnan**. Also called the technomancer, Temira is Head Healer and head of the Techno Centre. *Whilst apologies for the destruction of your race are overdue, I don't think stabbing you is going to help any*

Terrance Thorne – of Ronah. Anika Thorne's uncle. *Waste of space.*

Tobias – of Ronah. Son of Joana. One of the Returned. Also known as Toby. Deceased due to experimentation by Chamele.

Tommie – of Lissae's Mainland. Possibly related to Indijo of Ronah. Banished back to the Mainland by the Guardian.

Tormorylth – of ~~Lissae~~ *Ronah*. Tiny Q'Aralide. *Getting bigger all the time. And now golden. This is highly unprecedented, to have four goldens at the same time!*

Tuostinet – A creature as tall as three men, with claws as long as a Lissaen adult's torso tipping each finger. Long, curved horns sit on either side of the cat-like head. Fur covers the four limbs and powerful body. Only the three toes at the end of each limb are hairless.

U

Ulnanian – A race from Ulnan. The only known surviving member is Temira.

U'sala – A group of beings from all over the Realms who have banded together to protect the Realms from creatures who wish to change them for their own benefit. Currently, a small sub-set, led by Yessna, reside on Ronah.

U'tan – A race of extraordinarily powerful strategists who reside on Rataeo.

V

Vallan – A creature bred for its hide and meat. Vallan flesh is particularly delicious roasted.

Vannali – One of the sentient Shifting Islands on Lissae. She is home to the Weavers.

Varlee – of Rakemyst. Third in command of Elder SilverCloud's guards. One of the patrol members in Wolf's group. Spouse of Charin.

Vebnah – Goddess of the Element Air and wife of Na'reh.

Vren – of Talhan. Head of Vitreus Academy.

W

Weavers – A strong Innarnian race from Lissae. They reside on Vannali and usually keep to themselves. They are regarded as one of the oldest races and are often considered mythical beings as they rarely leave Vannali or allow visitors.

Wisara – Primarily ocean-dwelling beings whose bodies–although humanoid–look like the tangled roots of lotus flowers. Wisara tell the Tales of Lore. They travel the oceans and live in **Merthin**.

Wisp - A **Shadow Bringer**, sent by an unknown source to watch over **Shari Dawn**. *Why would you trust something like this? It is danger incarnate!*

Wolf Dawn – of Rakemyst. Mate of Belfar. Brother of Calem Dawn, and uncle to the thirteenth Altoriae. Commander of SilverCloud's guards. Previously known as LoneWolf Dawn.

Wubi – of the U'sala. Wielder of the spiked chain.

X

Xanderri – A cloud-like race relying on the bodies of their hosts to move around. *If they weren't already gone, I'd hunt them down and end them myself.*

Xani – of Talhan. Also called the technomancer, Xani was Head Healer and head of the Techno Centre. Deceased.

Y

Yessna – Commander of the U'sala. *Pain in my scales.*

Yvonne – of Ginorti. Part of the Satyr's Army.

Z

Zac Husdon – of Talhan. Formerly of Ronah. Techno apprentice.

Shari says they don't need permission? How do two males make hatchlings anyway?

Zana – of Rakemyst. Rakemyst's Linked. Eldest of the Linked, and an accomplished diplomat.

Zoemer – God of the Element Earth and husband of Rasshnae.

Z— Shari's palon. The only creature to be one of the Returned. See **Shadow**.

Map of Akoren

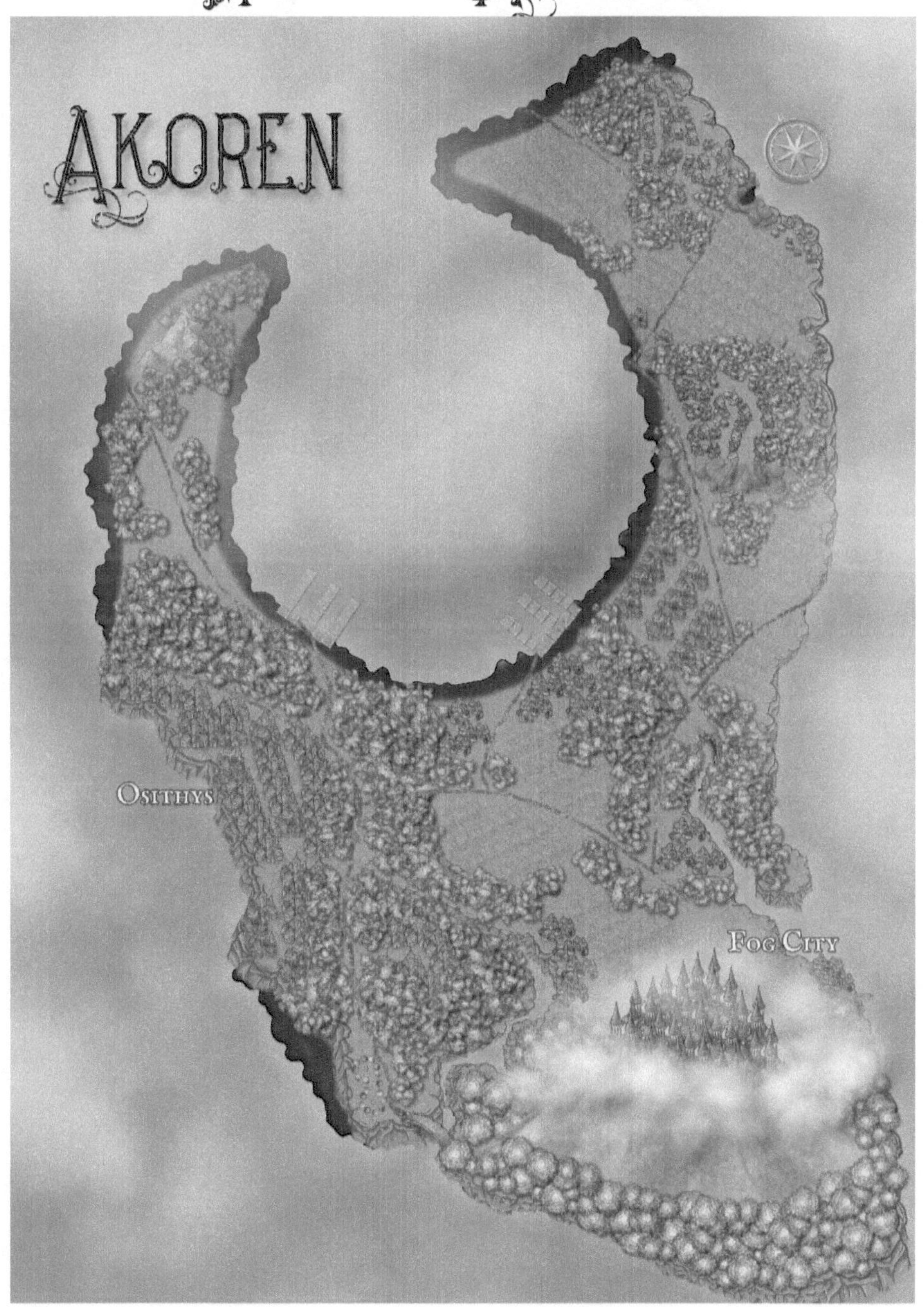

MAP OF
LISSAE
Sulanta
Opestila
Deep Sea
Vendalbara
Tevon
Yaston
Rohinda
Vutana
Kenorvia
Jinkor
Muhara
Neloni

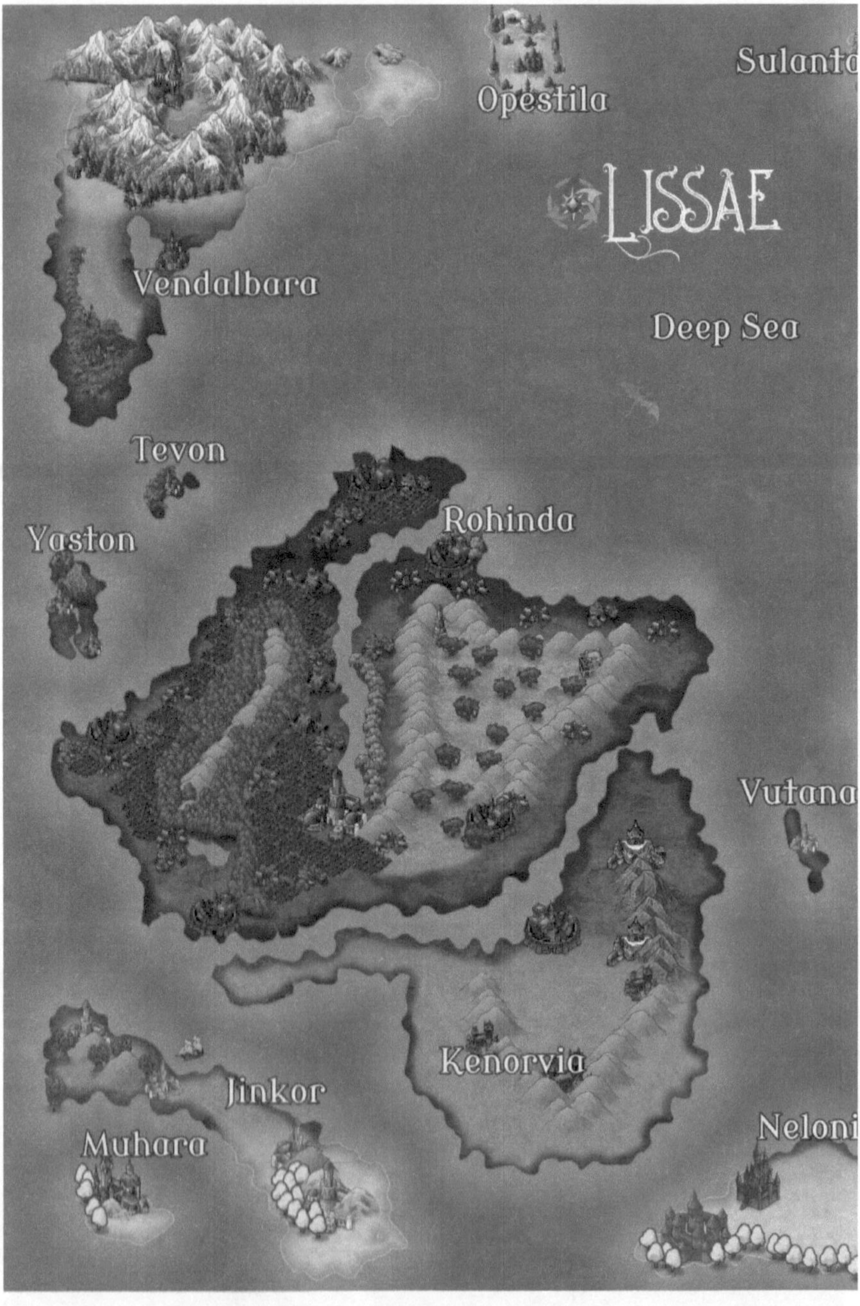

LISSAE

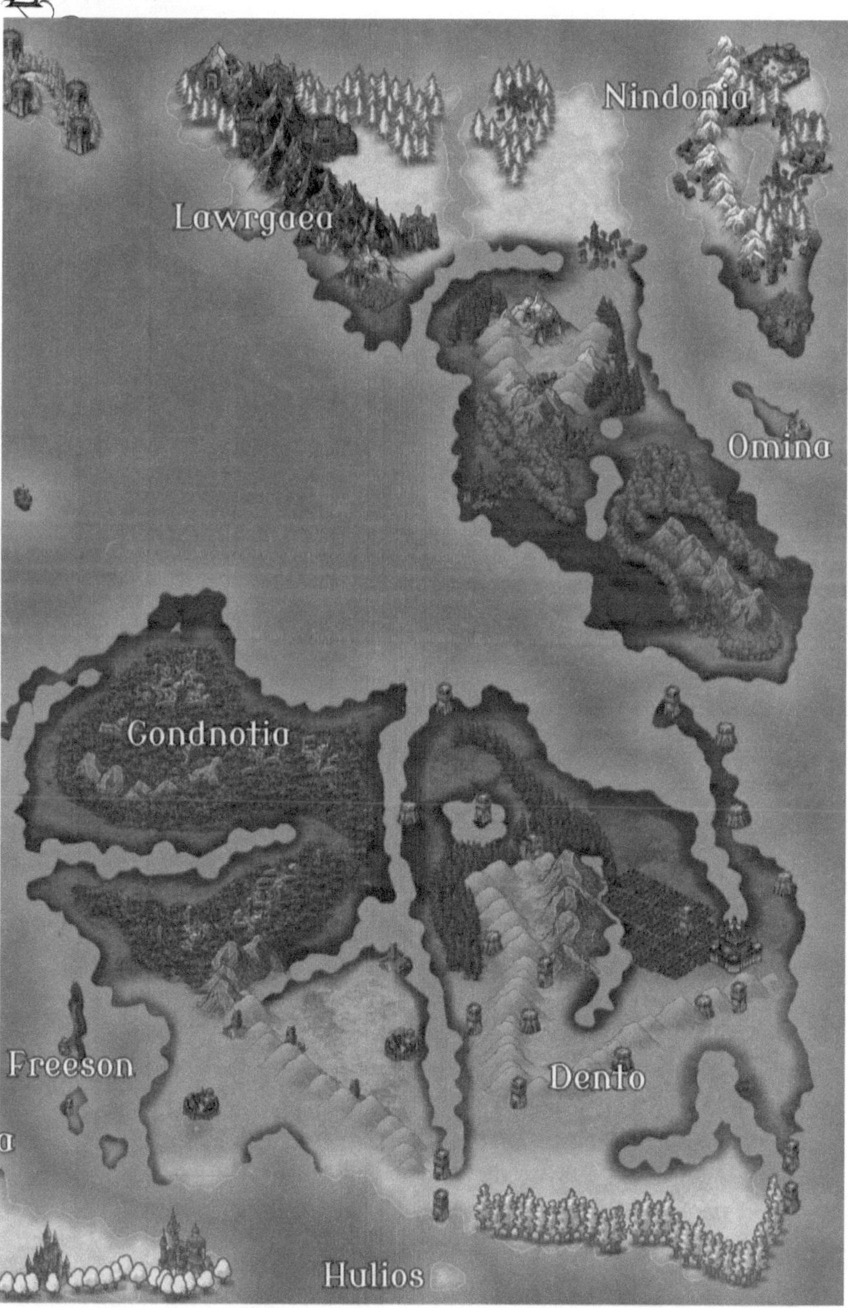

ENJOY THIS BOOK?

You can make a big difference.

Reviews are the most powerful tools in my arsenal when it comes to getting attention for my books. They help me gain visibility, and they can bring the Realm of Lissae to other readers who may appreciate the journey.

If you have enjoyed this book, I would be incredibly grateful if you could spend just a few minutes leaving a review (it can be as short as you like) at your favourite bookstore, or on the Goodreads page. You can jump right to the page by clicking below.

Thank you very much.

Find it in your preferred bookstore - books2read.com/akoren

Goodreads - goodreads.com/book/show/214103232-akoren

ACKNOWLEDGEMENTS

Another cliffhanger? Don't hate me! We're almost there.

This book would not have become what it was without the help of the amazing group of people who have rallied around me, kept me motivated, caffeinated, and going even when I wanted to stop.

To my amazing team of beta readers, you guys really are the greatest of all time. I love how, when I put out the call with the insane schedule I had planned for the rest of the series, you all rallied behind me. Jodie, Ruth, and Kathy, Lissae truly wouldn't be the same without you all.

A special shout out to my beautiful book wyrms. Every time I wanted to stop, and thought it was all too hard, your faces were the ones I pictured. That kept me going.

Anna from CREATING ink, I can't thank you enough for fine-tuning the manuscript. All mistakes in the final version are my own fault, and not of your making.

I have been sitting on this cover for two years now. Do you know how hard it's been not to share it?! I can't thank Vanesa enough for the stunning covers she continues to create. Lissae wouldn't look the same without you.

Special thanks to Corin, Ren, and Jasmine for some of the new character names.

Jodie—if ever there was a superwoman, you are it. Can I be like you when I grow up? (We'll ignore the fact that you are younger for the purpose of this question!)

Danielle, your encouragement has shaped the worlds both in the book and the one outside it. I'm so very honoured to be your friend.

To the amazing team at Sunshine Coast Libraries who always seem so excited to hear about what I've been up to in the writing world— endless gratitude for all your encouragement, particularly Gayle, Karen, and Codie.

I cannot forget you, the reader! Thank you for exploring the Realms within these pages. Until next time, I bid thee well.

And I promise, upon my keyboard, that Book 7 is *not* a cliffhanger!

About the Author

R. Lennard is the Australian author of the young adult fantasy series *Lissae*. She is an avid fantasy and sci-fi reader, and in her spare time, she works as a librarian. She enjoys learning about ancient civilisations, cosplaying, and drinking endless cups of tea.

Residing on the beautiful Sunshine Coast in Queensland, Australia, Rebecca enjoys the natural beauty of both the beach and the bush. She lives with her family and is ruled over by her cat.

Rebecca loves watching movies or TV shows and trying to figure out how they created particular special effects.

To find out more about Rebecca, head to rlennard.com

AFTER MORE TO READ?

What would you do when you had nothing to lose?

Orphaned, Jonathan Buan travels halfway around the Realm to defend his father's honour.

He finds more than he expected—more pain, more death, and more people to call his own.

Can he save them all, or will he become a demon's snack?

Find out what Jonathan was like before he became the Guardian.

Buy *Guardian* to bend the elements to your will today!

Available at: lissae.com/short-stories

When a sentient Realm asks you to be her protector,
how can you say no?

Shari Dawn appears to be just another teen, until a band of wandering Wisara visit her home—Ronah—a sentient, Shifting Island of Lissae.

Now her secret identity has been uncovered, Shari must learn how to control her powers, preparing to be tested in a prophecy passed down from the ancients, which will determine her role in the future of the Realm.

But sinister forces infect the dreams of Ronah's people. With a team she didn't want by her side, Shari must decide who lives and who dies.

The fate of the Realm is in her hands...

Buy *Ronah* and step into Lissae today!

Available at: lissae.com/ronah

How do you live after being eaten by a monster?

After he died, Collis found himself in a nightmarish Realm full of creatures who wanted to eat him. Waking up after the fiftieth time he'd died wasn't any easier than the first.

Stuck in a pocket Realm, Collis and the residents from Ronah must defend themselves against the deadliest creatures from across the Realms. But survival comes at a cost.

And if they die? They reform. Over and over. Just how are they going to escape?

Find out in *Returned.*

Available at: lissae.com/short-stories

A misplaced arrow could cause a war...

Wracked with guilt, Shari must face the joining of two Shifting Islands with her sword at the ready.

But as the search for the Guardian's next apprentice is still underway, fear strikes her heart. Not all the candidates are who they claim to be. And a fearsome new foe is out for revenge.

Can Shari lower her defences enough to let someone else in? Or will the decision cost her more than she's willing to give?

Buy *Rakemyst* and fly into Lissae today!

Available at: lissae.com/rakemyst

His choice could change the very fabric of the Realms...

The most feared being to walk the Dark Realms was once a mere hatchling. Scrawny, weak, and half-mortal, Sanithane strives to gain enough power to ensure his tormentors never bother him again.

But when his Queen sets an impossible task, Sanithane has to choose—his kin, or his life?

Find out the story behind the Golden Priest in *Shadows*.

Available at: lissae.com/short-stories

Something is watching them from the shadows...

After a devastating betrayal, Shari longs for life to return to the way things were.

But she has little time to dwell on normality. A disturbing new foe rises, and former enemies become allies in the fight to save Lissae.

Juggling school by day and patrolling by night, it will only take one slip up to bring everything crashing down. Shari must battle her way to the heart of her problems... or die trying.

Buy *Talhan* and discover the heart of Lissae today!

Available at: lissae.com/talhan

The clouds hang thick as the Light Realms start their attack...

Scooped up from the Portal, Shari must survive the Lightest of Realms. Can she find her way back to Lissae, before her Innarn is forcibly removed?

Having survived the Dark Conclave, Samuel returns to Lissae, alone. The Altoriae who went missing from his side holds the key to bringing back his race, but he's forbidden for searching for her.

Jonathan is struggling to keep the peace between those on the Shifting Islands and on the mainland.

Now his apprentice is back, they must decide—do they search for Shari, or prepare for war?

Buy *Ginorti* and discover the trees of Lissae today!
Available at:.lissae.com/ginorti

The dead don't stay that way for long...

In this heart-stopping conclusion to the series, Shari must navigate a world where the dead are returning and wreaking havoc on the living.

With the help of Jonathan and Samuel, she races against time to stop the influx of restless souls before they are overrun.

Grab your copy of Vannali today and immerse yourself in a world where the line between the living and the dead is anything but clear.

Vannali is the final novel of the Lissae series.

Buy *Vannali* and greet the dead today!

Available at: lissae.com/vannali

Reading Order

Guardian*

Ronah

Returned*

Rakemyst

Shadows*

Talhan

Guild*

Cantash

Sanctum*

Ginorti

Tempest*

Akoren

Weaver*

Vannali

Grace*

Lissae Chronicles*

The Altoriae's Handbook

*Part of the Lissae Chronicles

Keep up to date with the Lissae series and receive exclusive extras by signing up for the newsletter at:

lissae.com/welcome